Looking For Jamie

by

Angela Rigley

Dedication

I would like to thank the members of Eastwood Writers' Group for their help and support in getting my novel finished and to a higher standard than I could have managed on my own.

Looking For Jamie
By: Angela Rigley
ISBN: 978-1-877546-50-1

Bluewood Publishing Ltd
Christchurch, 8441, New Zealand
www.bluewoodpublishing.com

Special Note: This book contains UK Spellings.

To Caroline
Best Wishes
Angela Rigley

For other exciting books visit:

www.BluewoodPublishing.com

Chapter 1

The boy groaned as he made for the nearest tree to shelter from the approaching storm. Sinking into a pile of leaves, he tried to pull his rough brown coat around his frail body and tucked his blistered feet under him. Huddled into his clothes and trying to dredge some warmth from their meagre layers, a rasping cough hacked at his emaciated form. His coat, still damp from a previous shower, offered as little protection from the elements as his sodden shoes.

"What's this?" exclaimed Tom Briggs, the gamekeeper of the Brightmoor Estate, when Bridie, his black Labrador, unearthed what appeared to be a pile of old rags. "Well, blow me, if it isn't a child. What a sorry sight, to be sure!"

He looked around to check if the child was alone and, as there was no one else in sight, he picked him up and carried him the short distance to The Grange, Bridie yelping alongside him.

He pushed open the door of the large kitchen to find Nellie, the housekeeper, sitting at the table enjoying a snatched cup of tea with Freda. The cook was rather homely, but Nellie was dressed immaculately as usual in her black uniform, not a hair daring to peep from under her cap.

"What've you got there?" Putting down her cup she got up and went across to see what he was holding.

"It's a scrap of a child I found down by the roadside. He seems in a bad way."

"Give him here."

Tom gently placed the murmuring boy in her arms.

"We need to get these wet clothes off him or he'll catch his death of cold." Freda hastily unbuttoned the child's clothes and enfolded him in a warm blanket. "Poor little mite. I wonder who he is? I've never seen him before, have you?"

"Can't say that I have." Nellie peered at the child's face. "I can't see much beneath all that grime, but he doesn't look familiar." She turned to Tom. "Wasn't there anybody with him?"

"No, I couldn't see anyone."

"How strange!"

They all stood staring at the whimpering child, now swaddled like a new-born baby in the soft blanket.

"Let's get him into a bed. We can use the yellow bedroom. Nobody ever goes in there nowadays," the housekeeper suggested.

Tom opened the door for her and she carried the boy out.

"What do you make of that then? Where can he be from?" Tom took his pipe out of his pocket and placed it between his lips. "And, more to the point, what are you going to do with him?" He put some tobacco into the pipe before striking a match on the hearth and lighting it.

The cook chopped up a block of salt on the table. "I'm not sure, but Nellie will know what to do. We'll leave it in her capable hands." She scooped the salt into an enamel bin. "Would you like a cup of tea to warm you up before you go back on your rounds?"

"I wouldn't say no, and I don't suppose there's any of your fabulous seed cake to mop it up with? You know how partial I am to it."

The cook's round face beamed. "You're lucky, there's just one piece left." After washing her salty hands, she disappeared into the pantry to fetch the cake.

As she re-emerged, Nellie's voice could be heard through the cloud of grey smoke erupting from Tom's pipe. "You can put that smelly thing out," the housekeeper sputtered as she wafted the smoke away from her face.

"Sorry, I'm trying a new brand of baccy and it's stronger than my usual one." He tipped his pipe out onto the hearth. "How was the boy?"

"His breathing was easier when I tucked him up, and he's sleeping now, so we'll have to see how he is later, see if he can tell us anything."

He stood up and brushed the crumbs from his coat. "Well, I'd better be off. It wouldn't do for the master to catch me sitting here chatting. Do you think we should tell him about...?" He gestured with his head towards the ceiling.

"I don't think so, not yet a while. Wait to see what we find out first," replied Nellie. "He's still not over losing young Freddy like that, so I don't know what his reaction would be."

"Yes, I agree. Even though it happened two years ago, he's still grieving." Freda came out of the pantry with her arms full of vegetables. "But we can't keep him here indefinitely, can we?"

Nellie began to fold the clean clothes that had been drying on the overhead racks. "Perhaps he'll be able to tell us something when he wakes up. We'll let him have a good sleep first."

Tom nodded as he put his cap back on and went out, whistling for Bridie who, having lapped up a bowlful of water, had found a hedgehog to annoy. "Come on, girl, leave that flea-ridden creature alone. Let's get back to work."

* * * *

"Ruby, do watch what you're doing," Freda admonished the plain-faced parlour maid who had tripped and almost fallen over whilst making up the master's breakfast tray the following morning. "You've spilt half of that tea!"

"I'm sorry," cried the maid miserably. "It was my shoe lace." She bent down to tie it up. "I'll make a fresh pot."

"Well, hurry up about it. You know the master likes his breakfast on time."

Ruby wiped up the spilt tea before putting some more tealeaves into the pot, and pouring boiling water over them, with Freda's voice barely registering. She had heard it so many times before that she could almost repeat it word for word. 'I don't know how you come to be so clumsy. Not like your sister, she was the best maid we ever had. You wouldn't have found her with untied laces. It was such a pity what happened to her…'

After making sure the master had everything he needed for his breakfast, Ruby continued her morning chores, her plain face creased into its usual frown. She would never be able to live up to her sister's reputation.

She cleaned out the grate in the drawing room and laid the kindling, her melancholy diminishing as she set a match to the paper. The flames flickered, and within seconds were ablaze, so she set some logs on top and watched as a myriad of sparks cascaded down. She never ceased to get pleasure from this spectacle, no matter how many times she saw it, or how often she was chastised for taking too long about her chore, so she sat back on her haunches, spellbound.

Finally, deciding that she had enjoyed herself long enough for one day, she went back to the kitchen, where she bumped into Sam, the groom, and dropped the utensils she was carrying. As they both bent down to pick them up they banged heads.

"Sorry," Sam apologised, his cheeky face breaking into a grin.

"It's no laughing matter!" she cried petulantly, but he continued to grin.

"I can't help it, you've got black smuts all over your face." He took out his handkerchief and proceeded to wipe the soot off her cheeks. "Been making the fires?"

"Obviously!" She tried to wriggle away. "Anyway, what do you want?"

"So gracious, isn't she?" He turned to Freda who was plaiting the leavened dough she had kneaded earlier. The cook merely shook her head.

"Actually, I've come to see about the young waif Tom told me that he'd brought in last night."

"Yes, how is he?" Ruby asked, still wiping her face.

Nellie came in as she spoke and turned to the cook. "The poor lad, he thought I was his mother when I went in. His forehead's burning. Do you think we should call Doctor Abrahams?"

"Not yet. I'll prepare a poultice and try to reduce his temperature," replied Freda.

"Meanwhile, is that boiler ready, Ruby? There's a mountain of washing to be done."

* * * *

David Dalton wheeled Starlight round the small copse and pulled up, his breathing coming in short rasps, his handsome face glowing. He could always dispel his seemingly everyday feelings of malcontent and unhappiness by riding hard and forgetting the desperation he experienced ever since that fateful day over two years ago when the open carriage had overturned and his beloved wife, Elizabeth, and son, Frederick, had been catapulted out. The memory of his son's lifeless body lying in the dust still brought an unbearable pain to his chest and the only time he could put it to the back of his mind was when out riding.

Stroking Starlight's neck, he made soothing noises, although the strong, faithful steed was now used to the daily workout.

"Come on, my trusty friend, I suppose we'd better be getting back," he reluctantly decreed as he turned towards home at a more leisurely pace, his dark, brooding blue eyes scanning the surrounding countryside.

His lean frame fitted perfectly into the saddle, having been taught to ride before he could barely walk. He still remembered his first pony. He had loved and cherished her, but she had been taken from him, and the knowledge that she was very old scarcely diminished the sense of loss when she had died unexpectedly on his ninth birthday.

After handing the reins to the groom, he walked into the main hall, the centre of the great house, tapping his whip against his riding boots, and met Nellie, on her way upstairs with a bowl of hot broth.

"Who is that for?" He looked puzzled. "I wasn't aware that we had guests."

Nellie explained the situation, finishing with, "and we had no choice but to put the poor lad to bed overnight until he's well enough to tell us anything."

David paced up and down the hall, deep in thought. "Well, he can't possibly stay." He stopped pacing. "For a start, we don't have any facilities for a young child, and furthermore he must belong to someone. I don't want some irate farmer hammering on my door, accusing me of kidnapping his son."

"Tom's already making enquiries in the village, sir, so we should soon find out who he is. We can't turn him out, sir. He's such a pathetic little chap. I beg you to let him stay. We'll make sure he doesn't get in your way. You won't know he's here."

"Well…only because I know I can trust your judgement. I cannot recall any occasion when you've let me down, but make sure he goes as soon as possible."

Nellie carried on up the stairs as David entered his study, closing the door behind him. Leaning against it, his anguished face betrayed the remembered pain.

Why had this boy turned up now, just as he was beginning to control his grief? Perhaps he had been too hasty in allowing the boy to stay. Walking over to the decanter on the sideboard, he poured himself a brandy. It was rather early in the day for a drink but without hesitation he downed it in one gulp and then poured another, sighing deeply. The golden liquid shimmered in the sunlight as he twisted the glass between his shaking fingers.

Would this feeling of guilt ever leave him? If he hadn't been driving so fast they wouldn't have hit the boulder. Heaven knows how it got there in the middle of the road!

Opening the window he took a deep breath of the cool fresh air. A blackbird was singing lustily in the large oak outside, but that was the last thing he wanted to hear so he closed the window again, the sound of the cheerful bird adversely increasing his own melancholy.

* * * *

"Any news?" Freda asked Tom later that morning. She rubbed butter into the flour to make the pastry for an apple pie as she waited for an answer.

"Nobody knows anything about him, it's a real mystery. He seems to have appeared from nowhere. How is he?"

"Nellie's just gone up to him again with some more broth."

"If anyone can do anything with him, it's Nellie. She has a way with children. Do you remember how well she looked after the master after his parents died? She was like a second mother to him—even better than Nanny. I don't know how we would have managed without her."

"You've got a bit of a soft spot for her, haven't you, Tom?" teased Freda, adding some water to the pastry mix. "I've always thought so."

"A soft spot for whom?" Nellie suddenly materialised in the doorway.

Tom cleared his throat in embarrassment. "Um…that old mare, Margo, that the master never rides anymore," he improvised quickly. "She's been a bit neglected. She needs more exercising." Donning his cap, he bid a hasty retreat before Nellie could reply.

Nellie looked askance at Freda who seemed to be engrossed in her pie making so, with a shrug of her slender shoulders she walked over to the range to check the fire.

"Has Tom had any luck finding the boy's family? I didn't have time to ask him, he shot off in such a hurry."

"No, none at all."

* * * *

The boy stirred in the big bed and half opened his eyes. He couldn't think where he was. *I must still be dreaming*, he thought.

Looking round at the large tidy room, he ran his hand over the immaculate, sweet-smelling bedclothes. Where could he be? His aching head throbbed and his throat felt twice its normal size so he could barely swallow and, noticing a glass of water on the bedside table, he reached out for it, managing a mouthful before putting it back and falling back onto the soft pillows. His memory seemed to be playing tricks on him. Snippets of past events flickered though his mind as pictures in a picture book but they made no real sense. He saw a beautiful lady running towards him with her arms outstretched but, as he ran to be enfolded in them, a black cloud engulfed her and she disappeared.

"Mama, is that you? Don't leave me!" he wailed, reaching out his scrawny arms to capture her. Tears soaked his pillow as another image entered his fraught memory, of a young girl with blonde ringlets and big blue eyes. She was dancing around a garden surrounded by brightly coloured flowers, waving what looked like a rag doll, but then she too disappeared as if someone had drawn a curtain between them. He drifted off into a nightmare-ridden sleep.

When Nellie crept in to the bedroom again later she replaced the fallen counterpane and cooled his fevered brow with a damp flannel. Smoothing back his hair from his forehead, she could only guess at its colour beneath all the grime and wondered at the circumstances that had brought him to The Grange. She was remembering another boy, of similar age to this one. David had been a quiet, withdrawn child, rarely needing reprimanding and always behaving as expected. She had readily volunteered to raise him when his parents had both died within a few weeks of each other of the dreaded sickness that had killed half the neighbouring village. David himself had been very ill for a while but had survived and his sister, Annie, had somehow avoided the illness completely. Fortunately, a trust fund had been set up to deal with his financial needs and he had been away at boarding school during the term time.

The boy stirred and gazed with alarmed eyes at Nellie leaning over him.

"You're not me ma. Where am I?"

"Don't fret, lad, you're quite safe. You're at The Grange." She gave him a few spoonfuls of broth which he appeared to swallow with difficulty.

"'Ow did I get 'ere?"

"Well, that's what we'd like to know," replied Nellie. "Tom, our gamekeeper, found you lying by the roadside."

"I can't remember nothing, everything's fuzzy." He began to sob.

"Don't upset yourself, dear. Try and get some more rest." She tucked him up and he soon fell asleep again, so she left, closing the door quietly behind her.

Back in the kitchen, Ruby was washing up the dinner pots as Freda scrubbed the large table. Every grain of the old tree that had been chopped down to provide the wood needed to be scrupulously clean before she was satisfied with her task. She glanced at the half empty bowl that Nellie took to be washed.

"You've managed to get some down him then."

"Yes, a little."

"He is going to be all right, isn't he, Nellie?" Ruby's anxious eyes beseeched her. "My little brother James started off sick like that and he died a week later. You don't think he's going to die, do you?"

"No, I'm sure he isn't." Nellie went across and put her hand on Ruby's arm. "He's just weak from malnutrition and from being out in the cold and wet for so long. He'll soon rally round and be as right as rain, you mark my words. Now less of the long face, come on, give me a smile."

Ruby managed a half smile. She had a tendency to look on the dark side of life through her dull grey eyes, letting pessimism rule over any positive feelings that might creep in unwarily. Nellie and Freda worked hard to cure her of such fatalistic despondency and frequently succeeded, but they would never be able to persuade her to optimism, no matter how hard they tried.

* * * *

A few days later, the boy felt well enough to pull a blanket round him and sit on the window seat. He surveyed the scene below. What a surprise! Everywhere was covered in a thick blanket of pure white snow. He could see some footprints that had been left by a small animal and wondered whether it had been a rabbit or maybe a young fox. A robin caught his eye as it flew down and perched on the wall below and began to sing. Its mate joined it for a moment, but they were startled off by a large ginger tom that must have been hiding in the shadows, waiting to pounce. The snow had muffled its approach, but it was still too slow to catch the birds which quickly flew up into the trees and disappeared from view.

He was disappointed. The footprints had probably belonged to the cat after all.

Ruby entered with more broth and some biscuits. "What are you doing out of bed?"

He pointed out of the window and exclaimed, "You seen the snow? Ain't it exciting?"

She pulled a face. "Exciting – how can snow be exciting? It's cold and wet. I can't wait 'til it's all melted."

"If I was stronger, we could've gone out for a game of snowballs and built a snowman," he chirped, ignoring Ruby's outburst.

"I don't have time for such antics. I'm only a servant, you know. And you'd better get back into bed. Nellie'll have my guts for garters if you get poorly again. She'll only blame me for letting you get up."

After she had left, he ate as much of the soup as he could manage and drank the warm lemonade, even though his throat was still quite sore. The scene outside still enticed him and he wished that he could be out there playing in the soft snow.

He could resist no longer. He had to go. Images of a snowman flashed before his eyes. It had a large carrot for a nose and lumps of coal for his eyes. He moved falteringly towards the door, all his attention focused on reaching the snow-clad garden. How he reached the outside he would never be able to remember.

He gasped as cold air caught his breath and he stopped briefly in his tracks, then continued towards the snowman he thought he could see in the distance.

Why wasn't it getting any closer? It seemed to be getting further away instead. He blinked hard. Where had it gone now? It had disappeared. He spun around. Perhaps he was going in the wrong direction. He couldn't see it anywhere. Surely it had been over there by that tree – or was it that other tree?

* * * *

David was trying unsuccessfully to balance the accounts. He sat back, his hands behind his head, and stretched out his long legs. A huge sigh escaped him as he got up and poured a brandy. Walking over to the window, he studied the white landscape outside, wondering whether to risk riding out later. It had been snowing too heavily at first light, his usual hour for enjoying his favourite pastime.

A slight movement caught his eye. He leaned forward to take a closer look. It looked like a child wandering around the garden, dressed only in a white nightgown which blended in with the snowy environment. He looked again and for the smallest second thought it was Frederick, then reason took over and he remembered what Nellie had told him earlier in the week.

He rushed out of the room, almost knocking over a small occasional table in his haste, calling out for anyone to help, but it seemed as if the whole house was empty except for him. He would have to deal with the situation himself, so he ran out into the garden to the spot where he had last seen the child. But there was no sign of him. Had he been imagining it after all? He spun round and round, his eyes peeled. Then he saw the footprints in the snow at the same time as he heard a muffled cry from behind a pillar. He ran towards the sound and saw the boy huddled there, shivering uncontrollably. He picked him up quickly.

"My s-snowman d-disappeared," wailed the boy.

"Shh, shh!" crooned David, as he carried the weeping child into the house, not understanding what he was talking about. Nellie appeared as he entered the hall.

"I found this child wandering out in the snow, almost naked. Who's supposed to be looking after him?" he barked.

"I'm so sorry, sir, I've been searching the house for him since I discovered he wasn't in his bed."

She took the boy, who was unnaturally quiet by now, and hurried upstairs, rubbing his cold limbs in an effort to warm him up. She laid him in the bed, quickly wrapping him up in the fluffy blankets, and called to Ruby, who was hovering at the door, to bring a warm drink.

"What on earth were you trying to do, child?" she chided gently. "Just as you were recovering."

The boy looked up at her, his large brown eyes full of tears.

"I wanted…to go out to play…with Maisie…and the snowman. But when I got there…they'd gone," he explained between sobs.

"There, there." She took the warm chocolate drink from Ruby and held it for him to sip. "Drink this and then rest. No more exploits – promise?"

The boy nodded. He didn't want any more adventures – all he wanted to do was sleep.

David was waiting in the hall as Nellie descended the stairs. He didn't want to appear too eager for news of the boy's condition, but his expression must have betrayed him.

"I think he'll be all right," she said, patting his arm.

"Well, make sure it doesn't happen again," replied David. "Haven't you found his family yet?"

"No, we seem to hit a brick wall at every turn. We don't even have any leads to follow up."

Fortunately, the boy's physical condition was not too badly affected by the trauma in the snow. However, his mental state was still in turmoil. He began to have horrific nightmares, sometimes waking David at night with piercing screams. David would creep into his room and cradle the agitated child until his sobs subsided, stroking his forehead and humming snatches of half-remembered lullabies, almost forgotten until now. How his heart went out to the little boy who resembled his own beloved Frederick in size and colouring and who brought back so many memories – memories of nights such as these when Elizabeth was too drunk to notice that Frederick was unwell.

David kept the nightly escapades secret from the rest of the household. Apart from the fact that their rooms were too far away for them to hear anything, he didn't want anybody sensing his vulnerability. He had to appear as the cool, foreboding master of the house, a façade he needed to maintain at all costs.

One morning, after one of these occurrences of which the boy never seemed to have any recollections, David was eating his breakfast of liver and sausages when the boy walked in. He usually ate his breakfast in the kitchen with Nellie, but today he appeared unexpectedly in the dining room, still in his nightclothes.

David had authorised the removal of the trunk of Frederick's clothes from the attic so that he would be suitably clothed, as he was of a similar size, and the sight of him standing there resembling his son, even rubbing his eyes as Freddy had used to do, was almost more than David could bear.

He cleared the large lump in his throat and managed to say in a husky voice, "Good morning, young man. Would you like something to eat?"

The boy advanced to the table and stood looking in amazement at the trays of food arranged before him. "I've never seen so much food in me life. Is it all for you?"

"Well, yes, I suppose it is." David had never questioned the amount of food provided for him. "I'm sure I could share some with you if you would like. Here, sit down next to me."

While David spooned some sausages onto a plate, the child climbed onto a chair and hesitated only momentarily before tucking into the hot food. David watched him with an amused smile, and, as a stray splash of grease dripped down the boy's chin, he reached over and wiped it with his napkin, enjoying the role of fatherhood again.

The sound of a child's chatter and laughter had been missing for too long. It had been six months or so since his sister Annie had last visited with her two children, Sarah and George. They usually spent a few weeks at The Grange each summer. He might invite them to stay for the weekend. The children would be company for the boy – if he was still there, of course.

He was brought up short by the sight of the child licking his plate clean. "Would you like some more?"

"No ta, I'm full," the boy replied, getting down from the table. He began to walk out but turned back.

"I fink I remembered me name, but it might 'ave bin another dream, so I'm not sure."

"Well, what do you think it is?"

"Jamie."

"That's a nice name. Do you want us to call you that, anyway?"

The boy looked thoughtful. "Mm, it sounds right."

"So, Jamie, what are you going to do today? Nellie says you're recovering well."

"She don't let me do much, sir. She says I mustn't get too tired."

"I'll have a word with her and see what she thinks we could do, and, by the way, you don't need to call me 'sir'. You could call me…let me see…how about 'Uncle David'?"

Jamie took his time to consider with his head cocked to one side. "All right then…Uncle David," he replied after a moment. "But did you say 'what *we* could do'?"

"Yes, I don't have too much on, so I thought…that is, if you would like to do something with me…"

"Oh yes, sir, but I need to get dressed first. I can't do much in me nightclothes."

David smiled to himself. He was warming more and more to the youngster. "I'll meet you here in about half an hour then."

"But how will I know when half an hour's gone by? There ain't a clock in me bedroom, sir…I mean, Uncle David, so I won't know if I'm late."

"How thoughtless of me, I'm sorry. I'll come and find you then."

Dressing the boy proved an entertaining diversion for Nellie. Jamie recounted the previous half hour's events with such animation that her head was reeling.

"And he asked me if I wanted to do somefink with him today, and guess what? He told me to call him 'Uncle David'."

She nearly dropped the jug of water she was carrying, unsure which statement surprised her more. "He did what?"

"He told me to call him 'Uncle David'. Don't you think I should?"

"Well, if you're sure that's what he said."

"I fink so." He took off his nightshirt. "And I remembered me name."

"You did?" She had to put the jug down this time. This was one shock too many. "What is it?"

"Jamie."

"Oh, child, I'm so happy for you!" She wrapped him in her arms, uncaring that her cap was almost knocked off.

He wriggled out. "What d'yer think we could do today?"

"Well, nothing too strenuous, young man. I know I keep saying it, but you have been very poorly and I don't want you having any setbacks."

"But I feel so much better..." Jamie hesitated, his hands stilled from buttoning his shirt. He looked up with a forlorn expression. "How long d'yer think I'll be able to stay here?"

"Why, do you have anywhere else in mind?" Nellie asked light heartedly, wondering if Jamie would give any indication of whether he remembered where he lived.

"I...I wish I could remember how I got here, and what happened before I come. I see flashes of a pretty lady. Do you think she's me ma?"

One look at his crestfallen face and Nellie enfolded his thin little body to her bosom again.

"I don't know, darling, we're doing everything we can to find your family. But you can stay here as long as it takes." She gently pushed him away from her and looked directly into his eyes. "So don't you worry about a thing except getting yourself better."

Jamie managed a smile and began humming quietly as he continued dressing.

David appeared at the door as he was lacing up his boots.

"I wondered if it would be all right to take the boy for a short walk?" he asked Nellie. "The sun's shining and the snow's melted. Oh, and did he tell you he's remembered his name?"

"Yes, isn't it wonderful? But he'll need a warm coat. I'll go and find one. That goes for you, too, Master David. You're not too old to listen to good advice, you know."

David grinned. "Yes ma-am," he mocked, putting his arm around her shoulders. "I always feel like a child when you order me about."

"Get away with you." Nellie disappeared through the door in search of a coat for Jamie.

Both of them suitably attired in thick coats and warm scarves, they set off down the drive lined by tall horse chestnut trees on either side. The snow had practically disappeared. Just a few pockets of it lingered in hollows shielded from the sun's melting rays.

"Are you warm enough?" asked David.

Jamie nodded, breathing in deeply.

David followed suit. Suddenly, it felt good to be alive. The sunshine had dissipated any gloominess in him as well as in the atmosphere, and he felt vibrant.

"Race you to that clump of primroses," he called as, with a sudden spurt of energy, he ran headlong into the woods. Jamie followed and they came to a halt near a bridge over the stream that ran the length of the Estate on the east side.

"You…cheated," gasped Jamie, panting hard. "You said…the primroses…"

"I didn't say which ones—hey, are you all right?" David's worried frown revealed his anxiety as Jamie bent over, his breathing very uneasy.

"I'm just…a bit puffed…"

"I'm so sorry. You're still very weak, aren't you? Let's sit on this log while we catch our breaths."

Once he had recovered, Jamie asked, "Uncle David…d'yer think she's missing me?"

"Who?"

"Me ma. D'yer think she's wondering where I am?"

"I'm sure she is." David gently patted Jamie's knee. If only he could make things right for the tormented child. "We'll find her soon, I promise. Do you still not remember anything?"

"No, I keep trying, but only see blurry figures."

"The doctor said not to try too hard. It'll come back to you in time." He pushed the boy's cap further onto his head. "Feeling better now?"

"Yes. Is Nellie your mama?"

"Why, no, she's just my housekeeper."

"Don't you have a ma?"

"No, she died when I was about your age. How old do you think you are, by the way?"

"Not sure, how old are you?" enquired Jamie.

"You shouldn't ask adults their age, it's impolite, but if you promise to keep it a secret, I'll tell you."

Jamie nodded enthusiastically.

"I'm thirty-four, but remember it's a secret."

"That sounds very old, but you don't look old," replied Jamie, peering up into David's face, his head to one side.

"Well, thank you for that," grinned David, trying to keep a straight face.

He actually felt every day of his thirty-four years. He was not a vain man but he liked to look smart and keep up with the latest fashions, though he wasn't obsessive about it. His thick dark hair was brushed back off his face, and the high cheekbones above his gaunt cheeks emphasised the fullness of his sensuous lips. He knew most of the neighbourhood matrons considered him an ideal, handsome catch for their unmarried daughters but he himself could see nothing out of the ordinary when he looked in the mirror.

He stood up and they walked over to the bridge. They stood gazing down into the clear rushing water below and

David was reminded of one of the games he used to play as a child with his father. "Let's play 'stick boats'."

"What's that?"

"You drop sticks into the stream on this side of the bridge and then run over to the other side to see which one comes through first. That one's the winner."

They played the game happily for a while. Jamie won the most races and wouldn't let David forget it all the way back.

"I've had the greatest time!" Jamie exclaimed as they entered the house.

"My pleasure!" announced David smiling, as indeed it had been.

"Can we do it again tomorrow? Please," pleaded Jamie, his hands clasped together, as if in prayer.

"We'll have to see about that," announced Nellie, appearing from the kitchen. "I think you'd better have a nap now."

"Ah, but I'm not tired." Jamie tried to stifle a yawn.

The adults looked at each other, smiling knowingly as Nellie took Jamie's hand and led him upstairs.

David opened his study door but hesitated in the doorway. The walk with Jamie had filled him with an energy he felt disinclined to waste on an account book. He turned and crossed over to the morning room where the grand piano stood. It had been untouched, apart from the occasional wipe over with a duster, since Elizabeth had died.

She would play for hours, sometimes inviting him to join her, but he had preferred to sit and listen to her renditions of the famous composers, especially her favourite, Beethoven. Walking over to stroke the smooth maple wood before opening the lid, he could visualise Elizabeth's talented fingers deftly moving over the keys, and hear her beautiful soprano voice.

Sitting on her stool, he held his hands poised over the keys, motionless for a moment. Then he brought them down and began to play. All the pent-up emotion of the last few years was released in that outpouring of energy. He played as he had never played before – pieces he had not realised he knew by heart, but which were dredged from the recesses of his memory. On and on he played until, exhausted, he returned the lid to its habitually closed position and sat slumped with his head in his hands.

Chapter 2

David invited his sister Annie and her family to stay the following week.

Helping her down from the carriage, he asked how she was, regretting it immediately as she replied, "Well, you know how I suffer with my chest," and began to regale him with the thousand-and-one symptoms she seemed to suffer from.

The children were taken into the kitchen for some lemonade as the adults entered the parlour.

"Good of you to invite us, old chap," boomed Victor in his usual blustery way. "Sorry I can't stay long, though. You know how it is."

"How's the business coming on?" David poured them both a brandy. "Have you managed to contact that supplier I told you about?"

"Yes, I did, thank you, he's been marvellous. I've got customers queuing up for orders and we've even branched out with a new design for a lady's hat. Annie just adores it, don't you, dear?" Victor walked over to where Annie was already lounging on the striped chaise longue, her eyes partly closed.

"What?" she asked, looking up.

"We were talking about the business, dear, about how well it's taken off."

"Yes, I suppose it has, but the drawback is that I hardly ever see you nowadays. Only the other evening I needed your help when poor little Georgie fell and cut his knee. You were supposed to be home by six o'clock and when you hadn't arrived by seven I had to call Doctor Williams. You know how I hate to bother him, even though he's a family friend, but I couldn't cope on my own, what with all the packing and the household to organise."

"Yes, dear, I'm sorry. I've already explained why I was late, a customer kept me talking. I couldn't be rude and walk out, now could I?"

Annie merely shrugged, making no further rejoinder to her long-suffering husband as the sound of raised children's voices filtered through into the lounge.

"Yes I can!" David heard Jamie cry, as three dishevelled youngsters fell through the door.

"What's all the noise about?" he called above the din. "I hope you two aren't bothering Jamie. He's been very ill and mustn't be upset."

"George don't believe that I can count to a hundred," bawled Jamie. "But I can, can't I, Uncle David?"

A shocked silence stilled the room for a brief moment.

"Uncle David?" squealed Annie. "You let this little nobody call you 'Uncle David'?"

"Yes I do. And please remember he has a name!"

"Well, I don't think it's appropriate," sulked Annie. "It's too intimate, and it puts him on a par with my two little darlings. It's just doesn't seem right."

"I'm sorry if you disapprove, but I'm not changing my mind just to please you," retorted David.

"So, is it still all right?" squeaked Jamie, looking very unsure of himself.

"Yes, Jamie, the matter's settled."

Obviously beaten, Annie turned to her son. "Have you arranged your room to your liking, darling? I know it's rather small after your lovely bedroom at home but I'm sure you'll manage."

"It's a lovely room, mother, as you know," retorted Sarah. "It has the same blue furnishings as he has at home and the bed is even bigger than his own. I don't know why you have to criticise everything here." She turned to her uncle. "We both have beautiful rooms, as always, thank you, Uncle David."

David smiled at his niece. He had always favoured the pretty blonde-haired girl over her petulant brother. Her bright blue eyes lit up her freckled face whenever she smiled, which was quite often, as she was a naturally happy girl. He couldn't imagine how such a harridan as his sister could have begotten such a sweet, mild-tempered offspring. George, on the other hand, was growing up to be the mirror image of his bad-tempered mother and his pouting lips very rarely smiled.

"Now I don't want any arguing, any of you, do your hear?" David addressed the children.

"But…" began George.

"No buts. This is a peaceful house and that's how I want it to stay. Understand?"

"Yes, Uncle David," chorused George and Jamie in unison.

"Off with you, then, your tea should be ready." David shooed them out of the door, not missing the sly look George gave Jamie under his eyelashes, and hoping that they would soon settle their differences.

* * * *

Nellie looked at the downcast expression of the two boys and wondered what had been happening. She had been assigned to supervise the children's mealtimes in the absence of a nursery nurse, and was enjoying having children around the house again.

"What's with the glum faces?" She put some bread onto a toasting fork and held it in front of the fire. "Have you been falling out already?"

"Uncle David gave them a bit of a scolding." Sarah picked up the butter. "They deserved it, mind you."

"Jamie reckons he can count to a hundred, but he missed out sixty to sixty nine, so he can't." George pulled a face at Jamie.

"Only 'cos you made me say it too quick. I don't usually miss out no numbers," moaned Jamie as he sat down at the table.

23

"Don't forget you're bigger than Jamie so you should look after him, not fight with him. He's had a very rough time recently, you must make allowances for him," Nellie explained.

"That's more or less what Uncle David said." Sarah buttered the toast as Nellie took it off the toasting fork. "Do you want jam on yours, Jamie?"

"Yes please, if it's strawberry," replied Jamie, perking up. "Strawberry's me favourite."

"I thought you were supposed to have lost your memory, so how do you know that strawberry's your favourite?" George sneered.

Jamie hesitated. "I ain't sure. It's odd. I know me name's Jamie, and I like strawberry jam, but I can't seem to remember nothing important."

"Don't worry about it. The doctor says you'll remember one day," consoled Nellie.

"But how long's it goner take?" asked Jamie, his mouth full of toast.

"It'll take as long as it needs, so don't worry." Sarah seemed wise beyond her eleven years.

"Trust you to be on his side." George jumped up from his chair. "He can't even speak properly. We've only known him a short while, but you prefer him to me already." He stormed out of the kitchen.

"I don't want to cause no trouble." Jamie put down his drink. "D'yer think I should go and say sorry to him?"

"There's nothing to apologise for." Sarah wiped her mouth on her napkin. "He's always getting the sulks, he'll get over it."

"If you're sure." Jamie pushed his toast around his plate.

Nellie patted his shoulder. "Finish your bread while Sarah and I go and find him. He won't have gone far."

As Jamie ate the remnants of his tea after they had gone out, Freda entered the kitchen with her arms full of leeks and carrots. Jamie jumped off his stool and picked up the stray ones that she dropped en route and placed them in the sink.

"Thank you, my dear," said Freda. "You're looking better today. It must be having the company of other children. Much better than being on your own, isn't it?"

Jamie wasn't sure how to answer her. He was beginning to think that he had been happier before. There had been nothing but trouble since George had arrived and he had only been there a few hours.

He was tempted to stay there in the kitchen but Freda put paid to that idea. "Have you finished? Off you go then. I'm sure you can't wait to go and play."

So he had no option but to go and look for the others.

* * * *

The next day George found a bird's nest in the hedge that divided the herb garden from the vegetable garden. He had spotted a blackbird flying inside with a wriggling worm in its mouth and had crept over to take a peek. Five open mouths greeted him as the alarmed parent flew off, squawking.

Jamie and Sarah found him as he was about to reach in and touch the nest.

"What have you got there?" Sarah called, causing him to jump back. He had been so absorbed that he hadn't heard them approach.

Sarah parted the branches and looked inside. "It's a nest. What were you about to do, George? Surely you hadn't intended touching it, because if you had done, the parents might not have returned and those babies would have died."

"No, of course I wasn't going to touch them."

"Can I have a look?" asked Jamie.

"Just a quick one then, the parents will be getting agitated," replied Sarah.

Jamie peeped in. "Oh, I can see five babies."

Sarah pointed to a brown bird watching them from a branch above. "That's probably the mother over there. Come on, let's leave them in peace."

25

"Can we come back tomorrow and check that they're alright?" asked Jamie.

"As long as we don't disturb them." Sarah put back the branches to hide the nest before tiptoeing away. "Look there's the father. You can tell by his yellow beak and jet black plumage. He's going in to feed them."

"I've had enough of birds, can't we do something exciting?" George turned up his nose.

"Let's go down by the lake," suggested Jamie "There was a family of swans there last week. The babies, cyn...cyg..."

"You mean cygnets," advised Sarah.

"That's right—cygnets—looked really odd. Their feathers were brown instead of white. Come and see."

"Do we have to?" asked George, kicking in the grass beneath the hedge.

"I would like to, but you can stay here if you like." His sister turned towards the lake that was surrounded by large oaks and situated to the left of the house.

He hesitated momentarily, unsure whether to go with them. Perhaps there might be something interesting at the lake. He had better follow.

He caught up with them as they were chuckling at the antics of some ducklings trying to jump up the bank after their mother. The first duckling had already made it but the remaining two, slightly smaller than their stronger sibling, repeatedly slipped back into the water, sliding down the wet mud. Their mother must have realised their plight and returned to the water, leaving the first one alone on the bank. Quacking loudly, it ran along the bank until it found a shallow edge and jumped in, its wings flapping furiously.

"Poor thing, he thought he'd been left behind," laughed Sarah. "Didn't he look funny?"

"I don't think it's funny," moaned George, sticking out his bottom lip. "You left me behind."

"We weren't going to wait around while you made up your mind." she replied. "I knew you would follow eventually, you don't like being left out of anything, even if it's something you're not interested in."

"Look there!" shouted Jamie, interrupting the argument. "There's the cyn…gets I told you about."

George tried his hardest not to look in their direction but his natural curiosity got the better of him. "They do look rather odd," he admitted. "That one at the back has got white and brown feathers, and it looks even weirder."

They walked around the lake with Sarah pointing out to Jamie several of the birds and naming some of the flowers that grew along the edge.

"You're so clever," exclaimed Jamie, gazing up into her blue eyes. "I hope I'm as clever as you when I'm eleven."

"I'm not really," Sarah replied modestly. "I had a book on nature for Christmas and I'm really interested in anything like that so I've studied it 'til I know it inside out. Would you like to borrow it?"

"Pah, nature books, you wouldn't get me reading them." George raised his eyebrows, tired of listening to them fawning over each other. "They're for milksops."

He could tell that Jamie had been about to accept Sarah's offer but saw him shake his head. "Ha, got you there!" he said under his breath.

Sarah gave her brother a withering look, but he ignored her as he jumped up to catch a bough overhanging the water's edge. Dangling precariously, he taunted Jamie even further. "Come on, boy, let's see how tough you are. Climb this tree."

Before Jamie could reply, Sarah intervened. "Jamie isn't well enough to go climbing trees, you know full well. And you'd better come down now before you fall."

Jamie reached up to help him down but just at that moment there was a large crack and the branch that George had been playing on broke away, landing him unceremoniously in the cold water.

"Help me," he yelled, "I'm drowning!"

Sarah laughed. "If you stand up, you nincompoop, you'll see that the water's not deep." She waded in to rescue him. Jamie began to follow suit but Sarah pushed him back. "Don't you get wet, Jamie, I'll manage." She yanked at her brother's hand and pulled him upright. The surface of the water was level with his knees.

"I wasn't to know it was shallow," he retorted, knocking her hand away. "It could have been really deep and I might have drowned."

"Well, you will court danger," his sister replied. "So you should accept the consequences."

He had often heard their mother use that expression. He pulled a face as he waded out. Sarah was becoming just as bossy as her. "You don't care about me at all. I could have died. All you care about is precious Jamie."

He felt very sorry for himself and stalked off up the hill toward the house, not caring whether or not Sarah and Jamie were following.

Nellie was taking the washing off the line as the disgruntled trio appeared through the gate. "What's happened to you?" she asked.

"That Jamie tried to pull me off a branch and it broke, and I fell in the lake."

An astonished cry escaped Sarah's lips. "That's not true. Jamie was trying to help you down."

"No he wasn't, he pulled me in. You're always defending him," shouted George, pushing past her. "I bet you wish *he* was your brother and not me."

"I do when you tell lies like that," Sarah called after him.

He ran into the house, not wanting them to see the tears that had welled up at her words. He escaped to his bedroom where he changed into dry clothes. He then sat brooding on the edge of his bed, wondering how to regain his dignity. He would get even with them. They weren't going to make a fool of him!

He would have to think of a plot. Perhaps he could go back down to the lake after dinner and rig up some sort of a booby trap. He could then lure them down the following day and get his revenge.

Having resolved to get even, and with a half-hearted plan in his mind, he went back downstairs.

On the way, he met his uncle coming out of his study.

"Hello, young man. Why are you all alone? Have you fallen out with your sister again?"

"Not with Sarah, no, but that...I mean...Jamie. He tried to drown me earlier."

"What...?" started David.

He was interrupted by Nellie's appearance. "There you are, George. I was coming to get you some dry clothes but I see you've already changed."

"Yes, I'm not a baby. I found some in the cupboard."

"George tells me Jamie tried to drown him," interrupted David. "Do you know anything about it?"

"Well, I think that was a bit of an exaggeration," replied Nellie. "According to Sarah, George was hanging from a branch and Jamie tried to help him down when the branch broke and this young man here fell into the lake."

"He tried to pull me, not to help me, honestly, Uncle David. I thought I was going to drown." George abruptly burst into tears. "I was...so...scared." He gulped between sobs so convincingly that David pulled his nephew into his arms. If either Nellie or David could have seen George's expression as he hid his face in David's coat they would have realised that he was playacting.

All he could think of was getting Jamie into trouble. If he could convince David that Jamie wasn't the good little boy he thought he was, he might get rid of him.

"There now, don't get upset," soothed David. "Let's go and find a biscuit, shall we? I'm sure Freda will have some tucked away for emergencies such as this."

They wandered off towards the kitchen, George trying hard not to smirk. This could be his revenge, getting Jamie into trouble. He might not need the booby trap at the lake, although he would still bear it in mind.

* * * *

Meanwhile, Annie and Victor had had a day out at the Races. On their return, and before they could take off their coats and hand them to Pervis the butler, they were accosted by Sarah. She had seen their approach and wanted to tell her side of the story first.

"Mother, Father, George had an accident, and it wasn't Jamie's fault, but George is blaming him and—"

"Slow down, Sarah, you're babbling. Let us get into the house, and you can tell us the whole story," replied Annie, taking off her gloves.

"I'll let you deal with it, dear," said Victor, disappearing up the stairs. "I need to see David about an urgent matter."

Annie took Sarah into the lounge where the whole episode was related to her.

"Are you sure Jamie didn't pull him? It's not like George to tell lies," she said when Sarah had finished.

"I saw it happen, Mother, he was truly trying to help him."

"You do seem to have taken that boy's side against your own brother since we've been here. I'll have to hear George's version before I make up my mind."

"But, Mother…"

"No more until I've spoken to George. Now let me get changed. I've had a lovely day, the best day for a long time, and even made a profit of two shillings, but now you're determined to spoil it with your tittle-tattle." Annie flounced out of the room, leaving Sarah dejectedly biting her nails, a habit that caused her many chastisements.

* * * *

George brushed the biscuit crumbs from his shirtfront and wondered what to do next. If he could play on David's sympathy it would definitely be to his advantage. He would need an alternative plan though, in case Jamie was given the benefit of the doubt. He decided to take a walk down to the lake and see if anything cropped up that he could use as Plan B.

As he was about to go out through the door that led to the kitchen garden, his mother entered through the other door.

"There you are, darling. Sarah told me about your mishap. Are you alright?" She rushed over to hug him.

"Just about, mother." George found his weakest voice. "I thought I was going to drown. That Jamie ought to be punished, frightening me like that."

"Are you sure he really tried to pull you off? I mean, he doesn't seem the sort of boy who would deliberately try to hurt anyone."

"Don't you believe me either? Everyone's on his side." He stamped his foot and proceeded to turn on the waterworks again. "It's not fair!"

"Of course I believe you, darling. I just needed to make sure. We don't know anything about his background..." She stood aside to let him out. "You go and play now. I shall have to speak to Uncle David."

Walking away from his mother, George couldn't keep a grin from his face. He would have the last laugh!

* * * *

Jamie had earlier wandered out into the garden, wanting to be by himself. He decided to hide away in the secret den he had made before George and Sarah had come. He hadn't shown it to them, as he didn't want anyone else to know about it. It was down in the corner of the kitchen garden, hidden from view by a large bramble bush through which he had to crawl. He had been scratched more than once but it was worth it for the peace and solitude that he gained from being there. Just knowing that not another living soul knew of it made the secret even better.

He had discovered it one day when he had spotted a young rabbit hopping about near the raspberry canes and when it disappeared into the bramble bush, he followed on his hands and knees. When he came out the other side, he was delighted to discover a small recess, not quite high enough to stand up in, but wide enough to lie down if he curled up. The backdrop was an old oak tree, and as several of the roots were above the ground they formed a seat for which he had borrowed a cushion from the armchairs in his bedroom to make it more comfortable. He had also borrowed a picture book, which he could just see by the dappled sunlight that filtered through the branches above. These were enough, combined with the bramble bush that covered the top, to prevent rain coming in and soaking the den. One of the raindrops might occasionally seep through but all in all it was his haven.

Feeling miserable, he took the cushion from the seat, laid it on the ground and, resting his head on it, he curled into a ball and fell asleep.

He awoke with a stiff neck, a rumbling stomach and pins and needles in his hands. He crawled out and stretched, rubbing his sleepy eyes with his fists. Having no idea how long he had slept, he thought he had better get back to the house. He rounded the corner of the herb garden and saw Sarah sitting on a bench, crying, her head in her hands.

"What's up, Sarah?" He ran over to her.

"Oh, Jamie, thank goodness you're safe." She quickly dried her eyes. "Where on earth have you been? We thought you'd run away." She hugged him tightly.

"Run away? Why would you think that?" asked Jamie in bewilderment.

"Because of George's accusations. Come on, we'd better let them know you're all right. Everyone's been searching for you, even George. And he's admitted he made it up."

"I've found him," she called as they ran up the garden. "He's safe."

Nellie came running over and enfolded him in a huge embrace. "Thank God you're alright," she cried, almost in tears. "Let me look at you. Are you hurt? You look very pale. You must be starving, you've missed two meals, you know. Come on in and we'll make you a sandwich."

David also came hurrying over and Jamie grimaced, feeling guilty at putting everyone out.

As they entered the house they met Annie and George. "There you are." Annie shook a finger at him. "Where on earth have you been, causing all this fuss and inconvenience?"

"Leave him alone," David intervened. "The boy needs something to eat."

"Eat? He doesn't deserve feeding. He should be sent to bed without any supper for causing such a rumpus."

"I'm really sorry, Uncle David," cried Jamie. "I fell asleep. I wouldn't cause no fuss on purpose."

"There, there, don't upset yourself anymore," consoled David. "We were concerned for you, thinking that we had driven you away, but George has promised to apologise to you, haven't you, George?" He nudged his nephew forward. "He admits he was a little hasty."

George kept his head down, shifting uneasily from one foot to the other. "Sorry," he mumbled before he stalked out.

* * * *

George couldn't bear to hear them being so nice to Jamie any longer. The dressing down he had received from his uncle had been too humiliating. So the following day he decided to explore the lake on his own. He sat down beside the clear blue water and watched a kingfisher diving in and out of it. A bird after his own heart, the kingfisher, he thought, grabbing its prey and gobbling it up.

Then he spotted a moorhen with five black fluffy chicks trying to keep up with her. They stopped under a tree, and he thought it would be fun to catch one of the babies. He tiptoed over, not wanting to frighten them away, and climbed onto a branch. If he reached down he should be able to grab one.

Suddenly, he lost his hold and could feel himself falling. The water filled his mouth as he tried to shout for help, and he swallowed more water. He was falling deeper and deeper. Where was the bottom? Something ensnared his leg. He couldn't free it. He kicked wildly but to no avail. He was terrified. His lungs were bursting. He was going to die!

Before he knew what was happening, an arm grabbed him and pulled him up out of the water. He scrambled to the water's edge, where he lay, coughing and spluttering. Eventually, Sarah's voice pervaded his blocked ears.

"You stupid boy, you could have been killed. If Jamie hadn't seen you fall in, you would have drowned! You were lucky we were able to grab you in time."

Oh no, not Jamie! It would have to be him, of all people, who rescued me!

"Why didn't...you just leave me to die...?" he spluttered, feeling even more dejected than before.

"Don't be so—" Sarah began.

"Oh, shut up and leave me alone." He struggled to sit up. "You haven't even asked me if I'm all right. I could be dying of pneumonia for all you care!"

"Come on, up you get." Sarah relented as she and Jamie both took an arm to lift him, but he shrugged them off.

"I suppose you'll go running to tell Mother and Uncle David now to get me into more trouble."

"Aw, don't, Sarah." Jamie grabbed her hand and looked pleadingly up at her. "Don't get him into no more bother." Turning to George and pulling some greenery out of his hair, he asked, "You really hurt, George? Cos if you are, we'd have

34

to tell somebody. But if you're all right, we could sneak in the back way so nobody sees us."

George weighed up the alternatives. There was a distinct possibility he would get another telling off and he had had enough of them to last him a lifetime.

"I think I'll be all right…when I've got my breath back." He gave Sarah the most pathetic look that he could muster. "But I was really scared, you know. I thought I was going to die."

"All right then. We'll give you a minute and then we'll creep round the back and hope that nobody sees us." Sarah put her arm round him as he was shivering quite badly by this time.

"Let's go now, I'm really cold."

They all climbed the slope and hurried back to the house. Sarah sent Jamie to check that the coast was clear. Fortunately, there was nobody about and they were able to get upstairs without apprehension.

Chapter 3

"Go on then, lass, don't you want your freedom?" The warden held open the large prison door.

For the first time in almost six months, Tillie could look at the trees and hear the birds singing without envying them their freedom. Closing her eyes, she took a deep breath of the tangy, fresh air.

"Have you got anywhere to go?" the warden asked. So many of the inmates returned within weeks because, with no money and no means of support, they had to resort to thieving, so eventually got caught again. "Or any family to go to?"

"My sister's in service and I don't know where my brothers are. I'll manage though." Tillie didn't sound very convincing, even to herself, but she had to make the effort. "I need to get to Welton. Do you know which direction that's in?"

The warden pointed towards the south, so with her head in the air, she walked out into the unknown.

She walked for about a mile without meeting anyone. She didn't mind though, she wasn't prepared for company yet. The heat of the sun on her head and the sight of the blossom fading on the trees lifted her spirits. She sat down beside a stream, the babbling water meandering over the rocks reminding her how thirsty she was. Leaning over to take a scoop, she saw her reflection. How thin and pasty she looked, her auburn curls, growing again after being cropped when she had first been incarcerated, hanging lank and dull, and it seemed to her that her green eyes had lost their usual sparkle.

Looking up she saw that, further along, the stream opened out into a fairly large pool and it looked so inviting. Glancing around to check that no one was coming, she quickly took off her shabby brown dress and underclothes, and slipping off her shoes, she waded in. The cold water took her breath away but she persisted and within minutes was floating around like a mermaid.

The chill of the water eventually had her teeth chattering, so she climbed out and, using her petticoat, dried herself as best she could, then put her dress back on before lying down on a grassy mound where she soon fell asleep.

Awaking later, rather cold but refreshed, her usual optimism had rekindled and she was on her way, full of renewed vigour.

She came upon a family at the side of the road, the man looking very worried, scratching his head.

"Good day," she said. "Can I be of assistance?"

"Good day to you too," the man replied. "Well, as you see, a wheel's come off our cart. Don't know how I'm going to mend it. My wife here, Myrtle, is expecting our fourth child any day now, so I can't let her lift anything heavy, and I can't do it on my own."

The lady beside him was leaning back, with one hand on her hip and the other rubbing her large belly, giving credence to his words. Three grimy children sat on the top of the wagon and they all stared at her, munching on apples and bread.

"Perhaps I could help?" volunteered Tillie, thinking that maybe if she helped them they would offer her some of their food. "I could hold the cart with that branch if you rested it on something, while you put the wheel back on."

"What, a skinny thing like you? You don't look strong enough, but…"

Just then one of the children fell unceremoniously off the wagon. "What are you playing at, you young scamp?" cried his father. The child merely gave him a cheeky grin and began to clamber back on to the cart.

"Anyway, you boys had better get off there if I'm going to put this wheel back on." The man helped them down. "Now then…if you three lads and…this kind lady hold up the corner of the cart."

He lifted the branch for them and when they had it high enough he began to push the wheel on. It took all of Tillie's energy reserves to hold it up.

"Just a bit higher…"

She thought they weren't going to make it, she was exhausted, but just as she felt she couldn't carry on any longer, the branch dropped to the ground and the man cried, "Yes, we've done it!"

Tillie slumped breathless to the ground, utterly done in.

"I'll just make sure it doesn't come off again." The man secured the wheel, then wiped his brow with his sleeve. He turned to Tillie. "Thank you so much, young lady."

Tillie smiled weakly as her stomach gave an almighty growl.

"Say, have you eaten?" the wife asked. "We've got bread and cheese if you would like some?"

Tillie accepted the proffered food with gratitude. She tried to remember the woman's name. Some sort of herb, wasn't it?

"Well, thank you again. We would never have done it without you." The man ushered the boys back onto the cart. "We're off in the opposite direction, otherwise we could have squeezed you in."

"That's alright, thank you for the offer," replied Tillie. She had to find her son so she waved them goodbye.

Could it really be six months since she had been caught stealing the loaf of bread from the back of the bakery shop in Welton? Desperate, she had crept in, hoping that the baker would be too busy with his customers at the front of the shop. It hadn't even been a fresh loaf, when she had picked it up it had felt as hard as rock, but the baker had come through just as she had been about to make her getaway, and had handed her over to the law. She had pleaded with the authorities to find her son, whom she had left hiding in a barn, but they had ignored her pleas. They disbelieved that he indeed existed. Goodness knows what had happened to him or whether he was still alive. She had to find him.

The setting sun was turning the sky red. Scanning the horizon and wondering where she was going to spend the night, Tillie saw an old haystack in the corner of the meadow. Crawling into it she covered herself with the warm hay.

"One just has to make the most of the facilities that are available, that's my motto," she said aloud to a rabbit that had popped its head out of a nearby burrow. "No point being too proud to accept what's on offer."

* * * *

"I'm bored, I want to go home," wailed George some days later as the whole family were finishing their supper together.

"No, Mother, not yet," cried Sarah. "I'm really enjoying it here. We don't have to start lessons again for another week. Our governess said she'll be visiting her mother until next Sunday, didn't she?"

"Well, actually," intervened Victor, "I need to go home tomorrow anyway. I have to complete some business that I thought would wait, but I'm not so sure now."

His wife wiped her mouth with her napkin. "Well, we have had a lovely time and all good things must come to an end."

"But, Mother…" began Sarah.

"No, Sarah, we mustn't outstay our welcome."

Jamie and Sarah both pulled faces but the decision had been made, so the following day, their cases loaded onto the carriage, Sarah made her farewells to David and Jamie and reluctantly climbed up after George.

Annie gave David a peck on the cheek. "Thank you so much, you must come and visit us soon. It's so long since you last came."

"Yes, I will, when we've solved the mystery of this young one here." He nodded towards Jamie.

"Oh yes, of course. Not before then."

Jamie was trying to stop Lady, their young excitable golden retriever from climbing into the carriage after Sarah. He tried pulling and Sarah tried pushing her but she wouldn't budge. They were both laughing hysterically at the dog's antics until, with one command from David, she climbed down, her tail between her legs.

"Ne'mind, Lady, I'll take you for a walk instead," Jamie consoled her. "You can have a ride in a carriage another day." He managed to restrain the frisky dog whilst they said their final goodbyes.

Jamie's arms ached from waving when the carriage finally drove out of sight down the driveway. David put his hand on his shoulder. "You're going to miss them, aren't you?"

"Well, Sarah," replied Jamie with a wry smile.

"Yes, George can be a bit of a handful. Anyway, how should we occupy the rest of the day? How about…we build a tree house? I think I know just the tree."

"Aw, that'd be 'triffic." Clapping his hands, Jamie jumped up and down with delight.

"Come on then, let's go and check to see if it's suitable."

They made their way towards the woods that ran along the bottom of the lake with Jamie skipping along, firing questions about what a tree house should look like. They arrived in a clearing surrounded by gigantic oaks, two of which had large holes in their trunks, big enough for a child to stand up in.

"Wow!" exclaimed Jamie. "How come I ain't been here before?"

"Well, I've never shown it to George or Sarah either. Annie didn't like me coming down here when we were children. Our elder brother was killed falling from that tree over there and she always insisted the clearing was haunted, so she never came here herself and made me promise not to tell her children about it. Of course, I know it isn't haunted, but women have over-active imaginations."

"I shan't say nothing," replied Jamie feeling very honoured that he had been told such a secret.

"And you must not come down here on your own either."

"All right." agreed Jamie readily. "Is this the tree we're going to build the tree house in?"

"No, that's a little further on."

"But can I play here for a while first?"

"Of course, off you go," grinned David as Jamie climbed inside the hole. In his fertile imagination, he could picture all sorts of animals living in there.

After a while, he ran across to the other tree to see if it was any different. "Hey, this one's a lot bigger inside. Come and look."

David walked over, picking up Jamie's dropped cap on his way. He brushed down his trousers and then checked his pocket watch. "But it's time we got back. They'll be sending out a search party for us."

"But what about the tree house?" wailed Jamie.

"I'm afraid we'll have to leave that for another day. We don't have time to start now."

As they arrived back at the house, they saw a horse being taken round to the stables.

"I wonder who's that is," David muttered. "I wasn't expecting any visitors."

Pervis greeted them. "A young lady is waiting to see you, sir, in the lounge. She said her name is Miss Christine Wilson. She's moved into old Mr Larkin's house."

"I heard that it had been let," replied David. "Did you say *young?*"

"Yes, sir, and very attractive if I may say so." He looked down rather sheepishly. "Shall I take Jamie while you go in to see her?"

"Yes, if you would."

He entered the lounge where a beautiful woman stood in front of the fire screen, dressed in a red riding coat and black skirt, with a pert little hat perched precariously on the side of her head. Her blond hair had been scraped tightly into a bun, but several curls had escaped, framing her heart-shaped face. Dark lashes framed hazel eyes, which she fluttered at David as he approached, and a faint hint of a familiar perfume hung on the air.

David bowed, somewhat taken aback by the apparition before him. "Good day, madam. I apologise for not being here to greet you when you arrived. David Dalton."

"Good day, I'm Christine Wilson," replied the vision, bobbing a curtsey. Her velvety voice had just the faintest throatiness, enough for David to want to hear more. "I've moved into the house up on the hill, so I thought I would be neighbourly and come to invite you to an informal dinner party next week."

"Thank you, Miss Wilson." David showed her to a chair and they both sat down. "May I order some tea or coffee, or something stronger?"

"Thank you, Mr Dalton, I would love a cup of tea. I've been out riding all morning and called in on the spur of the moment."

"Have you been riding alone?" His brow puckered as he pulled the bell for tea.

"Oh yes, I do it all the time at home."

"Home?"

"Sorry, I mean at my parents'. They live in Derbyshire."

"And are you to be living here on your own as well?"

"No, my sister Grace is coming at the end of the week." She leaned forward, continuing in a whisper, "She and her husband are having a few marriage problems and need a break. They live with Will's parents who are very interfering." She straightened up, obviously feeling abashed at betraying a confidence. "But please don't broadcast the fact. I don't think they would like their business known to the whole world."

"Of course not," replied David, as Freda entered with the trolley. "Milk and sugar?"

"No sugar, thank you," Christine replied with an engaging smile. "Just a touch of milk."

David found it difficult to keep his hands from shaking as he poured the tea and handed her a cup. He had not felt like this since Elizabeth had died, and he had only known the lady a matter of minutes. His usual ice cool facade was beginning to melt and he wasn't sure he could handle it. Clearing his throat, he carried his drink over to the piano upon which stood a picture of Elizabeth and Frederick. He gazed at it, a far-off look in his eye.

"Was that your wife?" Christine enquired.

"Pardon…? Oh, yes, and Frederick, my son." He showed her the picture.

"He looked very much like you. I heard what happened to them, I'm so sorry."

"I bet they didn't tell you that it was my fault, that I killed them," he thundered, causing his cup to rattle in its saucer.

"Er, no, they said that it was a tragic accident." She stood up quickly, placing her unfinished drink on the table.

"Well, that was the verdict at the coroner's court. But what do they know? They weren't there." David looked at her with sadness. "You know, no one will ever take their place."

"No, of course not." Christine looked up at the clock. "Is that the time? I must be getting back," she gabbled, hurrying towards the door. "Don't forget the dinner invitation for next Thursday."

David politely opened the door and nodded. "Yes, thank you." He bowed his head as she hurried out into the hall where Pervis was waiting to see her out.

After she had gone, David poured himself a brandy and picked up the picture again. "Oh, my darling, I know you had your faults but I miss you so much. I feel so guilty at my reaction to Miss Wilson, so disloyal to your memory, but she probably won't want to speak to me again after my outburst."

* * * *

Tillie awoke as the sun rose in a magnificent golden sky. The wispy clouds were alight with a ruddy glow that lit up the heavens. She stretched, feeling so glad to be free. How she had missed the outdoors.

She needed a plan of action. It was no good wandering around aimlessly. The trouble was she didn't know the area at all. She had been taken to the prison in a windowless carriage, the journey taking what seemed to be hours, so she was probably miles away. She would ask at the next town.

She came to a field where some brown cows were peacefully chewing the cud. They looked up at her lethargically as she approached.

Feeling ravenous, she looked around for a container into which she could collect some milk. An old can laid nearby so she wiped it out as best she could with grass and twigs and knelt down next to the fattest cow in the herd. She had milked cows before so wasn't scared of the animals. To her delight, the cow didn't flinch from her grazing and Tillie was able to half fill the can. She poured the warm milk into her mouth, the can being too rusty to put her lips to it, and hardly spilt a drop. She wiped her mouth with the back of her hand and patted the cow gratefully.

"Thank you, Daisy, or whatever your name is. I needed that."

The cow turned her head and looked at Tillie as if she understood what she was saying. The expression on her face was almost a smile. Then she resumed her chewing. Tillie had to smile herself. Perhaps it was a good sign that nature seemed to be in sympathy with her.

She came to a village with a long row of plain cottages. A wizened old man appeared, seemingly from nowhere, leaning heavily on a stick.

"Hello," she called. "Could you tell me where this is?"

"This be the village of Darleymoor, of course. And who might you be?"

"My name is Matilda, but I'm usually called Tillie. I'm looking for the town of Welton. Do you know if it's hereabouts?"

A far-away look came into the old man's eyes, and he sidled up closer to her. "I had a sweetheart called Matilda once.

Pretty thing she was. Fair skin like you but with the most wonderful brown eyes you could lose yourself in. Died, she did, before we were wed. Never even got to…"

"Look, I don't mean to be rude." Tillie didn't like the glazed look in the old man's eyes and wanted to be away as quickly as possible. "But do you know if Welton is near here?"

"Aye. It be about twenty miles over yon ridge. But you won't get there today, not in them shoes. Why don't you come and have a cup of ale and something to eat in me cottage over there. You look like you could do with something in yer belly."

As tempting as the thought of food was, Tillie refused. By the gleam on his face it wasn't only food he wanted to put in her belly. "No thank you. I mustn't tarry."

She turned to walk away but her curiosity got the better of her. "By the way, why is this village so deserted? There doesn't seem to be anybody else around!"

"Ah, that be because them what aren't dead are hiding away from them what are. They don't want to catch what killed 'em."

"What was that?"

"Some say it was typhus fever, but nobody seems to know for sure."

"But doesn't the doctor know?"

"Doctor? We lost him first of all. He wasn't much help, was he, dying like that?"

"Then how come you aren't 'hiding away'?"

The man's face broke into a grin, showing black stumps where teeth used to be. "I suppose you could say I be the lucky one! I don't catch no diseases—never 'ave."

Tillie began to back away. The man's breath stank and he looked like a grinning devil. She felt very vulnerable and just wanted to be gone from the place. As she hurried away a curtain twitched in one of the houses opposite and she felt very sorry for the poor people holed up in their homes, too afraid to go out.

David was beginning to regret accepting the invitation to Christine Wilson's dinner party. His reaction to her had been instant and it bothered him. Had it been the scent of her perfume, so similar to the one Elizabeth used to wear, that had lingered even after she had gone?

Perhaps he could send a note with his apologies, saying that he had urgent business to attend to. But that would be the coward's way out, and he prided himself on being a man of courage.

Having changed his mind three times on which jacket to wear, he finally decided on the dark green one with the large lapels. It was his favourite. He might as well feel good if he was to endure a difficult evening. He had no idea how many people would be there. It was just an informal affair, Miss Wilson had said.

The party was already in full swing by the time he arrived. The house was buzzing with music and bright with colour.

"Mr David Dalton!" announced the butler as he entered the main room.

Everyone turned to look at him, many with expressions of surprise. After a moment's pause several people came over to shake his hand and declare how delighted they were to see him. Miss Wilson had been chatting to two ladies but as soon as the crowd dispersed around David he saw her steering them in his direction.

Should he apologise for his behaviour the previous week or act as if nothing had happened? He decided to take his cue from her.

"Hello again!"

She seems rather awkward but at least she's talking to me, he thought.

"So glad you could make it!" she continued. "May I introduce my sister, Mrs Grace Harrison?"

David bowed respectfully as he shook hands. "Mrs Harrison."

Her sister responded with a smile.

Stick to mundane conversation.

"This is a very fine gathering, Miss Wilson. I haven't seen this many people together for a long time."

"Yes, I thought it would be an ideal opportunity to get to know my new neighbours."

"Certainly."

A tall gentleman approached and spoke to her so David gratefully took his leave of the group and wandered off to mingle with the other guests, making small talk whenever required. When dinner was announced she reappeared, requesting him to partner one of her friends into the dining room. He found the lady very easy to talk to and the couple that were seated on his right were old acquaintances, so he was able to converse pleasantly throughout the meal.

The main course was salmon, his favourite, so by the time the ladies withdrew to the drawing room, leaving the men to their port and cigars, he found that he was actually enjoying himself. He didn't stay long, though, and made his getaway as soon as politeness allowed.

* * * *

Jamie missed Sarah terribly, but was not at all unhappy at George's departure. His strength was growing stronger day by day, as was his relationship with David, and he began to love him as a father. His memory had still not returned, but he occasionally recalled snatches of past times with his mother.

"I wish I could see her face more clear-like," he moaned as he threw a stone into the lake.

"I know, just give it time," consoled David. "I think we had better go and sit in the summer house as it looks ominously like rain, then you can do some more drawing."

Jamie had proven to have a natural artistic flair. It had soon been discovered that although he could count, he could barely read or write, so the whole household chipped in to help him whenever they had a spare moment. He had started doodling on the paper provided for writing practice, and had at first hidden his pictures, but Ruby had found them one day whilst tidying up.

"Did you draw these?" she had exclaimed, while Jamie had skulked behind the chair, afraid of being chastised for wasting paper. "They're brilliant!"

She had run to show them to Nellie who had immediately taken them to the master, dragging a bemused Jamie with her.

"This shows real talent," David had said, looking at each picture. "Have you really drawn these all by yourself?"

"Yes," Jamie was still hesitant of their reaction. "Do you really like 'em?"

"I certainly do. We shall have to ensure that you are encouraged to draw more often."

It was now quite normal to see Jamie with a wad of paper and a pencil, sketching anything and everything.

They sat down and David handed him a pencil. "That picture you drew of Lady was very good, you captured her so well."

"I loved drawing her. It was hard though, 'cos she wouldn't sit still." Jamie grinned as he tried to concentrate on his pencil marks, his tongue poking out.

"Freda was horrified at the picture you drew of her bending over the stove," laughed David.

"I didn't mean no harm."

"She knows that. She saw the funny side of it, eventually."

"P'raps I'd better not draw no more family portraits in case they gets me into trouble."

"Yes, that's probably a good idea," agreed David.

Jamie frequently reminded David that he had promised to build him a tree house, so, even though Freda and Nellie expressed their opposition to the scheme, stressing how dangerous it could be, one sunny morning his wish was granted. Enlisting Tom's help, planks of wood were carried down to the tree that David had singled out to be the most appropriate. Jamie carried the nails as he was eager to participate in the operation, and Ruby was also allowed to take part.

"We had a tree house when I was growing up, but my brothers would only let me and me sister go up in it on special occasions. We were so jealous," she reminisced to Jamie as they carried another load of supplies to the site.

"Where are they all now?"

"I don't know where my sister is. I haven't seen her since she left very suddenly—it must have been seven or eight years ago. My brothers both went into service as stable boys for a rich farmer the other side of Yorkshire. I sometimes get a birthday card from Matthew but haven't heard from Harry for a long while."

"What about your ma and pa?" Jamie wanted to know.

"Papa died in an accident down the mine when I was about seven, and that's why we all had to go out and earn our living. Mama wasn't very strong, and she never really got over it. She died a year after me and my sister came here."

"I can just about picture me ma, but I never had a pa."

"You must have had one once," argued Ruby. "Everyone has a father."

"Well, I don't remember one." Tears sprung up in his eyes as he ran on ahead.

"Hey, I didn't mean to upset you." She ran to catch up with him. "Come on, let's see how they're getting on."

After sawing and hammering all day, the men stood back and admired their handiwork. It consisted of a platform about four feet square, with slatted sides and a ladder leading up to the entrance.

"Can I sleep in it tonight?" Jamie began to climb the ladder.

"No, young man, I'm afraid not," replied David, wiping his brow with his handkerchief.

Stopping half way up, Jamie pouted.

"The weather's definitely not warm enough. But you can bring some cushions tomorrow and spend part of the day here if you wish."

Jamie brightened up a little but his face still showed his disappointment. He looked down beseechingly, but to no avail. "Well, can I stay for a while now?"

David took out his watch. "I'm afraid not, young man, we're going to be late for supper as it is. Cheer up. Nellie would never forgive me if you were to catch cold again. You wouldn't want me to get into trouble, now would you?"

"No," Jamie conceded, and climbed back down. He couldn't bear the thought of that happening.

Chapter 4

The following day Jamie was awake with the larks.

"What are you doing up so early?" asked Nellie when he ran into the kitchen. "Breakfast isn't ready yet."

"I ain't got time for no breakfast. I need some cushions for me tree house. Uncle David said I could spend the day there."

"Oh, he did, did he? Well I might have something to say about that."

"Aw, please, Nellie, I've been waiting me whole life for this day."

"Well…"

"Please…" he pleaded, his hands pressed together, sensing that she was weakening.

She raised her eyebrows in resignation and turned to Freda, who was frying liver and sausages on the old range. "You'd better find this young man something to eat please, Freda."

She turned back to Jamie who was hopping up and down with excitement. "You're not going without some food inside you, so sit down and eat what Freda gives you while I go and see what I can find in the way of cushions. I suppose we'd better make you some sandwiches for your lunch as well, if you're determined to stay there all day."

"Oh, thank you, thank you." Jamie climbed onto the nearest stool and gobbled down the food Freda placed in front of him, almost burning his mouth in his eagerness to be on his way.

Ten minutes later, armed with cushions and a blanket under one arm, a bag with sandwiches, a bottle of Freda's home-made lemonade and some books in the other, Jamie hurried down to the woods. Leaving the bag at the bottom of the tree, he clambered up the ladder, dragging the blanket behind him. He caught his foot in one of the folds on his way up, but managed to grab hold of a nearby branch just in time to save himself. He looked round nervously.

51

"Phew, good job nobody saw me do that," he exclaimed.

He arranged the cushions to make a seat with one at his back for padding. Too excited to read any of his books, he sat looking around. A bluetit came to rest on the branch at the side of him, its cheerful chirruping echoed in the distance by its mate. Jamie reached out to touch it but it was too wary and flew off into the woods.

It was so peaceful though. Jamie felt that this must be what heaven was like. For a split second, he thought he could see an angel hiding in a nearby tree but laughed when he realised it was a piece of white cloth caught on a branch. This was a hundred times better than his hideaway in the hedge, but he would still use that occasionally, if he didn't want to be found.

He looked around for his food and remembered he had left it at the foot of the ladder.

"Oh, fiddlesticks, I'll have to climb down and fetch it," he muttered as he leaned over the sill and saw it lying on the ground.

He climbed down, grabbed his bag, and clambered back up. He tucked into his feast of bread, cheese and ham, then finished it off with a juicy red apple he knew had been picked the previous autumn from the orchard. Wrapping up what was left, to save for later, he wiped his hand across his mouth and patted his full stomach.

The bluetit returned and swooped down to take advantage of a large crumb that he had dropped and then flew off quickly with it in its beak.

"I 'spose I'd better do some sums. I really want Uncle David to be proud of me so I gotta work hard."

Picking up the book David had prepared, he worked hard until he came to a particular sum that he just could not work out. He tried it various ways, but finally had to admit defeat. He felt like crying. "Uncle David'll be so disappointed in me."

He took another swig of lemonade. Perhaps he'd have more luck with the spelling words. At least he could learn them by heart. He began to recite the letters over and over again until he knew them perfectly.

"Now I'll try some writing."

Sitting chewing the end of his pencil, pondering what to write, he looked up and saw a squirrel above him, nibbling at a nut in its paw. He watched it until it licked its lips and ran down the tree to find another one.

"I know, I'll write a story about a squirrel," he exclaimed. "But how do you spell it? S-k-w-i-r-l. That looks 'bout right." So he began a story about a young squirrel called Sid, and his adventures, also drawing some pictures to go with the words. He was so engrossed that he didn't realise it was getting late until he heard Ruby calling from the bottom of the ladder.

A minute later her face appeared over the lintel. "Come on, it's time for tea. I won't try to climb in, it looks so cosy I might spoil it, so I'll wait for you at the bottom."

"I won't be long." Jamie packed up his books, then covered the cushions with the blanket, and with a final look round, he joined her.

"Weren't you bored up there all by yourself?" asked Ruby as they walked back. "I can't see any pleasure in sitting on your own all day."

"No, I weren't on me own really." He told her about all the animals and birds who had come to visit him.

"Tomorrow I might see a jay. I'd love to see a jay. I've see'd 'em in Uncle David's books, they've got blue feathers. Or even a golden eagle."

"I can't say I've ever seen anything like that. Wouldn't know one if I saw one."

"I could show you their pictures in the books, and then we could go out and look for 'em." Jamie looked up at her hopefully.

"I never have time to look at books. I work all the hours God gives and then I'm usually too tired to do anything but go to bed." Ruby wistfully shook her head.

"Don't you have no time off?"

"One afternoon a fortnight. I usually go and visit my grandmamma. She lives in a cottage up at Clandon."

"Is that far?"

"No, only about three miles."

Perhaps I could come with you one day, if Uncle David lets me."

"Well, she'd love to see you. I've told her all about you."

"Let's go and ask him now."

* * * *

David was pleased that he hadn't made a fool of himself at Christine Wilson's party, and he could rest assured that his integrity had remained intact. He had rather enjoyed the evening, actually, and decided that it was time to start socialising again, just in a small way to start with.

He went to find Nellie. "I think it's time I held a party for the estate workers like we used to when Elizabeth was alive. I know it's traditional to have one on May Day, but we've missed that, so do you think it could be arranged for next Sunday?"

"Oh yes. I think that would be a grand idea." Nellie put down the sheet she had been ironing. "I'll sort out the food with Freda and get Tom to spread the word around." David smiled as she scuttled off to the kitchen. It was so good to have happy faces around him.

* * * *

The morning dawned sunny and warm. The previous day had been very overcast with rain threatening, but the sky was now a brilliant blue. Every available person, including a few of the local villagers, was employed at setting up the long trestle tables out in the orchard before going to church.

"Please let me stay," pleaded Jamie when he was told it was time for him to get changed into his Sunday clothes ready for the service.

"There'll be plenty of time when we get back."

He realised that David was adamant, so begrudgingly did as he was told. He had started going to church each Sunday and actually quite enjoyed the singing and the prayers. He couldn't really understand the sermons, but he endured them by practising some simple mental arithmetic, receiving a glare from David when accidentally saying the answer aloud. The starched collar of his brown shirt dug into his neck and the heavy breeches were itchy, so he couldn't wait to get changed back into his loose everyday clothes as soon as they returned home.

Collecting Lady, he ran out to join the scene of activity.

"Can't you find anything useful to do?" cried Nellie as one of the tables was almost knocked over by the energetic pair. "There's a pile of spoons on the kitchen table. You should be able to carry them out without mishap."

Jamie ran back to the house and found the spoons. Concentrating on not dropping them, with Lady running around his legs, he almost bumped into David.

"Hey! Watch out, young man."

"Uncle David, Nellie's asked me to help."

David looked around at everybody scurrying hither and thither. "I suppose I had better pull my weight and get stuck in." Pulling up his shirtsleeves he hurried over to one of the tables that had not yet been covered, and proceeded to lay the white sheet that had been left there for that purpose.

The smell of baking filled the house the whole morning and by noon the tables were creaking under the weight of pies and breads and assorted sweetmeats.

At last it was ready. The estate workers began to arrive, dressed in their Sunday best, and soon everybody was tucking into the feast.

"This be the best spread we've had for many a long year," said one of the farm managers, raising his cup. "To the master!"

Everyone nodded in agreement and raised their drinks. "To the master!"

David stood up and gave a short speech about how pleased he was that the Estate was in such a good position financially, and that it was all due to their hard work, then they all raised their glasses again. "God save the Queen!" rang out from everyone's lips.

A group of fiddlers had been engaged for the entertainment, and as some people finished their meals they began to dance. Others urged on the dancers, clapping to the music, whilst some broke off into groups and played games. The festivities continued well into the evening, until the light began to fade. A few imbibed a glass too many of the excellent cider and had to be almost carried home, but everybody declared the day to be a resounding success.

As Nellie went round checking the orchard the following morning she was startled by a gangly youth unfolding himself from beneath a hedge. "My goodness, it's the new stable lad! Had a bit too much to drink, did we?" she laughed.

The lad yawned and stretched. "Me 'ead 'urts!" he groaned.

"That's not all that'll hurt if you don't get to work straight away. You're lucky most people are in a similar state after the great party we had. Go and splash some water on your face from that horse trough and try to sober up."

He did as Nellie bid and wandered off in the direction of the stables. She smiled to herself and shook her head as she continued to pick up discarded rubbish. She saw Jamie running towards her. "I've just seen that new stable lad with his hair all wet. He fell over twice 'cos he could hardly walk straight. It was so funny."

"Well, that's what happens when people drink too much. So, be warned, young man."

"Oh, I shan't never do nothing like that when I'm grown up. I don't want no one laughing at me!"

"It's easy to say that now," smiled Nellie as she ruffled Jamie's hair. "But if you keep that thought in your head as you get older, you shouldn't come to too much harm. Now, I think I've cleared it all up, but I'll leave you in charge of checking that nothing has been left behind while I take this rubbish back. Do you think you could manage that?"

"Oh yes, you can trust me and Lady."

They charged round the orchard and surrounding area, making sure everything had been cleared up, running in so many circles that Jamie got dizzy and collapsed in a heap, giggling.

Lying on the grass, recovering, he saw a slight movement out of the corner of his eye, and at the same time heard a faint mewing. He peered to see what had caught his attention. It moved again. Lady began to growl and crawl towards it. Jamie could just make out a brownish shape. "No, Lady!" he yelled desperately as he jumped up and overtook the dog. "Leave!"

He found a young fox cub with its paw caught in a piece of wire. "Oh, you poor thing, let's get you out o' there."

This was easier said than done. The cub had sharp little teeth and didn't seem at all grateful for what Jamie was trying to do. Snapping and snarling, it thwarted every effort he made to disentangle its injured leg from the wire. Lady was not helping the situation either, in fact she was making things worse by poking her nose at it and yelping.

"What are we going to do?" He looked around desperately. "We can't leave you 'ere. A fox, or somat'd soon catch you. Oh, you are a fox. Well, you know what I mean."

He managed to free the frightened animal when it was too exhausted to struggle any longer. He put it inside his jacket. "I'll prob'ly get into trouble for getting blood on me shirt, but I've got to get yer some help."

Lady was making a nuisance of herself. "Stop jumping up, you can't have it," he yelled. Looking around again, he had an idea. "I know, I'll find Tom. He's good with animals."

He knew the gamekeeper did his rounds in the mornings, looking for poachers, checking that the fences were still intact, and that sort of thing. He wondered whereabouts he would be. He headed towards the lake. From there he could see across the fields to the north, but there was no sign of Tom there, so he began to walk in the opposite direction. He hadn't been this far out before on his own.

"I think we might be lost." He looked down at Lady who was now trotting calmly beside him. "Where d' you think we should go now?"

The dog merely yelped and ran round in a circle.

"You ain't much help." He laughed, although he was beginning to get worried. After a short while he came across a paddock where he could see some horses cantering around. "I must be close to the house," he exclaimed with a huge sigh of relief, "there's Sam over there."

He ran over to the groom and showed him the sleeping animal inside his jacket.

"It's hurt, and I was looking for Tom to ask him if he could make it better. Do you know where he is?"

"No, haven't seen him this morning. Would you like me to have a look at it?"

Sam took the fox cub and it lay unmoving as he gently stroked it.

Taking one look at the groom's sombre face Jamie cried, "You will be able to save it, won't you?"

"I don't know, young man, the injury's pretty severe. But, tell you what, we'll find a box in the stables and make it comfortable, and see how it gets on."

Crossing over to the stables, they went into an unoccupied stall. It was so dusty that Jamie immediately began to sneeze.

"You soon get used to it," Sam explained as he found a box, filled it with straw and laid the cub in it. Showing no resistance it snuggled down.

"It's very young to be parted from its mother. But perhaps if we dip a glove in some milk we might be able to feed it."

"I'll go and find some milk," volunteered Jamie who was desperate to save the baby fox.

"And I know where I can lay my hands on an old glove."

Jamie ran over to the cowsheds. As luck would have it there were some churns outside and, lifting the lid off the first one, he saw that it was full. The smell of the warm milk rose to fill his nostrils. Dipping in the ladle that was hanging on the side, he couldn't resist having a drink before refilling it and hurrying back.

"I see you found some milk," laughed Sam, pointing to his chin.

Jamie wiped his face with the back of his sleeve and grinned. "I didn't think no one'd mind."

Dipping the glove in the milk, Sam then put it to the cub's mouth. It licked pathetically at it a few times and gave up, not knowing what to do with it.

"I'll try again later." Sam closed the door behind them. "After I've mucked out the other stalls."

"I'll come back after I've had me lunch," Jamie called as he ran off.

The fox cub began to thrive once it found out how to suckle the milk. Sam kept it secretly in the unused stable stall, where it slept contentedly in the box. Jamie went to check on it twice a day and even gave it a name, Rufus, after a fox in a book he had been reading. The Rufus in the book had survived many adventures and he hoped that his new pet would do the same.

* * * *

"Thank goodness, a signpost," muttered Tillie as she saw a fork in the road ahead. "I'll be able to tell if I'm going in the right direction." Reaching it, she could just make out the word 'Welton', but the distance was too indistinct. She looked around at her surroundings. Nothing but trees and fields as far as the eye could see to her left, but over a hill, in the direction to which the signpost pointed, she could just make out the top of a church spire.

It didn't look that far, she should make it before nightfall. It would be nice to get back to civilisation at last. Her stomach gave an almighty rumble to remind her how empty it was. All she had eaten that day were some berries found in the hedgerow and half a raw turnip. She didn't like cooked turnip very much and raw ones were even less palatable. The previous day she had found some wild strawberries. They had been delicious. Her mouth watered at the thought of them.

She quickened her pace and reached the first shop, the village bakery, just as the owner was closing the door.

"Please..." She hammered on the door in desperation.

"We're closed, can't you read the sign?"

"I only want some stale bread or cake. Please...I haven't eaten for days," Tillie begged her with tears streaming down her face.

Sighing, the shopkeeper reopened the door a little and Tillie fell into the shop, slumping on the floor almost unconscious.

"Hey. Get up, you're not fooling me."

Tillie could vaguely hear her but was too weak to respond. She felt herself being prodded with the tip of a shoe.

"What's the matter with you?"

Tillie could just make out an elderly lady with a shock of white hair. She tried to sit up. "I'm sorry. I'm just so hungry. If you could..." She collapsed onto the floor again before she could continue.

"Expect I'll regret this, I will, but I can't turn you out in this state. Let's get you in. No funny business, mind."

She helped Tillie into an armchair. "You sit there an' I'll make us a nice cup of tea. Name's Becky, by the way."

"I'm Tillie," was her weak reply.

A short while later Tillie sat back and patted her stomach. "That stew was delicious, but I hope I haven't had anybody else's share, I mean…"

"No, no," Becky explained as she started to clear the table. "Still always cook enough for two, I do. I can't get out of the habit since my Bert died. Stew was his special favourite. And it's no bother to cook 'cos I can leave it to 'stew' away on the back of the stove while I'm in the shop, I can." Straightening, she laughed at her own joke.

Tillie smiled as she piled the plates on top of each other. "What happened to him?" she asked more soberly.

Becky's face tightened. "Died last year…consumption," she replied with a tear in her eye. "Only ever had one child, we did, such a lovely little girl, long golden ringlets and big blue eyes, died of whooping cough, only three years old." She wiped her eyes with the corner of her apron. "God never blessed us with any more babies."

She carried the dishes over to the sink and began washing them, a faraway look in her eye. "But it wasn't for the lack of trying." She grinned ruefully before continuing. "So now I'm all on my own. Anyway, you're supposed to be telling me your troubles, not the other way round."

Tillie was too tired to respond. Sitting back in the cosy armchair, she felt herself being covered with a blanket before her eyes closed.

Awaking with a start a short time later, she thought for a split second that she was back in the prison. Then she realised she couldn't be, for she was far too comfy.

She wondered whether her last cellmate had survived. Having come into the prison with a slight cough a month ago, she had steadily gone downhill due to the unsanitary conditions. The hard labour they had to endure in the steamy laundry had actually been a respite from the unhealthy dampness in the cells. These factors, combined with the silence they were supposed to maintain and the monotonous diet, all contributed to the feeling of being in hell. She prayed with all her heart that she would never have to return there.

Once she had found her little boy she would somehow find a means of supporting them both so that she wouldn't have to steal ever again.

Drifting off to sleep once more, she dreamt that she was a rich lady dressed in a pink ball gown, living in a grand house, being waited on hand and foot by kindly servants, and she slept peacefully for the first time in a long while.

Chapter 5

It seemed as if the whole neighbourhood had gathered for the hunt. David was the Master of Fox Hounds, being the most influential land owner in the area. He knew he cut a handsome figure in his scarlet coat and black breeches and was proud of the fact. Surveying the colourful scene before him with excitement, he looked around at the other huntsmen, the masters and whippers-in, many of whom, like him, were dressed in scarlet coats, called 'pinks'.

An invitation had been sent out to all the neighbours, so he wondered whether Christine Wilson would be attending. Wheeling Starlight round, he saw her riding towards him with her sister at her side. Dressed in black coats with pink collars, pale breeches and black boots, they looked a pretty picture, happily chatting to each other.

"Good day to you, Miss Wilson, Mrs Harrison, I'm so glad you could make it," he called.

"We wouldn't have missed it for the world, Mr Dalton," replied Grace Harrison as they drew abreast with him. "Your hunts are renowned around these parts. We couldn't wait, could we, Christine?"

Her sister looked up and smiled. "No, we couldn't. It's all Grace has spoken about for the past week. I haven't been able to talk to her on any other subject."

"We haven't seen you since my sister's soirée," Grace Harrison addressed David again.

"No, I've been so busy with organising today's events that I haven't had time for anything else. I hope you enjoy the hunt. Have you attended one before?"

Christine was about to speak but Grace cut in again. "No, I haven't, that's why I'm so excited. Christine has, of course. I don't think there's anything she hasn't tried."

"What do you mean?" began Christine, glaring at her sister.

David could sense an argument ensuing so decided to make his getaway. "I can see my huntsman beckoning me, so must get everyone assembled. Do help yourselves to drinks. Perhaps we'll talk some more later."

As he rode through the throng of horses and hounds his excitement rose. The colours, the atmosphere and the sounds of the baying foxhounds, eager to be on their way, the anticipation of the kill and the sheer thrill of riding over the countryside in pursuit of their quarry, all contributed to the most memorable event of the season.

Everyone was ready. The huntsman sounded his horn and the cry of 'tally ho!' echoed around the valley. The charge was on. At the head of the main group David led the field, his hunter clearing the hedges with ease, followed by the other strong riders. Everyone wanted to be in at the kill so did their best to keep up, but a few stragglers kept up the rear with those who had come on foot. They rode for about an hour without seeing any prey, the hounds doing their best to flush out any unwary fox, but without success.

* * * *

Jamie was debating whether to visit Rufus before or after lunch. Seeing the mass of riders and hounds assembling at the front of the house, he recalled David's answer to his earlier plea to let him take part.

"Absolutely not, it is much too dangerous for children to come anywhere near."

Jamie had known deep down what the answer would be but he had had to try.

"However, I have been thinking of letting you learn to ride," David had continued. "We have a couple of ponies that would suit you. They're rather old but would be ideal for a child. Remind me tomorrow and I'll get Sam to sort things out."

Now if I go this morning, he thought, *I can tell Sam about the riding lessons as well as checking on Rufus,* so as soon as he saw the last huntsperson leave he ran down to the stables.

"I s'pose he's joined the hunt," he murmured when there was no sign of Sam. "He's never let me in on me own before, but I'm sure I'll be all right."

He tried to open the door and managed to create a gap small enough to squeeze through, but before he could get in, a body of red fur bounded out, almost knocking him over.

"Stop!" he shouted desperately as he chased after the young fox. "Rufus, come back!"

* * * *

"Good day to you," said Becky cheerfully the next morning as she turned from raking the fire.

Tillie yawned then jumped up, the smell of baking bread filling her nostrils. "Um...good day to you too. You should have woken me earlier."

"You were sleeping so contentedly, you were, I hadn't the heart to wake you."

"I did sleep really well, and I can't thank you enough for letting me stay the night."

"Well, I didn't really have no option, I didn't, seeing as how you fell asleep in my chair." The old lady grinned, her face red from the hot ovens. "To be truthful, it's nice to have someone to talk to, it is."

She put a fresh batch of bread rolls into the oven before making a pot of tea.

"So you don't know where your little lad is?" Becky asked later when Tillie explained why she was wandering the countryside and came to land in a heap in her doorway. "Oh, drat, there's the shop doorbell again. Pity I can't shut up for the day, but can't afford to do that, I can't, so finish your tea while I go and serve."

The steady stream of customers meant that Becky was too busy for Tillie to continue her narrative. Feeling guilty at sitting doing nothing, she ventured into the shop and asked if she could help in any way.

Becky pointed to some bread on the shelf behind her. "You could wrap those two loaves for Mrs Fletcher. She'll be here to collect them any minute, and I like to have them ready for her."

As she said this, she handed a ginger cake to a young girl in a ragged dress that had probably once been yellow but had obviously been handed down so many times that the colour had faded.

"There you are, deary, and don't go nibbling at it before you get home today. When I saw your grandpapa in the tavern last week he accused me of having mice."

Grinning as she handed over the money, the girl turned to go out, but before she reached the door it was opened forcefully by a large woman, dressed in a black coat and a fancy hat with red feathers.

"Ah, good day to you, Mrs Fletcher," Becky addressed the woman with a bow of her head. Tillie could see that there were other customers already waiting to be served but they all stood aside for her. *She must be someone of importance*, she thought.

"Your loaves, Mrs Fletcher. Would there be anything else today?" Becky didn't seem over-awed as she handed over the bread.

"I'll take two of your small fancy cakes and a large fruit pie, Rebecca, if you please," replied the customer in a very mannerly voice, which reinforced Tillie's previous opinion of her. She turned and peered at Tillie contemptuously through her pince-nez. "And who might this young woman be?"

"This is Tillie, a friend."

"It's short for Matilda." The woman had begun to screw up her nose, so Tillie thought that she might not look down on her with such disdain if she showed that she had a respectable name.

"Humph!" The red feathers bobbed up and down as Tillie was scrutinised again, but they soon lost interest. "Put it on my account, if you would be so kind, and have the same ready for me next week." Without a backward glance, she gathered up her purchases and flounced out of the shop. Everyone remaining breathed a collective sigh of relief and began chattering again.

"She thinks she's so high and mighty." One of the customers in the queue pulled a face at the departing harridan but Becky stuck up for her.

"She's a good customer, she is, and her bill is always paid on time."

"Don't know why she doesn't send one of her servants," another said.

Half-listening to them, Tillie could see out of the corner of her eye that the girl in the faded dress had been about to take a biscuit from the shelf, but she saw Tillie glance towards her and skulked out without it. Tillie didn't know whether to feel sorrier for the youngster, who was probably in the habit of doing this sort of thing and so in danger of being caught, or for Becky who must be losing money daily from pilferers. It had never occurred to her before to feel any compunction for the shopkeeper from whom she had tried to steal the loaf, and it seemed ironic that she was now indebted to a baker for her very life.

"I know it happens." Becky nodded when Tillie recounted the incident later. She reached into the hot oven to take out a fresh tray of steaming pies. "I often turn a blind eye, I do, depending on who it is. Folks round here don't have a lot of money, you know, and if I can help out a bit..." She smiled and shrugged her shoulders as she pointed to a tray of different shaped biscuits they had prepared earlier. "Pass me that tray, would you?"

Tillie handed it to her. The tantalising smell of the cooked pies set her mouth watering as she marvelled at how generous some people could be.

"You sure you feel well enough to be going?" Becky asked, concern etching her face when Tillie told her the following morning that she needed to be on her way. She had slept in the comfy armchair again.

"Yes, I must, and thank you for everything. I just have to find my son."

"I understand. I do hope that you find him safe. I'm going to miss you, I've really enjoyed having someone to talk to, I have. You must keep in touch."

"I certainly will. I need to return this, at least." Tillie picked up the tapestry bag that Becky had lent her. It contained a freshly laundered pink-striped muslin dress, the likes of which she hadn't seen in a long while. She hadn't the faintest idea when she would ever have the opportunity to wear it, but just knowing that she had it was enough to boost her self esteem.

"It doesn't fit me any longer, and never will again, so it might as well go to a good home." Becky had folded it carefully and placed it in the bag together with some clean undergarments.

Tillie was also wearing a dark blue dress of Becky's that was more appropriate for travelling in than the pink one, so the old brown one had been thrown away. She had momentarily considered retaining it as a keepsake but decided that that part of her life was well and truly over and she was making a new start.

After draping her thin shawl over her shoulders, she picked up the bread and cakes that the kindly baker had given her for the journey, then, giving her a large hug, she waved farewell.

As she walked, she recalled the story she had told Becky whilst they were eating the previous evening.

"A local farrier I hadn't seen before came to the house where I worked as the parlour maid, to shoe the master's horse," she had begun. "I was crying and he put his arm around my shoulders and led me into a barn. I went with him,

68

fool that I was. I didn't realise what he intended. I just thought he wanted to talk."

"How old were you?" Becky had asked.

"Fifteen, but I should still have known better. I fought him tooth and nail when he started to undress me, but I was no match for him."

"Why had you been crying?"

"I had just heard that my sweetheart had died in a freak accident. He was the youngest son of a neighbouring farmer and we were secretly planning to get married when he was of age, 'cos we knew his parents wouldn't approve of me." She stopped and Becky put her hand on her arm.

"We hadn't...you know," she had continued after a pause. "Much as he had wanted to. But I hadn't felt ready. Anyway, I thought if I pleaded with my attacker and explained that I was still intact he would stop, but it only seemed to excite him more."

"You poor love," Becky had said sympathetically. "Did you ever see him again?"

"No. By the time I realised I was expecting he'd left the area and nobody knew where he'd gone. I couldn't stay in my position at The Grange, so when I saw some gypsies passing through the neighbourhood I joined up with them and left my old life behind."

Remembering Becky's look of distress at her plight, her eyes filled with tears but brushing them aside she walked briskly on.

She arrived in the village of Welton in the late afternoon. The first building she came across was the church, and deciding that some divine intervention might help she entered into its dark interior. It was so peaceful and quiet. Kneeling down in the back pew she prayed as she had never prayed before. Calm enveloped her and she felt at ease. Hearing a sudden movement behind her, she turned to see a mouse scurrying across the floor, and as she stood up to go out, the sun shone brightly through the stained glass windows, bathing the whole church in a myriad of colours. She smiled, knowing that all would be well from now on.

* * * *

Jamie ran after the young fox as fast as he could, but had to give up when it disappeared out of sight into the distance.

"What am I going to do?" he yelled, raising his hands in the air and clasping them behind his head. Suddenly, he heard the sound of the hunt in the distance.

"Oh no!" he cried desperately as first one foxhound, then another, appeared from behind a group of trees. He stood transfixed for a moment, terrified that they would come after him, but they ran off in the opposite direction.

"I must find him before they do," he exclaimed as he sprang back into action. He knew it would be an impossible task but couldn't let his new pet be caught by the baying hounds. He wasn't sure what they would do with it but felt sure it would be something bad.

What could he do? He racked his brains. Then a brilliant idea occurred to him. If he could get Rufus's blanket and somehow give that to the dogs, it might put them off his scent.

He sprinted back to the stable and, gathering up the blanket, ran off in the direction he had seen the foxhounds going.

David was enjoying the hunt more than usual. He couldn't put his finger on the reason why. Perhaps it was his newfound feeling of bonhomie, but whatever it was, he gave in to it and rode with sheer delight and exhilaration. His dark eyes sparkling, he felt alive and reckless, and cleared obstacles higher than he would have previously thought possible.

I'd better not get too far ahead of the field though, he thought, looking around and finding himself almost alone, with just one or two fellow hunters in sight. He slowed down to let some of the others catch up.

"Hey, old fellow, I don't know what you have been taking but I'd like to try some of it," called Charlie Hodges, the huntsman, as he caught up. "Some of those hedges were positively unjumpable but you cleared them. How on earth did you do it?"

"I'm not really sure," replied David as others pulled alongside. "Just got carried away, I think. Anyway, any sign of a fox?"

"Not a one," replied Charlie, looking around at the others. "Has anyone seen anything like a fox?"

There was a general rumble of 'no's, and shaking of heads.

"They're all over the place usually." David reined in Starlight as he began to buck. "Today someone must have told them about us, and they've all gone into hiding."

They all laughed.

Christine and her sister trotted over. Grace's beaming face was ruddy from the wind. "Haven't enjoyed anything so much in my whole life," she exclaimed. "So glad you invited us."

"You're both very welcome." David looked at Christine to see how she was faring. Some of her golden curls had escaped from her hat and her hazel eyes lit up her glowing face.

She looked up at him and smiled. "Do you think we'll catch a fox today?" She attempted to push a curl back under her hat. "We've been out a long time without seeing one, haven't we?"

"Yes," Grace agreed as she wheeled her skittish horse around to face them again. "I thought the whole purpose of the hunt was to rid the countryside of vermin."

"Well, it doesn't look as if we are going to," replied David. "If everyone agrees I think we may as well call it a day."

Just then, the hounds that had been milling round sniffing in the leaves suddenly set up a loud yapping and they all turned to face one way. A fox had been sighted. This was what they had come for.

"Tally ho!" the yell went up and every man, woman and beast cantered off after it.

David kept abreast of Christine. They were moving too fast to hold any conversation, but he could see her glancing towards him every now and again. Grace galloped on ahead, giving her mare full rein.

They came to the end of the field where the fox had been sighted when suddenly the majority of the hounds turned and headed off in a different direction. Puzzled, the riders followed.

Then they saw the reason. A small boy was running at full pelt ahead of them, and the hounds were gaining on him.

"Isn't that...?" David heard Charlie utter.

"My God, it's Jamie," he cried in consternation. "What on earth...?" He didn't have time to complete the sentence as he dug his heels into Starlight's flanks and rode towards the boy at breakneck speed. Catching up with him just as the leading hound was about to pounce, he leaned down and scooped him up in one fluid movement.

The baying hounds attacked the blanket that Jamie had dropped as he was being hauled up, pulling it to shreds within seconds.

David wheeled Starlight round and pulled up as the rest of the riders gathered round.

"Is he hurt?" "Is he all right?" he could hear everyone asking. Panting and speechless he sat cradling Jamie in his arms.

"I didn't want them to catch Rufus," Jamie wailed.

"You could have been killed," gasped David, finding his voice. "I can't believe you did such a stupid thing."

"But Rufus was my pet. He escaped," Jamie tried to explain. "I couldn't let him get caught." He burst into tears, hiding his face in David's jacket.

"It doesn't look like there's any harm done." Christine leaned over and stroked Jamie's back. "Don't be too hard on him."

Hard on him, thought David, torn between relief and anger. *I could bloody kill him*. But, gritting his teeth, he turned to the crowd. "I think we've had enough amusement for one day, everybody, so I'll bid you all good day." He rode off towards the house, not caring whether or not the rest of the hunt carried on without him, with one arm around Jamie, who was still whimpering softly into his chest.

* * * *

I'm actually here in Welton at last, thought Tillie as she looked around her. *But where do I start?* She walked down the main street and paused outside the bakery shop from where she had stolen the loaf. Should she go in and explain? Peering through the window, she could see a man behind the counter, but he wasn't the same one who had caught her so there was no point. She continued down the street.

A little voice in her head kept telling her to go and check out the barn where she had left her son. This would be totally illogical. As if he would still be there six months later! But she had to do it, just to see if there were any clues as to what did happen to him.

Hurrying towards it, she saw a young child in the distance. Could it be him? She ran forward, but as the child turned round she could see that it wasn't even a boy, it was a girl wearing a white pinafore over a dark green dress.

Pull yourself together and remember the feeling you had back in the church, she said to herself, sighing. *It will all work out, just have patience.*

"Hello." Reaching the girl she bent down to her level. "My name's Tillie. What's yours?"

The girl looked up at her under her lashes and stuck her thumb in her mouth.

"I don't suppose you know a little boy called Jamie?" Tillie asked hopefully.

The green eyes continued to stare at her.

Tillie looked around to see if her mother was around, but there was nobody in sight. "Now what do I do?" she murmured. "I don't like the thought of her being out here on her own."

"Where do you live?" she tried. No response. "Where's your mama?"

The girl pointed with her free hand towards a cottage further down the street.

"Would you like me to take you to her?"

The child put her hand in Tillie's and started walking towards the cottage, still not saying a word, thumb still firmly in her mouth. As they approached, a harassed looking woman appeared.

"There you are," she cried, grabbing the girl and enfolding her in her apron. "I've been looking for you, dinner's ready."

She looked at Tillie warily. "Who are you, and what are you doing with our lass?"

"Pray, don't be alarmed, madam, I found your daughter wandering up the street alone, and thought I'd better bring her home. I didn't mean any harm, please believe me."

"It's all right," the woman conceded with a smile. "This little monkey here does have a habit of wandering off on her own, don't you?" She tickled the little girl under her chin, which made her giggle, but not enough to dislodge the thumb.

"Do I know you?" She looked again at Tillie. "You look vaguely familiar."

"Possibly, I lived here last year for a short time until…"

"Are we 'aving this dinner or what?" a man's voice bellowed from inside the cottage.

"Coming dear," shouted back the woman. "Must go," she said. "Doesn't do to keep his lordship waiting."

Hurrying inside, she dragged the little girl behind her, leaving Tillie annoyed at missing out on the chance to ask about her son. She walked towards the barn.

Memories returned when she passed the shell of a large house set back from the others. Hurrying past as fast as she could, trying to block them out, she reached the barn and pushed open the large doors. What a disappointment, it was empty apart from a pair of cooing doves perched high in the eaves. Not even a bale of hay.

"What did you expect?" she asked herself.

Leaving the barn after a final look around to ensure she hadn't missed anything, and back out in the sunshine, she decided she had better face her memories.

She and her son were supposed to have been making a fresh start after leaving the gypsy band they had been living with for the previous seven years. She and her friend Lucy had decided that they wanted some stability for their children, Jamie and Maisie, as they were weary of travelling around the countryside peddling pegs and whatever else they could lay their hands on to sell.

But it had all gone horribly wrong.

* * * *

David was so angry that he sent Jamie straight to his room. Nellie came running into his study as he helped himself to a large brandy to calm his shaking hands.

"What on earth's happened?" she cried. "I've just seen Jamie running upstairs in tears and couldn't get any sense out of him."

He couldn't trust himself to speak and turned away to stare out of the window. In the distance he could see one or two stragglers returning from the hunt and felt a faint twinge of remorse at his bad manners in leaving them the way he had. Finishing the drink he walked over to pour another.

"Are you going to tell me what's going on?" repeated Nellie, sounding more anxious this time.

David cast a ravaged look at her before polishing off the second drink in one gulp. "I thought..." He raised his stricken blue eyes to the ceiling. "I thought he was going to be killed. I couldn't bear to lose another one."

They heard the doorbell ring and David sighed as Pervis entered.

"Whoever it is, please send them away, Pervis. I'm not up to entertaining at the moment," he managed to say.

"It's Miss Wilson and Mrs Harrison, sir. They are enquiring after young master Jamie."

"Please tell them he's fine."

"Is that all, sir?" Pervis looked enquiringly at Nellie who shook her head and followed him out of the room when there was no further response.

Through a chink in the open door, David could see Christine and her sister in the hall. He knew it was the height of discourtesy not to receive them but in his present mood he couldn't be sure that he would be civil, let alone welcoming. He saw Christine look towards his door and he turned away, his handsome face creased with desolation. Nellie re-entered as he was about to pour out another drink. She took the decanter from his cold hands and placed it back on the table.

"Now then, are you going to tell me the full story? Miss Wilson and Mrs Harrison told me the basic facts, but they weren't sure of all the details."

"No more am I," replied David. "I just know that I snatched him from the claws of death in the nick of time."

He sat down, wringing his hands, trying to make sense of the day's happenings. "I have no idea what he was doing there, something about a pet called Rufus. Do you know anything about it?"

"Me? No, I haven't the faintest idea, but I'll get to the bottom of it, don't you worry. I think I'd better go up and check that he's all right." Looking at David's mud-spattered attire she suggested, "And perhaps you'd better get out of those dirty clothes and make yourself a bit more presentable."

He continued to sit with his arms resting on his knees, hands tightly clenched, staring down at his feet.

Nellie patted his shoulder. "Come on, now. I know you've had a nasty shock but..." David grabbed her, put his arms around her waist, and buried his face in her apron.

"There, there," she consoled him as if he was still a child, and raising his face she wiped his eyes with her apron. "It's good to know you can still release your emotions."

"Oh, Nellie, what would I do without you?" replied David ruefully as he stood up and ran his fingers through his black hair. "I'm sure I can trust you not to divulge this to anyone," he continued in a secretive voice. "It wouldn't do for anybody else to know that their master was so vulnerable."

"Of course, lad. You know you can rely on me to be the soul of discretion." Nellie opened the door and checked that there was nobody within hearing distance. "You get off upstairs while I get a bath organised for you, then I'll check on young Jamie."

Jamie had gone straight to his bedroom in tears. All he wanted to do was lie down but after taking one look at his filthy trousers he thought better of it. He didn't want to get into more trouble by dirtying the sheets, so hastily removing his muddy clothes, poured some water from the jug into the basin on the bedside table and washed his hands and face. This made him feel a lot better and braver.

He paced up and down, wearing only his underclothes, wondering what to do next. Then a horrible thought crossed his mind. "What if Uncle David throws me out?" he moaned. "I've never seen him so angry before. He might not want me here anymore!"

Where would he go? What would he do?

Suddenly, a faint memory surfaced at the back of his mind. He could see himself hiding in a barn, waiting. Waiting for what? He tried hard to remember, but couldn't. Pictures of his mother started dancing around inside his head until he thought it would burst. Covering it with his hands, and screwing his eyes up tightly, he curled up in a ball in the corner of the room.

"Oh, Jamie," he heard someone cry. "Don't distress yourself so!"

Hearing a familiar voice, Jamie assumed it belonged to the face in his mind.

"Oh, Mama, I waited and waited but you never came back!"

"Hush now, you're safe." He felt himself being enfolded in warm, soft arms and being rocked to sleep.

"I hope this doesn't set him back, he's been making such progress." Freda looked up from rolling pastry as Nellie recounted the incident on her return to the kitchen. "I've noticed a change in Ruby also, since he's been here, she seems a lot chirpier," she remarked as the maid went out humming. "It's bringing her out of her shell, having him around."

"I've noticed that, too," replied Nellie, opening a box of candles. "Now where did I put that candlestick? I'm sure I brought it in here." She searched the table, picking up utensils and bowls.

"You mean that one?" asked Freda pointing her floury finger at a large, gold candelabra on the sideboard.

"Oh, I'd lose my head if it wasn't screwed on," laughed Nellie, as she took out the remnants of the old candles and put them in a pan to melt down, then replaced them with new ones.

"I wonder if this means Master Jamie's regaining his memory. The doctor did say that it would return one day, didn't he?"

Tom entered as they were talking, took off his cloth cap and placed it on the table with his clay pipe. He filled a bowl with water and put it at the back door for Bridie. "Did I hear you say that the young lad's getting his memory back?" He sat down and took a large bite out of the slice of cake Freda placed before him. "That's good news, isn't it?" he mumbled, spitting crumbs all over the table.

"Tom Briggs, don't you have any manners?" retorted Freda as he swallowed the cake down with a drink of tea.

"Sorry, but you know how much I love your seed cake. You haven't made any for a while."

"That's because I have more important things to do than pander to your tastes," she replied, although she did look rather pleased at the compliment.

"Anyway, getting back to the boy...is he all right after that incident this afternoon with the fox?" Tom looked from Nellie to Freda as he drank the rest of his tea.

"Well, he's fine, physically. We were wondering if the shock had sparked off some memory," replied Nellie as she sat down beside him. "He was rambling when I went into him earlier."

"Do you know what happened?"

Nellie recounted what Christine Wilson had told her.

"She heard him say it was a pet?"

"That's what she said."

"Strange," mused Tom, scratching his head. "I can't imagine how he came to have a pet fox. Surely we would have known about it. Where did he keep it?"

They both shook their heads.

"Do you know if it survived, or was it caught?"

"Don't know that either," replied Nellie. "But...ah, Ruby," she called as the maid re-entered. "Have you put away that pile of laundry I gave you?"

"Yes," replied Ruby. "It's all done."

"Good girl. Now get this floor swept." Nellie looked askance at Tom. "It's a proper mess, all covered in crumbs."

"I'll be seeing you then." Tom quickly picked up his cap and pipe and left.

Ruby remained standing where she was, the broom motionless in her grasp. "D'yer think Master Jamie'll still be allowed to come with me to see my grandmamma next week?" she asked, her grey eyes full of concern.

"We'll have to ask the Master about that," replied Nellie.

"He's been so looking forward to it…me'n all." Ruby half-heartedly moved the broom over the stone flagged-floor. "I do hope he can still come. I'm really enjoying having him here."

* * * *

Tillie walked back to the burnt out house and stood in front of it, wrapping her arms tightly around her as memories came flooding back. Suddenly the sun glinted on something shiny in the ruins so, with an effort, she climbed over the debris to see what it could be. She had to move a charred tabletop and a chair leg to get close, and as she moved forward she trod on something soft. Looking down to see what it was, a moan escaped her lips.

"Oh, no, Maisie's rag doll, or what's left of it. How on earth did you survive?"

As she turned it over and stroked off the layers of debris, its remaining arm dropped off. Fighting off threatening tears, she resolutely tucked the rag doll under her arm, and continued to look for whatever it was that had caught her eye.

Now that she was on the inside of the rubble, she couldn't see anything sparkling, everything was dull and covered in ash. Had she imagined it? She kicked around in the ashes but the cloud of dust that was thrown up started her coughing.

Once she got her breath back, she peered into the darkness. There was the remains of the old lady's favourite chair, a tiny piece of red cushion still stuck to it. She could picture her sitting there with her embroidery in her hands, her glasses perched on the end of her nose, and the children sitting cross-legged in front of her, enthralled as she told them stories of her own childhood. Poor Mrs Curtis! Tillie prayed that she hadn't suffered.

Then she saw it again, the glint. This time she kept her gaze on the spot where she had seen it as she edged forward.

What could it be? Perhaps it was something of value. Her imagination ran wild. A ring? A bracelet? She knew Mrs Curtis had owned a lot of jewellery that shouldn't have burnt in the fire, so what would have become of it all? What would she do with it if she did find it? Would she be able to keep it?

She laughed out loud when she found it. No valuable piece of jewellery, no ruby necklace, only a copper kettle that had somehow escaped the ravages of the fire and lay exposed to the sun's rays.

Picking it up, she thought about the cups of tea she had made with it and licked her dry lips, thinking of what she would give to be able to make one now.

She glanced around once more to check if there was anything else that could be salvaged. Obviously someone had already been through the rubble, as she couldn't see anything recognisable, so she gingerly stepped back onto the street, carrying the kettle as if it was treasure.

She began to ask passers-by if they knew what had happened at the house, to find out what the local people knew.

"The widow set fire to the house in a fit of madness and everyone in it perished," one old man told her.

One lady stopped and blessed herself in front of the house. "Such a tragedy," she remarked as she turned to look at Tillie. Suddenly, her eyes opened wide as she seemed to recognise her. "Say, weren't you the new maid that worked here?" She paled visibly and began to back away as if she had seen a ghost.

"Yes, that's right," replied Tillie as she tried to catch at her arm. "Please don't be afraid. Did you think that everyone had died?"

"Yes, now please leave me alone." The woman hurried off down the street.

"Look, I don't want to frighten you," pleaded Tillie as she chased after her. "As you see, I'm alive and well, I'm not a ghost. Here, pinch me and see for yourself."

The lady slowed down and Tillie remembered who she was as she caught up with her. "You're Emily Thompson, the vicar's wife, aren't you?"

The vicar's wife nodded but still kept her head bowed as if she was afraid to look her in the eye.

"My name's Tillie Raven. I need to find my son. I'm sure you remember him, his name's Jamie. It's a long story, but after the fire we got split up and I haven't seen him since. I don't even know if he's alive."

Tillie saw her look up with compassion in her eyes and remained motionless, hoping that she would be able to help her.

Mrs Thompson sighed. "I think you'd better come with me, Miss Raven, and tell me what happened. Now I've recovered from the shock of seeing you alive, I think a drink would stand us both in good stead."

Tillie hesitated as she looked down at her dress and tried to rub off some of the ash that still stuck to the bottom of it.

"Don't worry about that, I've seen a lot worse, believe me."

Clutching the tapestry bag, the kettle and the charred rag doll, Tillie followed Emily Thompson up the street.

A little while later, her hands cupped around a warm, welcoming cup of tea, she said, "Please call me Tillie—Miss Raven sounds so formal."

"And you must call me Emily," replied her hostess, placing a plate of biscuits on the table. "I must apologise again for my behaviour back there. It was just such a shock."

"Please, there's no need. I'm sure I would have reacted in just the same way."

"You hadn't been in Welton long, had you?" Emily asked. Tillie shook her head.

"So, what brought you here in the first place?"

"I met Mrs Curtis's son when I was with the gypsies I'd been living with. He was a travelling musician, but of course you must know that. So entertaining he was, we had such a laugh. Anyway, we happened to encamp near Welton and he invited my friend Lucy and me to accompany him to visit his mother. When we arrived, we discovered that her maid had run off the previous day with the stable lad. I mentioned that I used to be a parlour maid and there and then she asked me to stay and work for her. What providence, I couldn't believe my luck."

"Pray, continue." Emily picked up a biscuit.

"Well, I begged her, rather presumptuously I suppose, to let Lucy stay as well, as I knew she and Maisie were unhappy at the camp, and she agreed. We settled in with her very quickly, especially the children. She couldn't do enough for them. Her son only stayed home a week or so and then went off travelling again. He couldn't stay in one place for long, he was a free spirit. I liked him a lot and at one time had hoped that...anyway..."

Emily took the bright orange tea cosy off the teapot and refilled the cups while Tillie looked around at the homely kitchen, remembering how good it had felt to live in a solid house once more after all those years on the road.

"Mrs Curtis had a set of spice tins like those," she said, pointing over to the shelf.

Emily looked over at the brightly coloured tins. "They're pretty, aren't they? They were a wedding present."

Nodding, Tillie sighed. "But I digress," she continued, "and I'm sure you have better things to do with your time than listen to me ranting on."

She began to stand up but Emily put her hand on her arm and gently pushed her back onto the chair.

"Not at all," she reassured her. "The vicar's out arranging a funeral and then he'll probably be visiting some of his sick parishioners, there seem to be quite a few of those lately, so I have plenty of time. Carry on."

Tillie continued her tale. "The old lady, Mrs Curtis, was rather forgetful. She would leave oil lamps burning all night and sometimes even candles. We would find them in the morning completely burned out, knowing full well they were new the previous day. Sometimes she forgot to go to bed and was still asleep in her chair when we came down in the morning, so Lucy and I took it in turns to make sure she was in bed and that candles were extinguished before we retired ourselves.

One night, however, she must have got up again without anyone hearing her. I was awoken by screams – chilling screams they were, I'd never heard anything like it in my life – so I jumped out of bed and ran to see what had caused them." Tillie shivered and pulled her shawl tightly around her.

Her head bowed, her voice barely audible, she continued. "Before I even got downstairs I could smell the smoke. It was choking. By the time I reached the bottom I could see flames erupting from the dining room. Inside, Mrs Curtis, her nightdress and her hair ablaze, was screaming like a banshee and then I saw Lucy running towards her holding out a blanket. I stood transfixed for a moment. What should I do? Should I go in there and help? Water, I thought, that's what's needed, so I rushed to the kitchen and filled two jugs. It seemed to take an eternity for them to fill. Then I ran back, water sloshing everywhere, but I couldn't even get near, the heat was so intense, so I just threw the whole jugs through the doorway. I felt so helpless. Then through the murk and smoke I heard Lucy murmuring, "The children!"

In my shocked state I had momentarily forgotten them, so, knowing there was nothing I could do for either her or Mrs Curtis, I ran upstairs and, shaking Jamie and Maisie awake, I grabbed some clothes and we escaped down the back stairs. Jamie fell and banged his head on the way down but I yanked him up and we ran for our lives."

A shudder shook her whole body as tears soaked her face. Emily stroked her hand across the table.

Tillie looked up at her with desolation etched into her face. "I should have saved Lucy and Mrs Curtis. It was my fault they died."

"Of course it wasn't, what else could you have done?"

"I don't know, but I'll go to my grave knowing that I ran out on them."

"At least you saved the children!"

"And myself."

"Look," continued the vicar's wife, passing her a handkerchief. "If you hadn't rescued the children, they would have perished as well. God saved you so that you could save them. Always remember that."

She pondered this for a minute. "I hadn't thought of it like that. Thank you," she replied at length, wiping her eyes and blowing loudly into the handkerchief. "I just..."

"No more now, shush," Emily put the cups into the sink before taking some potatoes out of the pantry. "And I insist that you stay for dinner."

Tillie began to protest but she continued. "A hot meal inside you will make you feel so much better."

"Everyone is so kind. I really don't deserve it," exclaimed Tillie, chopping up some extra carrots a few minutes later.

Emily raised her eyebrows and lifted her finger. "Uh...uh..."

She had to smile. Having been relieved of some of the guilt she had been carrying around for so long, she felt like a weight had been lifted from her.

"If you feel like continuing...but not if it'll upset you..." began her hostess as she turned from adding the extra vegetables to the hotpot in the oven. "I'm curious to know where the children are."

"It was Christmas Eve, and there was snow on the ground. I remember Mrs Curtis saying how lovely it was going to be to have a white Christmas."

"Everyone loves a white Christmas, don't they?"

"Well I used to, but not anymore.

"I'm sorry. I wasn't thinking."

There was silence for a moment before Tillie continued, "Everything that happened after we escaped the inferno is a bit of a blur. I know all I wanted to do was get away as far as possible from that hellhole. I dragged the children along, heedless of their cries and questions, just wanting to shut out everything that had happened. I found a barn close by and we holed up in there. I couldn't face anyone, I felt so guilty at deserting poor Lucy and Mrs Curtis. I knew everyone would blame me. Maisie kept asking where her mama was, but I just couldn't bring myself to tell her the truth, because that would have meant facing up to it. She somehow got the door open and ran out, calling for her mother. I just let her go. I didn't have the energy to stop her. I was numb. Jamie tried to call her back, but gave up and came back in and curled up next to me. Goodness knows what happened to her."

She shook her head. "Eventually, after a couple of days, Jamie's cries of hunger forced me to venture out. I waited for him to fall asleep and went to try and find some food. I knew he wouldn't have let me go without him if he'd been awake. But I got caught stealing a loaf and was taken into custody and then sent to prison. I haven't seen either of them since." She heaved a huge sigh. "Did you not hear anything about it?"

"No, nothing. I suppose there are so many cases going through the courts that one more went unnoticed. Didn't you explain to the judge what had happened? Surely he would have understood?"

"I tried, but it made no difference, and now I have to find Jamie, and Maisie as well, if either of them are still alive."

"It was presumed you all perished, although I did hear that the authorities never found all the bodies..."

Tillie shuddered and stood up.

Emily put out a restraining hand. "Let's set the table, the dinner should be ready by now." The kitchen door opened. "Ah, here's Edward, just in time!"

A large man with a thick thatch of fair hair entered. He looked more like a bear than a vicar. Acknowledging Tillie with a bow of his head, he walked over to his wife and, cupping her face with his big hands, he gave her a resounding kiss on the lips.

Tillie watched, fascinated. Somehow she hadn't expected a vicar to be so demonstrative.

"Dinner's almost ready, darling," Emily told him as she picked up a towel and walked over to the stove to take out the steaming food. "This is Miss Tillie Raven, by the way. You remember her? She worked for Mrs Curtis, at…you know…at the time of the fire?"

Tillie stood still, expecting a look of shock or horror from the cleric, but all she saw was a kindly smile.

"Yes, I know." He bowed his head. "Miss Raven," he acknowledged her before adding, "Yes, it's all over town, everyone's buzzing with the news." He turned and, taking her hand in his, he continued, "How are you?"

"Um, well, thank you," she replied in amazement.

"You say everyone knows she's here?" asked Emily, placing the dish on the table.

"Yes, old Mrs Penny saw you both walking down the street and she recognised Miss Raven."

While they enjoyed the meal, Emily explained to her husband how Tillie came to be in their kitchen, then said, "Trust Mrs Penny to see us. I expect you remember her, Tillie, she's…how can I put it delicately? She's Welton's answer to a town crier. Once she finds something out the whole town knows about it within a very short time."

They all laughed.

"She's a grand lady though, bless her," said Edward.

"Yes, she is. Even if she were not, you'd still find goodness in her," replied his wife. "You see the best in everyone, a perfect vicar."

She smiled up at him and he patted her hand. "Thank you, my dear."

As she stood up to clear the table he patted her belly. "I hope junior in here thinks so. I hope he'll think me a perfect father as well."

A gasp escaped Tillie. "Are you…?"

"Yes, we expect the happy event in the autumn."

"That's wonderful. You should have said something earlier, instead of letting me rattle on about my problems."

"Don't worry, that's what a vicar's wife is for." Emily piled up the dirty plates. "To be there for his flock when he's busy elsewhere. And anyway, I enjoy listening to other peoples' problems and trying to sort them out. It gives me great satisfaction."

"I can't think of a couple who suit your position more than you two," replied Tillie, her head to one side. "You're just...perfect."

They all laughed again.

"I've just had a thought," she exclaimed later as she helped dry the dishes. "If this Mrs Penny knows everything that goes on around here, she might know what happened to the children. Do you think it would be worth me going to visit her?"

Edward looked up from folding the tablecloth. "I think that would be a grand idea. Why didn't we think of it before?" He looked at his wife. "Do you have any more pressing matters to attend to this afternoon, my dear?"

"No, and even if I had, they would have to wait. What can be more important than finding those poor children?"

"Certainly, but would you mind accompanying Miss Raven on your own? Unfortunately I was told this morning that Farmer Brown died during the night, so I need to sort out his funeral. Yes, another one." He shook his head as Emily raised her eyebrows. "At this rate I shall have no parishioners left."

"You poor darling." Putting her arms around him, she gave him a hug. "You get off to Widow Brown then and I'll take Tillie to see Mrs Penny."

Chapter 6

Jamie awoke as a faint light was peeping through the curtains. He stretched and yawned. "I'm hungry."

Then he noticed that he wasn't wearing his nightclothes, and suddenly the events of the previous day came flooding back. Slumping back onto the pillows, he groaned.

"O 'eck, o 'eck!" he wailed. "What'm I goner do?"

He pulled the bed covers back over his head in a vain attempt to block out the memory, and lay there, thinking, *Uncle David was so angry…p'raps I better go and say sorry…before he turns me out.*

He jumped out of bed, dragged on some clean trousers and a shirt and ran down to the breakfast room. It was empty.

Was he too late, or too early? Perhaps the master wasn't even up yet. Dare he go up to his bedroom? Plucking up courage he went back upstairs and tentatively knocked on David's door.

A faint mumble came from within and Jamie didn't know whether it meant that he should go in or not. He hesitated for a moment before turning the knob and poking his head round the door. The curtains were still closed so the room was in darkness.

"Is that you, John?" a voice came from within. "It seems a trifle early."

Jamie crept through the doorway. "It's me, Uncle David. It's Jamie."

Silence.

"Uncle David?"

"Yes, Jamie, I heard you."

"Please, can I come in?"

"I suppose you better had."

Advancing towards the bed, as his eyes became accustomed to the darkness, Jamie saw David sit up.

"Open the curtains," ordered David. "There's no point lighting a candle if it's daylight outside. I presume it is daytime?"

"Yes, sir," replied Jamie, struggling with the curtains.

"That'll do. I can see well enough now."

Jamie stood in front of the bed, his head bowed and his hands behind his back, not knowing where to begin.

"Don't look so worried, I'm not going to beat you." David took off his nightcap and then patted a space on the bed beside him. "Sit down here."

"It ain't a beating I'm bovvered about, sir. I 'ad loadsa them before I come 'ere. Old Timmy Potts used to thrash all us kids in the gypsy camp when we got in his way."

"Is that so?"

"Yes, sir, honest, so I ain't…"

Suddenly, Jamie's face lit up and he jumped off the bed. "Hey, sir, that means I've remembered somat, don't it? There was the barn as well, that I remembered yesterday. D'yer think me memory's coming back?"

"Oh, Jamie! How can I stay mad at you? You're incorrigible."

"In—what?"

"Never mind." David shook his head. "But it's good news, if it means that your memory is returning."

A tap on the door made him look up. "Ah, here's John come to help me dress. You get yourself downstairs and tell Nellie you're having breakfast with me, and you can explain about yesterday's antics while we eat."

"There's just one thing…" began Jamie, as he was about to go out.

"We'll discuss it over breakfast, as I said."

"All right." He accepted that he would have to wait for the answer to what had been worrying him all morning.

Rushing down the stairs two steps at a time, he almost fell headlong but managed to regain his balance and reached the bottom of the stairs without further mishap. Bounding into the kitchen, he knocked into Ruby, causing her to drop the plate she was carrying. It bounced on the floor and somehow managed to remain intact, but the sausages it contained scattered everywhere.

"Oo!" He pulled up short of running into Freda, who was standing at the table ladling steaming mushrooms into a dish. "Sorry."

Bending down, he exchanged grimaces with Ruby as they began to pick up the sausages, and, gritting his teeth, he waited for the onslaught of rebuke from Freda.

Instead, all she said was, "You'd better give those sausages to the dogs, Ruby. I know my floor's clean but not clean enough to eat off."

Ruby went outside as Freda began to cook some more. "Now, my lad, I'd have thought that after yesterday's events you'd be a bit subdued, so what's brought on these high spirits? I'm sure they won't last long once the master's up and about."

"That's just it—I've already been in and see'd him. He wants me to have breakfast with him, so as I can tell him about Rufus."

"But he's not up yet...oh no, you haven't been and woken him up, have you? He'll be in a right mood if you have."

Nellie entered with her hands full. "Ah, there you are, Master Jamie," she emptied the washbowl down the sink and refilled the jug, "I've been looking for you."

"He's only been and woken the master," cried Freda. "And you know how he hates being disturbed early."

"But I told you, he's happy about it." Jamie jumped up and down. "Come wiv me, and see for yourself." He grabbed Nellie's hand and dragged her out of the kitchen and across the hall where they met David.

"I expected you to be there before me." David adjusted his cravat in the large ornate mirror on the wall. "Come on in, I expect you're starving."

"Yes, sir, I certainly am," replied Jamie, trying to adopt a posh accent, but not succeeding.

"Is breakfast ready?" David asked Nellie, who was standing in the doorway looking dumbstruck.

"Yes, yes of course." She jumped into action and hurried back to the kitchen.

"Right, young man, you'd better tell me everything," David began as Ruby brought in a tray of hot food and set it down on the table. As she walked past Jamie she winked at him. This set him off in a fit of giggles, which caused raised eyebrows from David.

"Sorry, sir!"

"And why are calling me 'sir' again?" asked David as he spooned kidney and bacon onto their plates. "I thought you were comfortable calling me 'Uncle David?'"

"I am, I am. I just thought you might not want me to after...you know...yesterday. You were so cross!"

"And I had good reason to be. I can still scarcely believe how foolhardy you were. What on earth were you thinking about?"

"Well, I had to save Rufus from the dogs, and—"

"Go on, tell me the whole story."

Jamie related the tale from start to finish.

"I can understand why you acted as you did," David said at length with a shake of his head. "But I still cannot condone putting your own life at risk in that manner. You have no idea how terrified I was for you. I really thought you were going to be killed by the hounds. That was why I was 'so cross', as you put it. I have grown to enjoy having you here and..." He heaved an enormous sigh and went across to pat Jamie on the head.

Now was the time to ask the burning question that had been plaguing him all morning. "What do you think happened to Rufus, Uncle David?" Jamie looked up, hoping for a favourable reply. "You don't think they caught him, do you?"

"I don't know, Jamie. I would like to say that they didn't, but in all reality I expect that they did. I'm sorry."

Jamie had considered this possibility but hadn't wanted to believe it. Hearing it spoken aloud made it come true. He tried to be brave but his bottom lip quivered and his eyes filled with tears. David held him close against him, stroking his hair until he recovered.

As Ruby came in to clear the table, the front doorbell rang.

"I suppose the whole neighbourhood will be arriving to find out how you are. Come on, lad, let's face the music." David took his hand and they walked towards the door.

The visitor was Christine Wilson, accompanied, as usual, by her sister.

"I beg you to forgive me for my behaviour yesterday, Miss Wilson, Mrs Harrison. It was unpardonable." David showed them into the drawing room after Jamie had gone off to find Lady.

"Please don't think any more about it," replied Christine, taking off her kid gloves.

"No, no, it was quite understandable, in the circumstances," echoed Grace before her sister could continue. Looking around at her plush surroundings as they sat down she remarked, "What a lovely room you have here, Mr Dalton. I do so love burgundy curtains and decor, don't I, Chrissie? I would have them in every room if fashion allowed it."

Christine half smiled, saying between clenched teeth, "Don't call me Chrissie, you know I can't abide it."

"Oh tosh, you liked it well enough when we were younger."

"Shall I ring for tea?" asked David quickly, eager to diffuse the situation.

"That would be lovely," replied the sisters together. They sat glaring at each other until Ruby arrived with the tea trolley.

"And how is young Master Jamie after his escapades?" asked Grace, as the maid began pouring the tea. "I hope he didn't suffer any lasting injuries."

"You asking me?" asked Ruby, pausing.

"No, no, you stupid girl, I was addressing your master."

"That will be all, thank you, Ruby," David intervened, praying that the visit was not going to be a long one. Ruby hurried out of the room without even curtseying.

"He's fine, thank you for asking," he continued as he passed the cups to his visitors. "It appears he was trying to save a young fox cub he had befriended. It had escaped from the stable where he had been nurturing it back to health, unbeknown to anyone except Sam. I shall have to have words with that groom of mine."

"At least there was no harm done," Christine smiled at David, "thanks to your swift reactions. It doesn't bear thinking about what could have happened…"

"I suppose you're right," he replied, marvelling how the brilliance of her hazel eyes lit up her whole face as she smiled.

"I hope you gave him a good dressing down," Grace scorned. "That's what he deserves. I understand he's not even your own son?"

"No, no, he's not related at all," replied David, tearing his gaze from her sister. "In fact, we don't know who he is." He then gave them a short resume of how Jamie had come to be living there.

"And he doesn't remember anything at all?" Grace raised her eyebrows.

"Well, actually, he did remember a small detail this morning, but the doctor says not to push him."

"I think you've gone far and above the call of duty. If it had been me I would have turned him out after his antics yesterday," she continued spitefully.

"Oh, Grace, how could you even think such a thing?" cried Christine in horror. "That's the difference between us. You always were the vicious one, even when we were children. I remember when you tried to pull the wings off that butterfly I had caught unintentionally in my bonnet. I cried for days."

Sniffing, she reached into her reticule and, taking out her handkerchief, she dabbed her eyes.

"Oh tosh," replied her sister with a shake of her head. "You always make a mountain out of the proverbial molehill. You know full well I didn't—" She looked up as if suddenly aware of her bad manners. "Anyway I'm sure Mr Dalton doesn't want to listen to our squabbles."

David had been looking from one sister to the other, trying to think of a way to intervene without appearing rude. He stood up. "Well, thank you, ladies, for taking the time to enquire about the boy. I'm sure you have pressing matters to attend to, your social engagements must keep you very busy."

The sisters also stood up. "Yes, yes, of course." Christine pulled her gloves back on. "We mustn't keep you from your...duties."

"Shall we see you at Major Wallace's ball on Saturday, Mr Dalton?" asked Grace as they went outside. "I hear it's going to be a grand event."

David looked towards Christine who seemed to be watching hopefully for his reply.

"I...um, I'm not sure yet," he muttered. He hadn't been planning on going but the thought of spending an evening in her company suddenly gave it some appeal, provided he could separate her from her vile sister.

"Most probably I will," he decided out loud, surprising himself. "Yes, I definitely will!"

"Until Saturday then," the vile sister called as the pair entered their carriage. Christine gave him an intimate wave as they drove off and he stood watching their departure, deep in thought.

I'm undoubtedly becoming more relaxed in her company, he decided. *If only I could get her without the sister. She's abominable! No wonder she and her husband are having marriage problems, you'd have to be a saint to put up with her. Poor Christine must be going through hell.*

He suddenly realised he had used her Christian name. Things were definitely looking up.

"Will I still be able to go and see Ruby's grandmamma next week?" Jamie asked the following day as he ate his breakfast in the kitchen. Looking up from peeling potatoes, Freda raised her eyebrows at Nellie. The housekeeper picked up the flatiron from the stand above the fire and continued to press the delicate tablecloth she had been concentrating on.

"You'd better go and ask the master yourself when he's finished his meal. It's entirely up to him."

Ruby came in with the remains of the master's breakfast.

"That sausage going spare?" asked Jamie, jumping down from the table and eyeing up the plate of leftover food she was carrying.

"Haven't you eaten enough, you little rascal?" laughed Freda.

"I didn't get no sausages today and I love them ones," he replied, digging his fork in before Ruby could take the plate away. He stuffed the prize into his mouth. "Can I have shom—?"

"Don't speak with your mouth full!" cried Freda.

"Remember your manners, if you please." Nellie wagged a finger at him. "Haven't you learnt anything since you've been here? I thought we had…Oh no!" she suddenly cried at the top of her voice.

"What's the matter?" Freda looked across to see what had caused the outburst. Nellie was holding up the tablecloth she had been ironing, revealing a large brown-rimmed hole. A horrified gasp escaped Ruby and Freda at the same time. Jamie looked from one to the other, totally bewildered at the sequence of events.

"What's up?" he asked.

"The master's favourite tablecloth, that's what's up," cried Nellie dabbing at the cloth with a damp sponge. "It's ruined! The mistress embroidered it for her trousseau before they were married. It was her pride and joy. Now it's gone up in smoke."

Jamie walked slowly over to examine the damage. "Were it my fault?" he asked as he looked at the brown patch Nellie stood staring at. "I'm sorry if it were my fault."

"Well, if she hadn't had to correct your bad manners it wouldn't have happened," began Freda but Nellie intervened. "I can't blame it on the boy, I should have been more careful."

"But..."

"No, Freda, I take full responsibility. I'll go and tell the master right away." She left the kitchen, its remaining occupants staring at each other in stunned silence.

Jamie was the first to break it. "'Spose I better not ask bout going to see your grandmamma." He turned with a grimace to Ruby who pulled a face back at him and shook her head.

"I think you'd better keep out of the way today," said Freda. "I know Nellie said she doesn't blame you but..."

He walked over to the window but was not quite tall enough to see out, so he opened the back door and put out his hand. "It ain't raining no more so I'll go down to me tree house. I'll be outta the way there, won't I? Would I be able to make some sandwiches?"

"Ruby'll make you some. You go and get your books."

* * * *

"I've been expecting you." Mrs Penny opened the door before they had chance to knock. Emily and Tillie looked at her in astonishment. "Yep, ever since I saw you walking down the street this morning, I knew you'd come knocking at my door."

"Weren't you shocked to see me, Mrs Penny?" asked Tillie as they were ushered into the little house. The front door led straight into the small lounge, where the walls were covered in shelves, creaking from piles of books of all sizes, many of them old, battered and covered in dust. Even a gypsy caravan looked large in comparison.

"Mm, not really," Mrs Penny's reply brought her thoughts back. "I had a feeling you'd come back some day."

"But didn't you think I was dead, as everyone else did?"

Her hostess merely shrugged as, removing yet more books and brushing cat hairs off the sofa, she gestured for them to sit down. Tillie noticed a small tabby cat curled up in the corner and, as they sat down, a large jet-black bundle of fluff jumped down from a shelf and landed on her knee, startling her. Raising her hands in the air she didn't know whether to stroke it or push it off.

"You're honoured." Mrs Penny picked up the cat and stroked it. "He doesn't take to everyone, you know." She buried her face in its soft fur. "May I introduce you to Labyrinth, the best friend anyone could have."

Tillie could feel hysteria looming up inside her and had to cough to stop herself from bursting out laughing.

"You may scoff, young lady, but a cat doesn't answer back or ridicule its betters. All it needs is food and water and lots of love..." She buried her face in its fur again. "Don't you, pussykins? Mama loves you, doesn't she?"

Tillie looked at Emily and could see that she too was having trouble keeping a straight face.

I'd better change the subject before we disgrace ourselves, she thought, so clearing her throat she began, "Mrs Penny...?"

There was a faint 'mm?' from the cat's fur.

"Um...Mrs Penny...we've come to ask if you know anything about my son Jamie or my friend's daughter Maisie."

"Ah!" Her hostess's face reappeared and the cat jumped down and ran out of the door.

"Ah," she repeated. "Now that's something else." Reaching up to one of the shelves, she took down one of the newer books and opened it. "Let me see."

She thumbed through the book, murmuring dates as she turned the pages. "When was the fire?"

Tillie opened her mouth to speak but was forestalled. "Oh yes, just before Christmas, I remember now. This is this year's diary. I need last year's."

As she replaced the diary and picked up a different one, Tillie was intrigued. "I don't wish to be rude, Mrs Penny, but what do you record in there?"

"Mm?" The long fingers continued turning the pages of the diary. "Here we are!" She looked up in triumph. "Oh, beg your pardon, did you ask me something?"

"It doesn't matter now. Does your diary tell you anything?"

"It says 'December twenty-fourth, Christmas Eve—a horrific fire at the home of Mrs Curtis. Everyone apparently...'" She peered at the writing. "I think it says 'perished'."

She looked at Emily and Tillie with her lips pursed. "Mm, obviously incorrect."

"But when we came in you said that you knew Tillie was alive." Emily frowned.

"Ah! That's because I saw her this morning."

The girls looked at each other in bewilderment.

"But..." began Emily.

"Mrs Penny," Tillie interrupted, putting her hand on Emily's arm in silent apology. "Does your diary say anything about Jamie or Maisie? Please, I have to know."

"Let me see..."

Tillie was feeling more and more frustrated at the slowness with which the old lady moved. *Actually*, she thought as she scrutinised her hostess leafing once more through the diary, *she probably isn't that old.* The bonnet, shawl and dress, all black, looked like widow's weeds and merely gave her the appearance of old age, and her long pointed nose reminded her of a witch in a story book she had once read as a girl.

"Here, 'December twenty-sixth—a young girl was seen hanging around near the burnt-out shell of the Curtis residence but when somebody approached her she ran off.'"

"Does it say where to, or if she was seen again?"

"No. I only know what I was told. I didn't see it myself."

"And nothing about Jamie?"

"Can't see anything here. Why, wasn't he with you?"

Tillie explained about how she had left him in the barn and been arrested. "Is that not in there either?"

"I don't record everyone's business. I ain't a journal," huffed Mrs Penny as she closed the book and hugged it to her bosom.

"I'm sorry, Mrs Penny, I apologise if I was rude. I'm just so desperate. I've come so close..." She put her head in her hands and burst into tears.

Emily put her arm around her while Mrs Penny flapped around, shaking her head.

"There, there," she repeated over and over again before delving into her pocket to produce a bottle of Sal Volatile which she held under Tillie's nose. "Take a sniff of this, it'll make you feel better."

Tillie took one whiff of the smelling salts. Screwing up her face in disgust she almost choked but they had the desired effect.

"That's it. Feel better now?"

She nodded. "I'm sorry for that but you must understand, I—"

"Lawks a livery!" Mrs Penny pressed her lips together. "It's just come to me! How could I have forgotten? There was talk of a young boy being found up at The Grange some months back. Nobody knew who he was. As far as I know he's still there. Now where did I put this year's diary?"

* * * *

Tillie and Emily walked back to the vicarage bubbling with excitement.

"I can't believe she didn't remember straight away." Emily opened the front door and they entered the lounge where she gestured to Tillie to sit down. "She usually knows everything that goes on. But I suppose it was six months ago and the hullabaloo will have died down. I wonder why I didn't hear of it, or Edward? He would have told me about it if he had."

A loud crash sounded from the direction of the hallway. "What on earth is that?" She jumped up and hurried out to see what had happened.

"Only me," came a muffled shout. Tillie couldn't contain her curiosity any longer and tiptoed after Emily.

"Where are you?" she heard her call.

"Over here." She peeped through the door and saw a head appear from a pile of coats, then Edward himself.

"I tripped over the umbrella stand, and when I reached out to save myself I pulled the coat rack off the wall," he explained with a grimace.

"Are you all right?"

"Yes, yes, no harm done." He shook his hands and feet. "Everything still in working order, except the coat rack, I'm afraid."

"Never mind that, it can soon be mended."

He brushed his hands down his trousers, and then retrieved his hat from the other end of the hall.

"We've only just returned." Emily kissed him after straightening his dog collar. "Were you coming or going?"

"Coming in. How did you fare with Mrs Penny?"

Realising they were coming back into the lounge, Tillie quickly sat back down on the sofa. She didn't wish to be caught eavesdropping.

"Rather well, didn't we, Tillie?" a smiling Emily replied as they came in.

Edward nodded to Tillie. "Good day, Miss Raven."

"Good day, vicar. Yes, we did very well indeed, I'm thrilled to say."

"We think we might know where Jamie is." Emily sat down again. "Do you remember hearing about a boy being found up at The Grange just after Christmas?"

Shaking his head, her husband pursed his lips. "I don't think so. But then the Grange isn't in my jurisdiction."

"Where exactly is this Grange?" asked Tillie. "Is it far?"

"It's some miles north. My jurisdiction covers the south of the county." He turned to Emily. "You do mean the one on the Brightmoor Estate?"

"Yes, I don't think there are any other Granges around here, are there?"

"The Brightmoor Estate!" screeched Tillie. "That's where..." She looked at Edward then at Emily. "Are you sure?"

Emily hesitated. "Well, that's what Mrs Penny said, didn't she? The Grange?"

"She did, but I never imagined it would be the same one." She jumped up. "I have to get there straightaway. Please excuse me." She ran towards the door.

"You can't go now. It's practically dark." Emily rushed after her. "Even if you knew the way you'd never get there tonight." She turned to her husband. "Tell her, Edward. It would be foolhardy."

"But I'm so close," wailed Tillie.

"My dear, listen to Emily." Edward walked over and placed his hand gently on her shoulder. "Stay here and get a good night's rest and I'll arrange a carriage to take you there in the morning. If this boy is your son, he'll need you to be fit and rested. You won't want to arrive dishevelled and ragged, now do you?"

Tillie shook her head. She knew what he said made sense, but to have come so far and now be thwarted by the time of day was almost too much to bear.

Chapter 7

"Now you behave yourself, young man," Nellie chided. Jamie had been granted permission to visit Ruby's grandmother. "We don't want you disgracing yourself, do we?"

"I'll be on my best be'aviour," he replied.

"That sounds posh." Ruby bent down to lace up her boots. "Grandmamma'll think you're nobility if you talk to her like that."

Jamie laughed. "I couldn't keep it up for long, so there ain't no worry bout that."

Nellie straightened his jacket and, licking her fingers, she smoothed down his hair before placing his cap on straight. "You'll do. And remember to stay by Ruby's side all the way, no running off and hiding. I know what you're like, playing tricks on people."

"I'll be good, promise."

"Off you go then, the pair of you." She handed Ruby a basket that Freda had prepared for them to take.

The maid peeked under the cover. "Preserves and cake. She'll be thrilled."

As they passed the stables Sam came out to greet them. "Have you recovered from that incident with Rufus, young master Jamie?"

"Yes, but I heard you got into trouble."

"Who told you that?"

"I heard Tom telling Freda."

"Yes," chorused Ruby. "Me'n all."

"It wasn't much, I just got told, in no uncertain terms, not to harbour any more stray wild animals." Sam tweaked her bonnet. "I haven't seen this before. Is it a new one? It makes a nice change from your usual mop cap."

Ruby blushed and lowered her eyes. "Fancy you noticing."

"You'd be surprised what I notice." The groom winked before turning away. "Enjoy your walk."

103

They walked quite a way, with Jamie pointing out various birds that he had learnt about, until they came to a stile. Ruby climbed over first and waited for Jamie to follow. The ground around it was very muddy, and he slipped and fell, his chin coming down with a thud on the step, and he ended up flat on his face in the mud.

"Oh, my!" Dropping the basket, Ruby clamboured back over the stile. "Are you hurt?"

Jamie stood up and blinked. He could feel blood oozing from his lip.

"Oh, my," she repeated. "What we gonna do? There's nobody around to help." She studied his face. "Do you think you could walk as far as Grandmamma's cottage, it's only over the other side of this field and through the copse?" She began to dab at his lip with the corner of her petticoat. "It'd be quicker than going back."

"Yes, all right." He tried to be brave as he brushed some of the mud off his clothes.

"If you could see yourself, Master Jamie." Ruby looked him up and down with a faint smile. "If it weren't for the fact that you got a cut lip, I'd be having a proper laugh right now at the state you're in."

Jamie tried to smile as well. "Ouch, that 'urt!" he yelped, dabbing at his lip.

"Sorry. Come on, let's get there quick." She grabbed his arm and helped him over the stile. "Grandmamma keeps all sorts of herbs and potions. She'll soon patch you up." Picking up the basket she hurried on. "I never like crossing this field. Once a big, black bull chased me. I only just made it to the other side." She looked around. "It don't appear to be here today though, thank God."

Jamie gasped at the blasphemy. "You shouldn't swear," he said between closed lips.

"I know, but you won't tell anyone, will you? Especially Grandmamma."

Jamie shook his head. He didn't want to get her into trouble.

They made it to the end of the copse without further mishap, and he had to shield his eyes as they emerged into the sunlight.

"That's her cottage, look, the second one along." Ruby pointed down towards a row of small cottages. "There she is. Can you see her, sitting on the doorstep?"

Jamie could see a lady in a black dress and white apron with a white cap on the back of her head. There was a basket on her knee, and others at her feet. Ruby waved and received a wave in return. They ran the remaining distance and as Ruby was being enfolded in a hug Jamie hung back, conscious of his filthy condition.

The old lady held out her arms to him but stopped. "My goodness, what's happened to you? They didn't send you out in this state, surely?"

"No, no." Ruby laughed. "He had his Sunday best on when we left. Looks more like his Saturday worst now!" She doubled up in a fit of giggles.

"It doesn't look funny to me, young lady," chided her grandmother as she examined Jamie's face. "The poor lamb's hurt himself. Come on in and we'll get you cleaned up."

She shooed them inside the cottage and sat Jamie down on a stool in the kitchen, then she turned to Ruby who had by this time recovered her composure. "Make yourself useful, girl. Pour some water into that basin, and pass me a towel."

A few minutes later, his face washed and his lip soothed with homemade ointment, Jamie felt a lot better. He tried smiling and found it didn't hurt nearly as much as before.

"We can't do a lot with your clothes." Grandmother looked down at the muddy mess. "We'll have to make do with sponging off as much as we can." Looking into his face, she appeared to be contemplating his features, then she shook her head and continued wiping off the mud.

"I 'ope I don't get into trouble for getting messy." Jamie sighed. "I only just got over the last bit of bovver."

"Are you a naughty boy then?"

"I don't mean to be, things just happen."

"He ain't a bad lad at all. Just gets into some scrapes." Ruby unloaded the contents of the basket onto the table beside them. "There's some of your favourite pears here, Grandmamma, and a fruit cake. I watched Freda making that yesterday, and she says she'll show me how to make a cake one of these days. Then I'll be able to make you one, all on my own."

"You're a good girl, Ruby. Your ma'd be proud of you." Her grandmother looked into Jamie's face again. "That's who he reminds me of...or more to the point...your sister. I thought I could see a resemblance to someone, but I couldn't put my finger on it."

Jamie looked from one to the other. "How can I look like your sister? I'm a boy. I don't want to look like no woman."

"No," Ruby laughed, "you just remind Grandmamma of her, that's all. Come to think of it..." She peered into his face as well. "It's true—you do look a bit like her. Ain't that queer? I hadn't noticed that before."

The old lady stroked his face. "Don't you remember anything about your past?"

"Only a bit. I remembered last week that I used to get thrashed by Timmy, one of the gypsies." He rubbed his shoulder, grimacing. "Can't really see his face though, just feel the beatings. Sometimes it were round me 'ear. That stung." He rubbed the side of his head as well.

"Gypsies?"

"Them what I lived with."

The old lady looked questioningly at Ruby but she merely shrugged her shoulders. "Nothing else? Not your ma or pa?"

"He ain't got a pa. He told me before." The maid finished emptying the basket. "I told him everyone has a pa but he wouldn't believe me."

106

"All right, Ruby, thank you."

"I remember being left in a barn and it was cold, but nowt else." Jamie screwed up his face.

"You poor lamb." Grandmother gave him a hug. "Let's get you fed. You'll feel a lot better then."

* * * *

"John, please lay my clothes out early this evening," David asked his valet as he was being shaved on the morning of Major Wallace's ball. "I'll need extra time to prepare myself."

"Certainly, sir, the green jacket or the brown one?"

"The brown one, I think, and the new fawn trousers. I want to look my best tonight."

"Of course, sir. But if I may be so bold, you always look good, whatever you wear."

"Thank you, John. That's because a good tailor like mine is worth his weight in gold."

John wiped his face with the warm towel. "Will that be all for now, sir?"

"Yes, thank you."

He took one final look in the mirror. *I don't suppose the sister will be indisposed. That would be too much to hope for,* he thought before descending the stairs to start the day's activities.

There was a chill in the air so he was glad he had decided to travel the short distance to the Major's house with the top of his landau closed. A house ablaze with light welcomed him as he pulled up.

The butler took his hat and gloves, and he looked around, surprised at how many people were already there.

"Ah, Dalton." A booming voice heralded the host. "So glad you could make it."

A large jolly fellow, with red cheeks and a ginger walrus moustache, shook his hand vigorously.

"Good of you to invite me, Major."

"Good turnout, what?"

"It certainly is." David looked around at the guests already dancing or standing talking in small groups. "I thought to be one of the first, but it appears that others had the same idea."

"They don't want to miss out on any gossip." The Major nudged David in the ribs and winked. "Are you acquainted with that lady over there?" He gestured towards a small lady in a becoming yellow dress dancing with one of the local bucks. David shook his head.

"Pray, excuse me, I must catch up on the news of her sister's husband." The Major made off, leaving David to search for Christine Wilson.

It didn't look as if she was there yet so he helped himself to a drink and stood watching the colourful dancers, quite content to be a mere spectator. His foot began to tap to the lively music being provided by a band of local musicians.

A disturbance at the door attracted his attention. His heart sank as he recognised the cause. Grace Harrison was having an altercation with the butler.

"You stupid man," he heard her shout. "Can't you be more careful? This hat cost more than you probably earn in a year and you've ruined it."

A hush descended as everybody in the room turned towards the group. David craned his neck but couldn't see Christine amongst them. The dancers resumed their gavot and the murmur of voices soon increased to the level it had been before and still there was no sign of her.

"Mr Dalton." Grace appeared at his side. Donning the semblance of a smile, he turned to acknowledge her.

"Mrs Harrison."

"I'm sorry to be the bearer of bad news, Mr Dalton, but I'm afraid my sister is indisposed and unable to attend. She's really disappointed, she had been so looking forward to coming."

"Nothing serious, I hope." He tried not to show his disappointment.

"No, just a bad head cold, but I told her it was unwise to venture out when one is not feeling well so she has taken to her bed with a warm toddy." She waved her fan coquettishly at him. "I don't have any dances marked on my card yet so if you're short of a partner I would be happy to mark you down for the next one."

It would be impolite to refuse, so, bowing politely and gritting his teeth, he took her arm and escorted her onto the dance area.

She talked non-stop throughout the dance, not seeming to require a response, so he was relieved when it ended and he showed her to a seat. He knew that he should ask if she required some food but, bad manners or not, he made his escape without doing so, out of the French doors onto the balcony.

The cool night air was a balm after the tobacco-filled atmosphere inside. He sighed, frustrated at the turn of events. Tonight would have been a perfect opportunity to get to know Christine better. He hoped she was not very poorly, and decided that he would call on her in a few days, by which time the illness should have abated.

Rejoining the party, he was inundated with requests to play cards or join in debates about world affairs so the evening passed quickly enough.

However, his evening was to get even worse. On arriving home he found that a messenger had just arrived with an urgent letter. He recognised the handwriting immediately as Annie's. What could be so pressing to be sending missives so late in the day? He ripped it open quickly.

My dearest brother, the letter began. Alarm bells rang even louder at the unaccustomed endearment.

I apologise for writing to you with such urgency, but I desperately require your assistance and beg that you hasten here to Harrogate instantly.

The truth of the matter is, this morning I slipped over on some spilt milk in the kitchen, and I am now laid up with a broken ankle. The

109

doctor advises that I have complete rest, but Victor is away in France on some business venture and I do not know when he will return.

You know I would not, in normal circumstances, put you to so much trouble, but I have no option but to fall on your good nature and elicit your immediate help.

I await a favourable reply, and do please excuse any irregularities in my writing. They are due to the constant pain I am suffering.

Your affectionate sister,

Annie.

David sighed as he folded the letter. As his sister stated, he had no option but to do as she requested. He quickly penned a reply and paid off the messenger, instructing him to take it straight away. His own journey would have to await the morning, as it was impractical to leave before then. He had bags to pack and business affairs to sort out at the very least.

Hurrying upstairs, he began sorting through his wardrobe to see which clothes he would want John to pack in the morning, when he stopped and raised his hands behind his head.

What about Jamie? What should he do with him? Would he suffer a setback if he was left behind? But would it be worse for him to be taken along?

He paced up and down, trying to decide the best course of action. Finally he came to the conclusion that it was too late to make any rational decision. He would ask Nellie in the morning for her opinion.

* * * *

"Please, please let me come with you, Uncle David." Jamie had come downstairs and found David discussing the trip to Harrogate with Nellie in the hall. "I'd love to see Sarah again."

"But you didn't get on with George, when they were here." Nellie fastened a button on his shirt.

"I can keep outta his way."

"You'd have to be on your best behaviour the whole time." She looked at David for confirmation. "Mrs Smythe will be in pain so she'll have even less patience than usual."

David nodded in agreement. "Yes, Nellie's right, Jamie. Now think hard."

"I'll be good."

David raised his eyebrows.

"Please." Jamie pressed his hands together and looked up with wide appealing eyes.

"You'd better pack him some clothes then, Nellie. It looks like the little monkey's got his way again." He ruffled the boy's hair.

"Aw, fanks." Jamie jumped up and down in excitement.

"But what about my grandmamma?" wailed Ruby, who had been on her way to clear out the fireplace in the morning room. "You promised you'd go and see her again."

Jamie's shoulders slumped. "Oh yes, I did."

"I'm sure your grandmother will understand, Ruby," David told her.

The maid did not look convinced as her bottom lip stuck out. "And what about Lady?" she moaned, seeming to be trying every ruse she could think of to prevent Jamie from going. "You won't be able to take her with you."

"You definitely will not be able to take Lady. That is a fact." David raised his eyebrows again. "So, do you want to reconsider?"

Jamie was torn, but made his decision. "I really do want to see Sarah."

"Right then, young man, as soon as you've finished your breakfast you can gather up the books and things that you want to take, while I put my affairs in order. I've arranged for the carriage to be at the front of the house at ten o'clock, so make sure you're ready."

* * * *

"Why don't you wait in the nursery?" Freda asked after Jamie had almost knocked her over, running in to pick up a pencil he had dropped earlier under the kitchen table, and banging his head scrambling to pick it up.

"'Cos I might miss Uncle David." He rubbed his head and grimaced in pain. "He might go without me if I'm not ready for him."

"He wouldn't do that, he's a man of his word. If he says he'll take you, then he will." Eventually Nellie sat him on a stool in the hall to prevent him getting under everybody's feet.

Ruby was still sulking though. "Grandmamma will be so disappointed," she said as she came across him swinging his legs back and forth. "I'll miss you, too. It was good to have someone to talk to when we went last time." She gave him a light punch in his belly. "Even if that someone was a pain in the bum." She smiled as she touched his face. "Is your lip better now?"

"Ruby, have those bedroom floors been mopped?" The housekeeper's voice came from the top of the stairs.

The maid pulled a face at Jamie as she rearranged the mops and dusters in her arms and hurried up the stairs.

Hearing the carriage pull up at the front door, Jamie jumped down from his stool and, with an effort, opened the door and ran out. He ventured over to the nearside horse, a sleek grey mare. He was rather unsure about such large horses as he had not dared broach the subject of riding lessons since his trouble with Rufus. He put out his hand to stroke the horse's mane just as it threw back its head and neighed. He jumped back in fright at the sight of the enormous teeth.

"That'll teach you to go near Fallon on your own," he heard David laugh behind him.

He drew Jamie close to the horse again. "She's quite tame as long as you don't startle her." He stroked the shiny neck and was rewarded with a nuzzle, then he handed Jamie a carrot. "Open your hand out flat and offer it to her."

Jamie cautiously held out the carrot but the horse's mouth was wet and it dribbled spittle on him. He pulled back his arm and dropped the carrot.

"Ugh! It's slimy!"

David chuckled. "Try one more time."

He picked up the carrot and held it out again. This time it was the horse's tongue that tickled his fingers and made him drop it.

"Never mind." David gave the carrot to the horse while Pervis loaded the last of the bags onto the back of the carriage. "In you get. It's time we were on our way."

Nellie had come out to see them off and Jamie waved to Ruby whom he spotted watching from an upstairs bedroom. He felt sorry for her, she always had to work so hard.

The journey passed quickly enough, with David pointing out one or two places of interest on the way. Jamie prattled away, quite happy to get an occasional response. They stopped for lunch at a coaching inn and were soon on their way again.

"T'in't far now, is it?" cried Jamie craning his neck to read a milestone. "I just see'd a sign what said: '*Harrogate 2 miles*'. At least, I think it said 'Harrogate'. It began with a *h* and had a *g* in it."

"You're quite right," replied David, surveying his whereabouts. "We should be there in about twenty minutes." He took out his pocket watch and smiled. "We've made very good time."

"I can't wait to see Sarah." Jamie was even more excited now that they were on the last leg of the journey. "Does she know I'm coming?"

"No. I haven't even told Mrs Smythe. When I sent the letter last night, I hadn't considered bringing you along." He leaned forward and put his hand on Jamie's knee. "You'd better be prepared for a frosty welcome, my lad."

* * * *

"If you wish it, I could postpone my ladies' meeting and accompany you," said Emily, as Tillie tried to force down the breakfast that her friend had insisted she eat.

"No, no, you've done so much for me already." Standing up, Tillie wrapped her shawl around her shoulders. "I wouldn't dream of taking up any more of your time."

"I'm only too pleased that I could be of assistance. You will let me know how you fare, won't you? I can't wait to find out. Perhaps I should put my ladies off…" Emily turned to Edward who had just come in. "What do you think, darling?"

"Sorry, my dear, I didn't hear the question," he said as he tripped over a chair leg, dropping the pile of books he had been carrying.

"Do you think I should put off the ladies' meeting and go with Tillie?" She pushed the offending chair back under the table and helped her husband pick up the books.

"That has to be your decision, my dear." The vicar straightened his clothing. "But I'm afraid I won't be able to go."

"No, no, I wouldn't expect it. You've done more than enough, arranging the carriage for me." Tillie turned and reached out to Emily. "Please don't put yourself out, I'll be fine."

"It would be to satisfy her own curiosity as much as for your benefit." Edward smiled. "I know my wife, her inquisitive nature can sometimes get the better of her."

"Oh, Edward." Emily tapped him playfully on the arm and grinned. "But I suppose he's right." She gave Tillie a gentle push towards the door. "Don't let us hold you up a moment longer then. You get off and find that son of yours. Go on, shoo!"

Tillie didn't need any further bidding. She climbed into the carriage and waved goodbye.

She seemed to be doing a lot of that lately, waving goodbye. But hopefully this would be the last time. She began to wonder what she would do if the child at the Grange wasn't

Jamie. It had to be, though. Surely there couldn't be that many small boys rambling about the area on their own, could there?

Then it occurred to her that, even if it was Jamie, he might not want to see her. He probably thought that she had abandoned him.

Or worse still, they might not allow her to see him. They weren't to know that she hadn't done it intentionally.

Wringing her hands and jigging her legs up and down in consternation, she moaned aloud.

"You all right, miss?" the driver called over his shoulder.

"Yes, thank you," Tillie called back, trying to pull herself together. She had come this far, she wasn't going to be put off now.

"Nearly there. Look to your right when we pass these trees."

Tillie did as she was bid and saw The Grange in its full glory. The windows lit up by the early morning sun's rays gave it a magical look. Old memories returned as she recalled happier times when she had lived as the maid at this very house. If only that blacksmith hadn't arrived, she might still have been here. But then she wouldn't have had Jamie. She couldn't imagine life without him now. She jiggled up and down again, praying that everything was going to work out.

She wondered if her sister Ruby was still there. She hadn't been in touch since she'd left. If only she had realised she had been living so close, when she had been with Mrs Curtis.

I know what I can do. She clapped her hands as a solution presented itself. *I'll pretend I've come to visit Ruby, then sound out the situation while I talk to her. If the boy is Jamie, he'll recognise me, and if he isn't…well…*she didn't want to think of that.

I'll need to make up a story though, about why I don't have my child with me, as they'll all know why I left. But I'm sure I'll think of something.

Feeling more positive, she began humming. Turning round, the driver smiled and joined in, so by the time they drew up at the door it was a cheerful duo that Pervis greeted.

Tillie recognised the butler straightaway but kept her face hidden under the bonnet Emily had given her. The driver helped her down and passed Pervis the tapestry bag that was now even fuller, thanks also to the vicar's wife's generosity.

She walked in through the large door, her stomach not just fluttering but turning somersaults as she took in the dark old oak-panelled walls and the magnificent chandelier above her ablaze with fluttering candles.

"Who may I ask is calling?" asked Pervis. "I'm afraid the master is away from home."

Tillie handed him her bonnet. Breathing in the familiar smells and atmosphere of the house she felt that she had come home. "I've come to see Ruby. Does she still work here?"

She suddenly realised what a faux-pas she had made. What had she been thinking? She shouldn't have come to the front door, she should have used the back kitchen entrance, but she'd been so fraught it hadn't occurred to her. She could have crept in secretly. Still, too late to back out now and thank goodness the master was away, she would have felt stupid, being announced.

"My goodness, if it isn't Tillie Raven!" Pervis interrupted her thoughts. "Come here, let me look at you!" The butler obviously hadn't noticed her blunder. Stretching out to put his hands on her shoulders, a broad grin creased his usually sombre face.

Nellie came running down the stairs, probably alerted by the unusual shouting.

"Nellie, look who's here." He turned Tillie to face her.

"Why, Tillie, it is you! I thought I'd heard wrong. I can't believe it. Wait 'til Ruby finds out."

At that moment Ruby slouched into the hall with her hands full of baskets of kindling wood. She stopped to look at the visitor.

"Oh, my God!" she yelled, dropping the baskets, scattering the wood all over the floor. "Oh, my!"

The sisters ran into each other's arms, tears streaming down their cheeks. They hugged for a moment, pulled away and looked into each other's faces, then hugged again. By this time Freda had come out and joined them. Tillie was passed round from one to the other, hugging everyone in turn.

A voice called from the kitchen. "Where is everybody?"

"Out here, Tom," they all cried.

"Well, well, Tillie Raven, as I live and breathe!" He hurried over and embraced her also.

Clinging onto Tillie's hand and dancing round her, Ruby's usually miserable face had changed into the picture of happiness. "What are you doing here, and where have you been, and...?"

"Slow down, Ruby, let your poor sister catch her breath." Nellie turned to Tillie. "She's never been the same since you left, you know...but never mind that now, come and tell us all about yourself."

They all trooped into the kitchen and Freda made a large pot of tea.

"Don't let me get you into trouble." Tillie looking round at everybody as they sat happily drinking tea and eating large slices of Freda's cake.

"The master's away so he won't know we're not working," Nellie reassured her. "Not that he'd mind. You always were his favourite. I seem to remember he had rather a soft spot for you. We've had a few maids since you left but none of them have stayed long. In fact we've managed without one for over a year now."

"Will the master be away long?" Tillie's outward smile belied her inner turmoil.

"Don't know. He had an urgent call from his sister, Annie – you remember her?"

Tillie nodded, forcing another bite of cake into her dry mouth.

"She's laid up with a splinter or something..." began Tom.

"Now, now!" admonished Nellie, wagging a finger at him. "Less of that! She's broken her leg, or her ankle. Anyway he's had to take off up to Harrogate to look after her."

"I've been wondering why her husband couldn't do that." Ruby scraped up some of the crumbs from the table.

"He's away abroad on business, I think."

"And does anyone else live here now?" Tillie picked up her cup, even though it was now empty, trying to act as casually as she could.

"Well, there's John, of course. If the master has to stay any length of time up at Harrogate he'll have to join him there, but he's remained here for the time being."

Tillie began to sweat. She closed her eyes, not knowing how much longer she could bear the tension inside her.

"And there's Jamie…"

There it was, the announcement she had been praying for. The room went black. Knocking her head on the table, she fell forward in a faint.

* * * *

The house was on a hill, the end one in a row of four, with steps leading up to the front door. David tugged the bell pull on the wall and Jamie heard a corresponding clanging inside. He did his best to remain out of sight, hidden behind David.

A servant opened the door. "The mistress is expecting you, sir, if you would like to come this way."

They entered a large drawing room with pictures hung around the walls. Jamie remained behind David, trying not to be seen as he looked up at them. Then he heard, "Took your time, didn't you? I expected you hours ago."

Peeping out, he saw Annie sitting up on a sofa, her legs covered with a pink blanket.

"Oh, my God!" she screeched. He grimaced as he quickly hid again, but it was too late.

"Surely that isn't who I think it is?" Peeping under David's elbow he saw her put her palm up to her head, and fall back on the pillows. "As if I don't have enough to contend with, you bring that urchin to plague me. How could you do this to me?"

"Good day to you too, Annie." David ignored her outburst, moving forward to greet her. Jamie clung on to the back of his jacket. He had been warned to expect a frosty welcome, but nothing like this. He'd only thought about Sarah, forgetting quite what an ogre her mother was.

David continued, "I'm not going into details now about why I brought the boy, but if you want me to stay, then you'll have to put up with him as well."

He pulled Jamie out from behind him. "Say good day to Mrs Smythe, Jamie. Let's be civilised about this."

He hesitated for a moment, then bowed and said in a low voice, "Good day, ma-am," before looking up at David, who nodded confirmation that he had done the right thing.

"You can't surely expect me to be civil when I'm in so much pain," Annie bleated with her nose in the air. "I'll never forgive you for this."

"Be that as it may." David bent forward to plump up her pillows. "But I'm here now, or *we're* here now, so would a drink be too much to ask for, after our long journey, sister dear?"

Giving David a snooty look, she picked up a hand bell from the table at her side and rang it. A young maid entered.

"Katy, bring some tea for Mr Dalton and myself. Oh, and take this...child and find him some lemonade or something." She shooed Jamie away with her hand.

He looked up at David who nodded. "Yes, Jamie, go with Katy. I'll come and find you later."

Perhaps it wasn't such a good idea to come, Jamie thought as he followed the maid to the kitchen, but once seated at the table and sipping his drink while she took the tray of tea to the drawing room, he felt a lot better.

"What's your name?" Katy poured herself a drink on her return, and took a large gulp of it.

"Jamie." At least she was friendly. He looked around. "Where's Sarah?"

"At school, George too. They should be home soon. D'yer know her then?"

"Yes, they all come to stay with Uncle David a while back. Didn't they tell you bout it?"

"No, I've only been here a couple of weeks."

"Oh." Jamie sipped some more of his drink. Then he remembered something that Sarah had said. "But I thought they had a...what do yer call it? A govaniness."

"Oh, she were sacked before I came. Don't know the ins and outs of it, but now they have to go to school, whether they like it or not."

"I wonder what it's like at school. Did you ever go?"

"Me? Nah. Me oldest brother went to the ragged school for a bit, but he didn't like it so me pa said he didn't have to go again cos, anyway, he needs him on the farm. And he says there's no point in us girls learning stuff when we could be out earning money."

"You got lots'a brothers and sisters, then?"

"Ten...eleven if you count the new baby that'll be arriving in a couple of weeks." She took some potatoes out of the pantry and began to peel them. "You got any?"

"No, I don't think so."

"Don't you know?"

"I lost me memory."

"Oh." She continued to peel the vegetables with a puzzled look on her face.

Just then he heard the front door open and Sarah's voice crying, "Uncle David! Mother said you were coming."

He could only hear muffled voices after that and was longing for her to come in, for he knew he daren't go back into the drawing room. He sat jiggling on the edge of his chair staring at the door.

"Why don't you go in to her?" Katy began chopping up some onions.

"Oh no. I got to keep out her way, she hates me."

"Who, Sarah?"

"No, Mrs high-and-mighty Smythe."

Katy snorted, leaned over and whispered. "I know what you mean." Straightening, she looked around guiltily, putting her hand up to her mouth. "I um…don't tell no one I said that, will you?"

"Course not." Jamie also looked around. "I wouldn't let Sarah hear me say this, either, but her ma's the most…what's the horriblest word I could use? Well, the most horriblest person I ever knew."

"Mm, if me ma didn't need me money…"

Jamie's patience was wearing thin. He jumped down from the chair. "Surely Sarah knows I'm here by now. Why ain't she come in to see me?"

"Perhaps she's been ordered not to."

"S'pose so." As he said this the door opened wide and he ran towards it eagerly.

"What's the hurry, little urchin?" It was George, not Sarah. Jamie tried to suppress a moan. "You going somewhere? Like back where you came from, maybe? Don't know why Uncle David brought you, 'cos you're not welcome."

He hadn't changed. In fact, now he was on his own territory he was worse.

"Pour me a drink, then." He turned to Katy who had her hands full of onion peelings. "Do what you're paid for."

The harassed maid dropped the peel on the table and quickly picked up the jug.

"I don't want it tasting of onions, stupid girl. Wipe your hands first."

Jamie gasped. How could anyone be so unkind? "Shall I do it?" He reached over to take the jug from her.

"Pah, it would taste even worse if a beggar like you did it."

"George, why do you always have to be so obnoxious?" Jamie hadn't heard her come in.

He ran towards the door. "Sarah!"

She opened her arms and embraced him warmly. "Take no notice of him. He's still as awful as ever." She gestured towards her brother who was helping himself to a biscuit from the tin on the dresser.

"I just knew it," George said with his mouth full. "As soon as I heard that the little runt was here, I knew you'd be all over him."

"George, stop it! Your jealousy'll get the better of you one of these days."

"Huh, me jealous? Of that little—"

"Enough!"

"You can't tell me what to do! You're—"

"Maybe not, but I can," David shouted from the passage.

Jamie had been watching the pair arguing, thinking that perhaps it was not so bad after all, having no brothers or sisters.

"I could hear you squabbling from the drawing room," David bawled as he marched into the kitchen. "Don't you think your mother could do without it at this unfortunate time?"

"You shouldn't have brought him then," mumbled George under his breath.

"I beg your pardon, young man, perhaps your father let's you get away with cheek like that but I won't. While I'm here you will see that you behave in a polite and gracious manner to everyone, Jamie included. Understood?"

George put down his unfinished drink and, murmuring under his breath, stalked across the room.

"Excuse me, I'm waiting for an answer." David folded his arms.

"Yes, Uncle David." George kept his head down as he shuffled over to the door, poking his tongue out at Jamie behind his uncle's back as he went out.

Katy had been standing goggle-eyed, with an onion in one hand and a knife in the other. Jamie smiled at her. She didn't

122

look any older than Sarah, her fair, straggly hair peeping out from the mop cap on the back of her head.

"Katy was saying…" he began. A pair of terrified violet eyes silently beseeched him. She looked as if she was crying. He wondered why but continued, "She was telling me that she has ten brothers and sisters, Uncle David. Can you imagine that?" The violet eyes closed and her face relaxed.

Surely she didn't think I was going to tell on her about what we were saying before? he thought. *I wouldn't do that, not in a million years.*

"I didn't know that, Katy, you never told me." Sarah put the dirty glasses beside the sink. "That must be fun…or perhaps not." She smiled wryly. "Not if they're all like…" she indicated with her head towards the door.

Picking up a carrot, she began to cut it up. "Would you like me to help you prepare the dinner again?"

"Why, where's cook?" asked David, looking around.

"She walked out the day before yesterday. She and Mama had an argument about the way she cooked the beef or something, and she upped and left."

"So who's been…?" He swept his arm in an arc around the kitchen.

"Katy, but I help as much as I can."

"This is atrocious! How can young Katy here be expected to cook for the whole family, as well as doing all her other chores?"

"She doesn't mind, do you Katy?"

"Not at all, sir, I'm used to cooking for a lot." The maid bobbed her head.

"That's not the point." David opened the pantry door and peered inside. "It looks as if we could do with some more provisions. It's practically empty in here." He took his watch out of his pocket and opened it. "It's too late to go shopping today." He turned back to Katy. "Do you have all you need for dinner tonight?"

"Yes, sir. That's if you don't mind hotchpotch."

"I love hotchpotch." Taking off his jacket and hanging it over the back of a chair, he rolled up his sleeves and picked up a carrot.

"If you show me where the knives are, I'll help. What do I do with this?"

A stunned silence greeted his words. The two girls looked at him, goggle-eyed in amazement.

Jamie looked from one to the other, wondering why they looked so shocked. "I could help as well."

The clanging of a hand bell was heard from the drawing room. Wiping her hands down her apron, Katy started towards the door.

David put out a hand and stopped her. "No, I'll go." He put down the carrot he had been waving in the air. "I need a word with my sister, anyway. You carry on here as best you can and I'll return when I've sorted a few things out." Rolling down his sleeves, he put his jacket back on.

He turned to Jamie on his way out. "I'm sure they'll find you something to do that won't get you into trouble. Just don't get in the way or cause them more work."

"Sure thing, sir!"

David smiled and shook his head.

The bell rang again, more urgently.

"I'm coming." David sighed, rolling his eyes as he went out. "Give me a chance!"

Chapter 8

When Tillie came to she was lying in a soft bed. For a second she curled up in its luxuriousness then sat bolt upright. A warm hand gently pushed her back onto the pillows and she turned to see Ruby smiling at her.

"Oh Ruby, how I've missed you!" she whispered, reaching out to her. "How've you been?"

"Never mind me, what about you?" Her sister wrapped her arms around her. They rocked backwards and forwards, while Tillie tried to decide how much of her predicament she should share.

The door opened and Nellie came in. "Thank goodness you're awake. You had us worried back there."

"I'm fine now, just a slight headache." Tillie tried to extricate herself gently from Ruby's arms. "I...um..."

"No need for explanations now." Nellie patted her shoulder. "Would you like something to eat?" She smoothed out the wrinkled bedcovers. "Something light? A bowl of Freda's potato and leek soup?"

"I'll get it." Ruby started towards the door.

"That would be lovely, just what I need." Tillie looked at the pair of familiar faces before her. "You can't imagine how much I've missed you all. I should have come home years ago but I didn't know if I would be welcome, after..."

She realised that she had called it 'home', but didn't amend it as that had been how she had considered The Grange when she had first settled in, and how she had always thought of it since.

"As I said, explanations later," Nellie said, before turning to Ruby who was still hovering in the doorway. "Soup, Ruby!"

"Yes...but..." She rushed back towards Tillie and grabbed her hand. "I just can't believe you're back!" she wailed before running from the room in tears.

"Poor Ruby," Nellie and Tillie said at the same time, making them both smile.

"You're looking better. I was really worried about you earlier, fainting like that." Nellie plumped up the pillows, making Tillie more comfortable. Straightening, she looked directly at her. "You're not…with child, are you?"

Before Tillie could reply she added, "But that's none of my business. I apologise, I shouldn't have…"

"That's all right, Nellie. And no, I'm not," Tillie reassured her with a shake of her head. *Should I take her into my confidence now?* she deliberated, but was saved from committing herself when Ruby reappeared.

"Now you go and get some for yourself," Nellie said to the maid as she placed the tray of hot soup in front of the patient. "You've been up here all day. Now that you know your sister's all right you can stop worrying."

"If you're sure you don't mind?" Ruby looked from one to the other uncertainly. "I am a bit peckish, and that soup smells so delicious."

"Of course you must go, Ruby." Tillie put the spoon to her mouth. "Mmm, it's lovely. Go on, shoo!" She remembered Emily using this expression and rather liked it.

"I'll leave you to enjoy your meal in peace," said Nellie after Ruby had left. "When you feel up to it, just come downstairs. The master's away, as you know, so there's nobody here to bother you."

"What about this Jamie?"

"Oh, he's only a young boy that we took in. Nobody knows who he is, and he's lost his memory so even he doesn't know."

"Oh." Tillie tried her hardest to eat calmly. "And isn't he here?"

"No, the master took him up to Harrogate with him. I could tell he was reluctant to do so, but young Jamie can be very persuasive when he wants something."

It had to be her Jamie. 'Persuasive' was definitely how she would describe him, but she wondered why he had wanted to go to Harrogate. Well, at least he seemed to be well and happy.

After Nellie had left she forced down the remains of her meal and, setting the tray to one side, she sighed. She seemed fated never to see her little boy again, and all she wanted to do was look into his big brown eyes and cuddle him.

Wrapping her arms around her body as if she was rocking a tiny baby, tears ran down her face. She gave in to them, letting all her frustrations and disappointments wash out, then, drawing the covers over her head, she curled up and fell asleep again.

* * * *

"And where do you think the little beggar's going to sleep? You obviously didn't think this through. Oh…I still can't believe you could inflict such misery on me in my time of need."

David stood patiently listening to his sister ranting and raving. He raised his eyes to the ceiling and took a deep breath. "For heaven's sake, Ann, don't be so melodramatic! He can sleep in with me. It won't be a hardship."

"Don't call me Ann! You know I much prefer to be called Annie," she whined. "I'm sure you only do it to provoke me."

"All right, Annie! Anyway, why didn't you tell me you didn't have a cook? How can you expect that poor girl in there, with all her other duties to perform, to cook for everyone, as well as be at your beck and call?"

"It was her fault I slipped in the first place. If she hadn't spilt the milk I wouldn't be lying here now. Oh, the pain!" Grimacing, she leaned forward and rubbed her leg. David couldn't be sure how much she was suffering and how much she was faking, but decided to give her the benefit of the doubt.

"Well, I'm here now, and I'll help all I can." He paced up and down while his sister lay back and closed her eyes. "I shall have to get some organisation into the household. Do you know anyone who could lend you a cook until a replacement can be arranged?"

"No."

"Katy says she can manage tonight, but we'll have to sort something out tomorrow."

"Yes, all right, if you say so. I'll leave it all in your capable hands." She lifted her hand up to her head. "Could you leave me now, I'm a trifle tired." She yawned as if to prove the point.

"Of course. Is there anything you require before I go?"

"No, just make sure you close the door quietly on your way out."

What had she expected him to do? Slam it? Gritting his teeth to prevent a sarcastic retort escaping, he closed the door as quietly as he could and went to the kitchen where he found Katy on her own.

"Where's Jamie?" he asked.

"Oh, Sarah took him for a walk down to the park, sir. George was…" she looked up at him as if unsure how to phrase the explanation. "He was…"

"I can well imagine what George was doing," he reassured her. "Did she say how long they'd be?"

"No, sir, she didn't."

"I thought she was supposed to be helping you prepare the dinner."

"Oh, she did, sir. It's all done." She pointed towards the range, inside which he assumed the dinner must be cooking, for he couldn't see anything on the top.

"That's splendid, well done!"

"Thank you, sir." Katy curtsied and grinned at the compliment.

Poor kid, she had probably never been praised for anything before, he thought.

"We need a cook urgently, not that you're not doing a grand job, because you are, believe me." He reassured her with his hand on her arm. "But it's not fair to heap all this extra work on you when you have your other tasks."

He began walking around the kitchen, picking up utensils and turning them over to examine them, wondering what they were used for.

"I know someone...sir," Katy stuttered, her eyes wide and uncertain.

"You do?"

"Me auntie, sir, she's staying over on the other side of town."

"And can she cook?"

"Oh yes, sir. She was head cook up at the Mansion House before the old man died. The house is empty now, 'til the new master moves in, so she's got no work...sir."

David heaved a sigh of relief. "Right, do you think you could go over first thing in the morning and arrange for her to come and see me?"

"Yes, sir. Certainly, sir." She curtsied, smiling.

That was one problem solved. What was next on the agenda?

* * * *

Tillie awoke to the sound of birdsong, and could see daylight. She must have slept right through.

She'd missed Jamie by a hair's breadth. Screwing up her toes in frustration, she felt like weeping. But that wouldn't solve anything. She looked around at the décor, wondering whose room she was in. The washstand with the blue jug and bowl were the usual ones found in most bedrooms, so that didn't give her any clues. She sat up, trying to remember which room was decorated with pink wallpaper and gold stripes. Wasn't the mistress's room pink and gold? But surely they wouldn't have put her in there? But she couldn't remember any other room having those colours. Perhaps it had been decorated since she left, but, no, it didn't look like it, there were one or two worn patches over by the window.

She remembered that when she had left, Elizabeth had been expecting a baby, but nobody had mentioned her or the child, or any other siblings. They must have all gone to Harrogate, but it would be a bit of an upheaval to take the whole family unless they were planning on staying quite a while.

And that still didn't explain why she was in this room.

Pushing back the covers, she swung her legs out and stepped onto the bedside rug, wriggling her toes in the soft rags and enjoying the luxury of having something warm and cosy to stand on after all those years on the road.

After a quick wash she opened the tapestry bag that someone must have brought up for her while she was asleep. It seemed a pity to get something else dirty when the blue one she had been wearing was still all right so she put that on and closed the bag up again.

She didn't know if anyone else would be up and about yet, but knowing that they all rose fairly early she suspected that someone would be. It wouldn't matter if they weren't, she knew her way around. She couldn't find her shoes so assumed that Nellie had probably taken them to be cleaned as they had been rather muddy. Ah, Nellie, what a brick she was.

The door opened and the object of her thoughts appeared. "Ah, you're up already." Nellie smiled as she came into the room. "Here are your shoes."

"I was looking for them. Thank you so much, not just for the shoes, but for…for just…being you."

She put her arms round the housekeeper who grunted a denial and wriggled away, saying, "Oh, you haven't changed."

She held Tillie at arm's length, looking into her eyes. "You always were a lovely-natured girl." She paused for a moment and then continued, "I can sense that something's troubling you though. Do you want to talk?"

Tillie sucked in her cheeks and shook her head slowly.

"Don't worry, there's plenty of time." Nellie patted her cheek. "Come down when you're ready."

"Yes, I just need to do my hair."

"There's the mistress's silver brush and comb set there on the dressing table. You can use that."

So I was right, Tillie thought, wrinkling her eyebrows in bewilderment as the housekeeper picked up the brush and ran her hand over the soft bristles. *It is the mistress's room.*

"The master couldn't bear to part with them after..." Nellie continued. Then she looked up. "Of course, you won't know..."

"Know what?"

Putting the brush back down, Nellie sighed as she lined it up with its partner. "There was a horrific accident, about two years ago. The wheel of the carriage caught a boulder in the road and they—that's the mistress, their young son, Freddy, and the master himself—were all catapulted out. Freddy was killed instantly."

Gasping in disbelief, Tillie reached out, but Nellie shook her head, seemingly unable to continue for a moment, so she entwined her hands in front of her, waiting in silence for the distressed housekeeper to continue.

"I'm sorry. It still gets you here." Nellie punched her stomach.

Tillie tried to think of some words of comfort but her shocked brain couldn't come up with anything appropriate.

Nellie continued. "Yes, Freddy was killed on the spot. The doctor said he wouldn't have suffered though, and the mistress was taken to hospital where she died two days later."

"And the master?"

"He got off with a few cuts and bruises. He still berates himself about it. It seemed to make it worse for him that he wasn't injured."

"I'm so sorry. It must have been awful."

"That's putting it mildly. He's only just begun to get his life back on track."

Tillie sat back down on the bed, digesting the upsetting information as Nellie took out a white handkerchief from her apron pocket and blew her nose loudly.

"Were there any other children?" She remembered what she had been thinking about earlier.

"No, they had twin girls when Freddy was about two, but they both died in infancy and the mistress never carried another baby full term."

"That is such a sad story, the poor master! I suppose that's why he's taken in the stray boy, as a substitute for his own son."

Pursing her lips, Nellie shrugged her shoulders.

Tillie continued. "Do you think it would be too bold of me to ask if I could stay until he returns, to give him my condolences?"

"I'm sure that wouldn't be a problem. He'd be very pleased to see you, because, as I said earlier, you were always his favourite." With a questioning look she asked, "But what about your own life? Or are you...running away from something?"

Tillie couldn't look her in the eye. She turned and walked over to the window, wondering what to tell her.

"Something like that," she mumbled non-committedly. She was uneasy telling the white lie, so kept her back to the knowing housekeeper.

Brushing her hair after Nellie left, she thought how difficult it was going to be to take Jamie away, once he returned from Harrogate. It seemed as if the master had grown attached to him, and that was why he had taken him up there.

This could be a problem, but then again, perhaps it could work in her favour.

* * * *

132

"I didn't know whether you were still staying with Uncle David." Sarah took Jamie's hand as they walked towards the park situated at the end of the street. "Whenever I ask mother, when she gets a letter from him, she just tells me it's none of my business."

Jamie smiled up at her, his heart full as he looked into her bright blue eyes. "Uncle David always tells me how you are, when he gets a letter. But he didn't tell me you had to go to no school, though. Is it awful?"

"No, it's not bad. There are some friendly girls there, and yesterday I was chosen to be ink monitor."

"What's that?"

"It's when the best behaved child is chosen to give out the inkwells." Sarah looked very proud of herself, making Jamie wonder why inkwells, whatever they were, should make her stick out her chest. "And I enjoy playing games at lunch time, especially hopscotch and blind man's bluff."

"Can't say as I've ever played them. We used to play spinning top."

Stopping suddenly, Sarah's eyes lit up. "Does that mean you've got your memory back?"

"Not really, I just remember some things now'n again."

"Oh." Sarah looked disappointed. "Never mind, here we are." She walked on ahead through the gate, so Jamie followed her, trying hard to remember something really important to impress her, but could bring nothing to mind.

His disappointment was soon forgotten when they entered the park and he was stopped in his tracks at the sights and sounds of the people out enjoying the evening sunshine. There were ladies dressed in colourful costumes, men on horseback, carriages pulled by teams of matching horses, and couples walking arm in arm.

"Come on, let's go down to the lake and see the swans," called Sarah, who had started to walk ahead. Stopping when Jamie didn't follow her, she walked back to him.

"What's the matter?" she asked, looking back at the throng of people.

Jamie shook his head in amazement. "I never seen such a sight," he exclaimed. "All these fancy people, all in one place!"

She smiled just as a tall man on a brown horse rode up to them, took off his hat and bowed.

"Good day to you, young Sarah," he called. "I hope your father is well."

"Yes, thank you, sir," Sarah curtseyed.

"My regards to your mother."

As the man rode away, a frantic shout of "Whoa!" made Jamie turn, and he saw a carriage careering towards them. The wide, frightened eyes of a young lady pulling on the reins of a white horse stared out at him. Without thinking he jumped back, dragging Sarah with him, and fell to the ground just in time to see the spinning wheels rush past, inches away from them.

He lay breathless, his chest heaving, trying to gulp in some air.

"You all right?" he managed to gasp. There was no reply. He sat up and looked at Sarah anxiously.

The rider who had spoken to her came running up, pulling his horse behind him. "Are you hurt?" he asked.

"I'm not, but I don't know bout Sarah." Jamie shook her but there was no response.

The man bent down and turned her face towards him. Jamie could see a red patch on her pink bonnet and touched it, gasping, as he looked at his finger and realised that it was smeared with blood.

"Sarah!" he wailed.

George appeared from behind him, as if out of nowhere. "Get out of the way," he yelled, shoving Jamie to one side. "How could you do it? I saw you push her."

"Now then, master George," began the man, "that's not what happened at all. I saw this young…"

"You shut up," George cried, leaning over his sister.

Sarah stirred.

"Sarah!" Jamie cried again, trying to get closer to her but he was thrust away once more, this time more violently, and he fell back on the grass.

People started gathering round. "We'd better get help," someone said.

A voice from the back of the crowd shouted, "Here, use my carriage," and a large well-dressed man with a pink cravat stepped forward.

He bent to pick Sarah up but George yelled, "Leave her alone!"

Sarah tried to sit up. "I want to go home," she moaned, so George helped the man with the pink cravat get her into the carriage, while Jamie looked on, feeling helpless. The man then turned to the boys. "I'm afraid there's only room for one of you."

"It doesn't matter about him." George climbed in before Jamie could get near. "A carriage is too good for him, he can walk back."

"Will you be all right, J—?" Sarah tried to lean out to him, but her brother cut her off.

"Course he will, a vagabond like him. Let's go."

The driver gave Jamie a concerned look but he urged his horse on and the carriage moved off, leaving Jamie surrounded by hundreds of faces, all talking at once, all asking him questions about what had happened. The babble was getting louder and louder, closing in on him. He was suffocating. He put his hands up to his throbbing head, feeling as if it was going to burst. He heard a muffled voice in his ear as someone put an arm on his shoulder, but he shrugged it off and ran. He ran and ran, not knowing where he was going, only wanting to get away.

* * * *

135

David heard the carriage draw up at the front door and looked out of the window to see who it was. "My God, it's Sarah and George. What on earth are they doing in a carriage with a strange man?"

Annie had been dozing but soon sat up at his exclamation. "My Sarah?"

"Of course, how many other Sarah's do we know?"

"Help me up, I need to see."

David helped his sister to her feet and, with his arm round her back and her right arm round his shoulder, he helped her shuffle to the door.

The manservant had by this time opened the front door. George came bursting in first.

"Mama, Sarah's been hurt and…and she's got blood on her head and…"

Propping Annie up against the wall, David ran out to help his niece.

Sarah started to speak.

"Shh, don't try to talk." David lifted her out of the carriage and carried her into the house.

"Oh, my!" wailed Annie on seeing her daughter up close. "What have they done to you? And just look at your lovely bonnet."

"Is that all you can think about, her bonnet?" cried David angrily, brushing past his sister and almost knocking her over as she stood leaning precariously against the wall. "You never cease to amaze me."

He lowered Sarah onto the bed in the lounge and called Katy to fetch a bowl of warm water and some disinfectant, while George stared goggle-eyed at his sister, his hands on his head, as David removed her bonnet.

Annie's voice was heard from the hall. "Georgie, come and help me. I'm stuck."

David looked back at his nephew who stared, transfixed and unmoving. "Go and help your mother, George, I'll see to

Sarah." For a brief moment he considered leaving his sister where she was but thought better of it.

"It doesn't matter now," Annie's voice came from behind him. "This nice gentleman has helped me in, as everybody else chose to desert me."

David turned to the man who had brought his niece home and shook his hand. "We owe you a debt of gratitude, sir."

"Glad to be of service, sir." The man bowed.

Katy stood hesitantly at the door. "'Scuse me, sir."

"Yes, Katy, have you brought the water and disinfectant?"

"Um…" the maid fidgeted nervously.

"What?"

"Sir, I don't know what disinc—tant is, sir."

David sighed as he turned to Annie, who was attempting to sit down on a chair. "Don't you use disinfectant in this house?"

"You mean that stuff that's supposed to kill germs? I don't need that, I run a clean house," she replied haughtily.

David sighed again, deciding this was not the appropriate moment to share the benefits of keeping germs at bay. He turned back to Katy. "Just bring some warm water and a clean flannel, thank you Katy," he instructed before putting out his hand to his visitor. "Excuse me, sir, I do apologise." He waved his hand around the room, not pointing at anything in particular. "I cannot thank you enough for bringing my niece home safely."

"It was the least I could do, in the circumstances. I don't think she's too badly hurt."

"I'll be fine, there's no need to fuss," said Sarah. "I'm just worried about Jamie."

David looked around him, suddenly registering that Jamie wasn't there.

"Pah!" Annie began. "Don't worry about—"

"Where is Jamie?" David cried, ignoring his sister. He turned to the man whose pink cravat made him blink. "Come to think of it, he wasn't in the carriage, was he?"

"No, if you mean the other boy, unfortunately there wasn't room for him, so we had to leave him in the park, but I'm sure he'll find his own way home."

"But he doesn't know his way. He and I only arrived this afternoon."

Annie banged her hand sharply on the table. "Stop concerning yourself over that ragamuffin. For goodness sake, it's your niece you need to worry about, not some runaway you've taken in off the street."

"I could go and look for him," the man volunteered, backing out, obviously eager to depart. "If that would help."

"No, no, sir." Annie put out her hand to him. "We wouldn't want to put you to any more bother."

"Well, if you're sure." He looked at David as if for confirmation.

David had to agree, much as he would have welcomed the man's help. "Yes, sir, we mustn't detain you any longer, I'm sure you're a busy man." Shaking his hand once more, he showed him out. "Thank you once again."

"Here's my card, in case you need me further." The man handed over a business card as he climbed into his carriage. "Good day to you."

"Good day to you, sir," replied David, tapping the card as he looked anxiously up and down the street to see if there was any sign of Jamie. There was only an old couple strolling along, but no sign of a young boy. He looked up at the sky as the carriage departed. The sun was getting lower, it would soon be setting. How would he find his way in the dark? As Annie had pointed out, his first obligation was to Sarah, but what should he do about his protégé?

* * * *

Tillie was greeted enthusiastically when she entered the kitchen. Ruby was like a Cheshire cat, her face set in a constant grin. "I still can't believe you're back," she repeated every few minutes.

"It does feel good." Tillie looked around at all the familiar faces before sitting down at the table and tucking into the plate of food Freda put in front of her.

"You never did have an ounce of spare flesh on you." The cook spooned some more mushrooms onto the plate. "Now you're even thinner. Didn't they feed you where you've been?"

Tillie cast an anxious look at Nellie who had been about to go out of the door but she turned back. "We'll hear what's happened to Tillie later, when she's got her strength back. For the time being, we'll not pry. She'll tell us when she's ready."

Tillie cast a grateful smile and, realising she had bacon fat dribbling down her chin, got up to wipe it off on a towel. "That was delicious. The best meal I've had in ages. Thank you." She rubbed her hands together. "Now what can I do to help?"

"Don't even think about anything like that." Nellie had still not gone back out. She looked at Ruby, who was still grinning, a duster hanging loosely in her hand, and suggested, "Why don't you both go for a walk somewhere? Perhaps go to see your grandmother?"

"Oh yes, could we?" cried Ruby, jumping up and down like a small child. Then her face fell. "But what about my chores? I still have—"

"We can manage, don't worry. It's not every day you find a long lost sister, so go on, go out and enjoy yourselves!"

They both hugged her while Freda looked on, smiling.

"I'll wear my new yellow bonnet again." Ruby was still grinning as she ran out to get changed.

"She really has missed you." Nellie smiled ruefully at Tillie as she bent down to pick up a spoon that Ruby had knocked off the table. "But I'm sure you'll make up for it now you're back. You stay as long as you want."

It didn't take long for Ruby to get changed out of her maid's uniform into her beige walking dress and they were soon out of the door with another basket of Freda's baking to take with them.

Ruby skipped along like the little girl Tillie remembered her as. She had missed her sister terribly, as they had been very close, especially after their parents had died.

"Do you like my new bonnet?" Ruby asked, putting her hands behind her head to show it off better.

"Yes, it's very pretty," replied Tillie, smiling.

"I bought it from a shop in town, they had a sale on. I'd been saving up for ages." She did another twirl. "Isn't it the finest hat you ever saw? It didn't have the lace when I bought it. I sewed that on to make it look fancier." She looked down shyly and blushed. "Sam likes it."

"Who's Sam?" Tillie noticed the blush and wondered if her sister had lost her heart.

"He's the head groom."

"And do you especially like him?"

Ruby shrugged, looking coy. "He makes me laugh."

"And is he your sweetheart?"

"Oh no, nothing like that."

As they passed near the stables Tillie noticed Ruby craning her neck. They both jumped as a voice came from behind them. "Looking for anyone in particular?"

"Sam Wright, you frightened the living daylights out of me!" Ruby began to blush again. "How did you get there without us seeing you?"

"Ah, I saw you coming from way back there and I hid." He gestured towards her sister. "Are you going to introduce me to this delectable lady?"

Ruby's smile disappeared immediately. "She's..." she began with a pout.

Tillie intervened, "I'm Tillie, Ruby's sister. You must be the groom she's been talking so much about."

"She has, has she? What's she been saying about me then? Nothing bad, I hope?"

"Oh no, only good things. I think she…" She stopped on seeing the pleading look on Ruby's face, and decided to change the subject. She looked over to the edge of the field. "Oh, look at those lovely flowers. Shall we pick some for Grandmother?"

She started towards them, linking arms with Ruby who urged, "Please don't say anything."

"I won't," she whispered back.

"Are you the sister who used to work here?" Sam asked on catching them up. "Ruby says good things about you, too."

"Ruby never has anything bad to say about anyone. She's the kindest, sweetest girl in the world." If she couldn't tell him that her sister liked him, then she could at least sing her praises.

"Yes. I think you're right," replied Sam, looking at Ruby again with his head on one side. "Say, I hear Jamie's gone to Harrogate with the master. Any idea when they'll be back?"

"No. Mrs Smythe's broken her ankle," replied Ruby, still looking rather despondent. "So it could be a while." She turned to Tillie more cheerfully. "I took Jamie with me last time I went to see Grandmamma and she loved him. You'd love him too, he's really special."

Tillie's heart began to pound. How could she bear the waiting any longer? If only something would happen to bring him back!

"Grandmamma thought he looked a bit like you," continued Ruby, clearly oblivious to her sister's inner turmoil.

Tillie stood up and put out her hand to take the flowers Sam and Ruby had picked, not wanting to pursue that line of conversation. "I think that's enough, Grandmamma should be pleased with these." She arranged them all into a pretty posy. "Pleased to meet you, Sam, we'd better be off now."

"Goodbye, Sam," called Ruby, her gaze lingering as he began to walk away.

"Goodbye Ruby," he called, "and you, Tillie. See you again soon."

As they walked on Ruby seemed rather wistful. "He seems to like you."

"He doesn't even know me, and I have no intention of letting him do so, so don't look so worried." She took her sister's arm and they skipped along until they came to the stile.

"Jamie slipped over here." Ruby pointed to the place where he had fallen. "I know I shouldn't have, 'cos he cut his lip, but I had to laugh, 'cos he was covered in mud from head to toe, poor little mite."

"You always did have a peculiar sense of humour." Tillie climbed over the stile after her sister.

"I can't help it. It was always me being told off when we were children, wasn't it? You were always the goody-goody." She looked down. "But then Papa died, and we came here, and though it was hard work, at least I felt safe and part of a family again. Then you left me as well. I was so alone and lost. I thought I'd never be happy again. Nellie's always telling me to cheer up, and 'til Jamie came there was nothing to be cheery about." She flung her arms in the air. "But now you're here as well…"

Tillie threw her arms around her sister. "Oh, Ruby, I'm so sorry. But it wasn't easy for me either."

"Of course, how selfish of me." Ruby came to a stop, frowning. "You still haven't told me what happened…"

"Let's not talk about that now. I know Grandmamma will give me the first degree when we get there, so let's just enjoy the walk."

She still hadn't thought up a reason for turning up unexpectedly. Perhaps it wasn't such a good idea to be going to see her grandmother. The wise old woman was sure to worm out the truth, and she would certainly recognise the anguish in her eyes.

Chapter 9

As soon as they exited the copse, Tillie could see her grandmother in the distance, sitting at her door with a basket on her knee. "She still does her basket-weaving then?"

"Yes, all the time." Ruby stopped with a mischievous gleam in her eye. "I know, let's creep up on her and give her a surprise. She's not expecting us so we could go round that way." She pointed to a lane that ran behind the cottages. "And come up behind her."

"Trust you to think of that," Tillie replied, still trying to decide what story to tell, so her mind wasn't really engaged, but if Ruby wanted to play a trick she would go along with it to please her.

"Come on then, before she looks up and sees us." Ruby pulled Tillie by the arm, almost knocking the flowers out of her hand.

"Mind the posy." Rearranging it, she hitched up her dress, and they ran across the field, skirting a small brook at the bottom, and down onto the lane.

As they slowed down to a walking pace a neighbour saw them and beckoned them over. "It's Ruby, isn't it? Going to see your grandmother? You don't usually come this way."

"I know," Ruby replied with a gleeful grin. "But we've got a surprise for her." She pointed to her sister. "So we're going to sneak up behind her."

The old lady peered at Tillie but obviously didn't recognise her. She turned back to Ruby. "Well, I wanted to warn you that your grandmother has been proper poorly. She had a right nasty turn day before yesterday."

"But we saw her from up there—" Ruby pointed up to the copse they had come from, "—and she looked fine."

"Possibly she did from far away." The woman shook her head. "But I tell you, she's not well."

The girls looked at each other in consternation then looked up the lane towards the cottage.

"Has she seen a doctor?" Tillie turned back to ask.

"Nay, she won't. She's as stubborn as a mule."

"We'd better hurry up and get to her then. Thank you for warning us." They began running, all thoughts of creeping up on her gone from their minds.

Grandmother was sitting slumped in her chair. She looked up slowly as the sisters approached, and half smiled.

"Grandmamma!" Ruby bent down to put her arm around the old lady's shoulders. "Shouldn't you be in your bed?"

"What for?" Her grandmother shook her head. "Beds are for sleeping in or dying in…and I ain't in the mood for either." She then screwed up her face and looked at Tillie. "You've brought the boy again. Hope he hasn't fallen this time." Her head slumped onto her chest.

Tillie was at a loss to know what to do as Ruby looked at her, her own anguish mirrored on her face. Dropping the flowers, she picked up her grandmother's shawl from the ground where it had fallen and gently wrapped it around her frail shoulders, feeling the scrawny bones beneath.

"Would you like a cup of tea, Grandmamma?" She couldn't think what else to say. A slight nod was her response so she hurried into the cottage, followed by Ruby.

"She thinks you're Jamie," Ruby cried, tears falling down her cheeks as she placed the basket of food on the table before making up the fire that had almost gone out. "How could she not see that you're wearing a dress? What are we goner do?"

"I don't know," wailed Tillie as she made the tea, then refilled the kettle and put it back on its hook over the fire. "I just don't know."

With shaking hands, she carried the tray outside and placed it on a small table that Ruby brought out.

"Here you are, Grandmamma. Here's your tea. I've put lots of sugar in it to give you some energy."

Grandmother managed a feeble smile. "It'll take more than sugar," she rued. She could barely hold the cup so Tillie took it from her and raised it to her lips.

"You're not Jamie, are you?" she studied Tillie's face again.

"It's Tillie," cried Ruby with tears in her eyes. "You know—my sister, Tillie."

"Ah," was the reply.

"She's come to surprise you."

"That's good."

Ruby looked at her sister in desperation. "We've got to do something."

"I've been thinking. What if we could get her to The Grange somehow? I'm sure Nellie wouldn't mind, would she, if we took her there?"

"That's a great idea. But…how can we get her there?"

They looked up and down the lane, trying to come up with a solution.

"Need a pee!" the old lady suddenly cried. The sisters looked at each other and burst out laughing. "What's so funny? Need a pee, now."

"All right, Grandmamma." Ruby bent down to help her up. They put the unfinished tea to one side and helped her into the cottage. Tillie found her chamber pot under the bed. It was almost full.

"Phaw," she exclaimed, gagging.

"Make haste!" cried the old lady.

She hurried out, trying not to spill any of the contents, and emptied it down the outside privvy, then with much ado, wading through petticoats and underclothes, they managed to help the old lady onto it, leaning her against the front of the armchair for support.

"Don't need an audience."

"Just call us when you've finished then."

Tillie held her nose as they went back outside. "Phew, how long has she been wearing those clothes? They don't half stink!"

"Aye," agreed Ruby. "Come to think of it, she was wearing that dress last time I came, and the time before that. She probably hasn't changed her underclothes since then either."

"Didn't you notice that she was a bit…smelly?"

"Well, no. She seemed fine. What with all the bother of getting Jamie cleaned up, I didn't notice. Anyway, old ladies always whiff a bit, don't they?"

"I suppose so…but we've got to sort her out. Do you think that lady who spoke to us earlier would know anyone in the village who could help?"

"Shall I go and find her again?"

"Yes, while I help Grandmamma get cleaned up."

* * * *

As he re-entered, David heard his sister's strident voice. "My goodness, David, your own niece is lying on her deathbed and all you care about is that—"

Before she could finish he heard Sarah wail, "I'm not going to die, am I, mother?"

He hurried in. "Now see what you've done with your exaggerations," he reproved his sister, resting a reassuring hand on his niece's shoulder. "No, Sarah. You're not going to die. Your mother is just being her usual unthinking, callous self. Pray, do not take any notice of her."

"How can you say such things about me?" Annie put her hand up to her forehead. "Especially when I'm so incapacitated and in such pain."

"Oh, Annie, cut the dramatics! We have more important issues here."

He turned his back on her as Sarah asked anxiously, "Do you think Jamie'll be all right?"

"…Yes." David hoped she didn't notice the pause. He didn't want to lie to her, but she needed comforting at this time, so he couldn't let her know his concerns. "But let's check you over first."

"I'm fine," she replied, sitting up straighter on the bed.

"I need to make sure of that. Let me look." He could see a small cut on the side of her forehead. It didn't look bad now that it had been bathed. He looked into her eyes. "Are you sure you feel—?"

"She's told you she's all right," retorted her mother, "and you've assured her that she's going to live, so stop fussing."

David raised his eyes and sucked in his breath, trying to keep his composure. He already felt concerned about Jamie, and his sister's seemingly uncaring attitude wasn't helping.

Sarah began to get up. "Honestly, Uncle David, I'm just a little tired. Perhaps Katy could help me up to bed."

"I'll help her." George had been hovering nearby.

"That's a good idea, darling." She took his hand. "And then you may as well get to bed yourself. It is rather late and you have school in the morning."

"Do I have to go to school tomorrow?"

"Yes, George, you do have to go," David barked. "But I don't think Sarah should, not until she feels better."

"That's not fair!"

"Just get to bed, George. I can't take any more of your arguments," thundered his exasperated uncle. "Do as you're told for once in your life." He ran his hands through his hair, trying hard not to lose his temper and slap the boy.

George slumped out of the room, so Katy helped Sarah off the bed and took her upstairs.

"Did you need to be so hard on little Georgie?" whined Annie, trying to get up from the chair.

David went over to help her back onto the bed, having calmed down somewhat. "I apologise if you think I was too harsh, but he…anyway, I'm going out for a while, I don't know how long I will be."

"I suppose you're going to look for that boy."

"Yes, I am. We cannot just leave him out there all night." Annie opened her mouth to speak but he forestalled her. "No

147

matter what you think of him, he is my responsibility and I have to find him before anything untoward happens to him."

He went out into the hall, ignoring his sister's mumbling and donned his hat and overcoat. Taking one of Victor's canes from the umbrella stand, he went out and made straight for the park. There were still several people there but he couldn't see any children. They would all be tucked up safely in their beds, not like poor Jamie. He covered the whole of the park from top to bottom, his eyes scanning every path as he went, calling Jamie's name every now and again and even occasionally looking under hedges and up trees, but with no success.

By this time the park was almost empty, the last few carriages making their way out. He walked over to the other exit and looked up and down the street that it led out into. Perhaps Jamie had got confused and gone out that way.

A young couple were approaching.

"Excuse me, I'm sorry to bother you, but have you seen a young boy hereabouts at all?" he asked.

They looked at each other and both shook their heads. "No, sir. What does he look like?" asked the man.

If you haven't seen a boy, what does it matter what he looks like? thought David, but he remained polite. "Small and fair, wearing a brown jacket and blue shirt."

"No, we haven't seen anyone like that," the man replied, looking to his partner for confirmation.

She shook her head. "Sorry."

"Thank you for your time. Good day." David doffed his hat and bowed.

"Sorry we couldn't be of any assistance," repeated the man. "Good day to you." They continued their walk.

He thought of looking for a policeman, but knew that if he found one, he wouldn't be interested in a runaway boy.

He saw a lamplighter doing his rounds and waited for him to light the one above him before taking out his pocket watch to check the time. Ten o'clock. There was no point staying out in the gloom any longer but he might as well ask if the man had seen the youngster.

"Aye, I did see a young boy matching that description a while back. Let me think." The man had a broad Yorkshire accent. David could hardly contain himself as the man stood pondering, scratching his chin. "Aye, t'was earlier this evening. There was an accident—a young girl—she got knocked down by a runaway horse. I think he were wi' her. Yep, that's when I saw him."

"And did you see what happened to him?"

"Nay, there was such a to-do, everybody all clamouring round, like, to have a nosy, thou knows warr it's like."

"So you didn't see where he went?"

"Nay."

"Well, thank you for your time. I'd better let you get on with your job."

"Rait you are. Can't keep grand folks in't dark, can we?" The lamplighter carried on down the street chuckling to himself, leaving David as frustrated as ever. He retraced his steps across the park, which was now in complete darkness, so if Jamie had been there he wouldn't have seen him. It was hard keeping to the path but once his eyes became accustomed to the dark he soon found himself at the exit onto his sister's street, and as it had already been lit up he was able to get to the house safely.

There was still a candle alight in the hall and he went in after having one last look up and down the road. The drawing room was in darkness so, assuming Annie was asleep, he picked up the candle and crept quietly upstairs, hoping that he would find Jamie already there.

He entered his bedroom but was devastated to find it empty. Uttering a curse, he went back out onto the landing, wondering what to do next.

Perhaps he and George had made up and Jamie was in with him. He eased open his nephew's bedroom door, but found George sound asleep, his blankets sprawled all over the floor. David picked them up and covered him over without waking him, before checking under the bed and in the wardrobe—anywhere that a small boy could be hiding.

Next he went into Annie and Victor's room, knowing that his sister was downstairs. Again he checked everywhere in there but the tidiness had not been disturbed, so that left Sarah's room. He knew the pair got on well but didn't think they would go so far as sharing a room, but he had to be sure.

He opened the door and entered just as the flame on his candle spluttered and died. He gave an exasperated moan, having been so absorbed in his task he hadn't noticed it had burned right down. He was in complete darkness and as he backed out the bed creaked and he heard Sarah ask groggily, "Is that you, Mama?"

"No, it's me...Uncle David," he whispered. "Sorry I disturbed you. Go back to sleep."

"Is Jamie back yet?"

He hesitated, not wanting to worry her, but he knew that if he told her the truth she would want to get up and look for him. Mumbling something incoherent, he closed the door behind him, hoping that it would satisfy her in her semi wakefulness.

Cautiously he felt his way downstairs to the kitchen but, after bumping into a chair, he decided to abandon his quest before he woke the whole household. There were only the servants quarters left to search anyway, and he couldn't very well go wandering up there, even if he found a candle.

He sat down on the chair, at a loss as to what to do next. Sitting in the darkness, his heart went out to Jamie. If he himself felt disorientated, how much worse must it be for the youngster?

Perhaps somebody had found him. He wouldn't be able to tell them where he was staying, as he didn't know the address, so they would have to wait until daylight, when he would be able to recognise the house.

He stood up and began to feel his way towards the stairs. He might as well go to bed now as he felt sure that there would be a knock on the door first thing in the morning and Jamie would be standing there as bold as brass, a grin on his cheeky face.

* * * *

After Ruby had disappeared up the lane, Tillie went back into the cottage. The sight of her grandmother, with her head lolling forward and her tongue half out, brought tears to her eyes. She nudged her shoulder. "Grandmamma."

"Uh!" The old lady raised her head a little.

"Shall we get you into the chair?"

"Have I finished?"

Tillie had to smile. "I don't know... have you?"

"Think so."

"Put your arms round my shoulders then." She bent down and lifted her up, and after pulling up her drawers, she swivelled her round and deposited her into the armchair.

"Wait there while I get you some water for a wash. Don't go away," she said in a vain attempt at humour.

A nod and a slight grin, then a weak reply, "I won't."

Tillie sighed. Her grandmother's sense of humour had been one of her most endearing characteristics. At least that hadn't completely vanished.

After taking the chamber pot outside and emptying it again, she returned and poured some water into a bowl, then picked up a flannel and a towel.

"Put your hands in this." She placed the bowl on her grandmother's lap. "A nice wash'll make you feel better."

The old lady swished her hands around in the water and looked up at Tillie with a half smile. "Mmm, lovely."

Tillie's heart almost broke at the sight of the once vibrant and lively woman now reduced to the state of having to be helped to have a simple wash. "Feel better?" she croaked, dabbing at the wrinkled face with the flannel.

"Mmm."

After a few minutes she put the bowl of water to one side and asked, "Would you like me to brush your hair?"

Another faint nod, so Tillie found a hairbrush beside the bed and, removing the pins from the thick white hair, she brushed each long strand, receiving the occasional grunt if the brush caught on a particularly matted tangle. Once it was smooth and lug-free she plaited it, having found some ribbon to complete the job.

"There, Grandmamma." She stood back, surveying her handiwork. "Does that feel good?"

Grandmother smiled, closed her eyes and rested her head back on the chair, so Tillie took the bowl back to the sink, trying hard to keep tears at bay.

She looked out of the window, thinking about her son—how her wise old grandmother had recognised his likeness to her, without even knowing who he was—and wondering how much longer it would be before she saw him again. Her reverie was disturbed when she thought she heard a voice from the chair and she hurried back over.

"Grandmamma, did you say something?"

There was no response. The lined face was still, eyes closed, mouth half open.

Tillie's heart sank. She gently nudged her shoulder.

No movement. Not a flicker.

She stroked the soft cheek to see if she could feel any sign of life at all but there was nothing.

"Oh, no," she moaned as she sat down on the floor, resting her head on the gnarled old hands, now unmoving where before they had never been still. She sat like that, not knowing for how long, time seeming to stand still, saying the few prayers she knew by heart, and some she only half remembered.

"Got to make sure you get to heaven," she whispered as she stroked the dead, bony hand.

How was she going to tell Ruby? Suddenly she heard footsteps outside, but before she could warn her, her sister had rushed into the cottage followed by a young man.

"I've found..." Ruby began, but she stopped on seeing the scene before her. "Tillie?" She edged across to the chair. "Is everything all right?"

Shaking her head, Tillie took her sister's hands in her own.

Ruby yanked her hands away and bent down to touch her beloved grandmother. "She's just asleep." She touched her again.

Tillie shook her head. "No, Ruby, we have to face it. She's..." She couldn't bring herself to say the dreaded word and flung her arms around her sister. They clung to each other, sobbing, until Tillie heard the young man who had accompanied Ruby clear his throat behind her. She had forgotten he was there. She looked over and saw him standing in the doorway, twiddling his cap around in his hands.

"Is Mrs Raven dead, then?" he asked artlessly. Tillie nodded, not trusting herself to speak yet.

"Shall I call me ma? She'll know what to do."

Tillie nodded again. Whoever his mother was, she was bound to be of help. Tillie hadn't a clue what to do next.

* * * *

Out of breath, Jamie found himself in a street lined by tall trees. He bent forward, hands on knees, taking in great gulps of air, before taking off his cap and wiping his wet forehead. He peeped behind him, expecting the hordes of people to have followed him, feeling sure that he had heard their footsteps after him, but he was alone. His shoulders slumped in relief as a sigh escaped him and he sat on a wall for a while to recover.

What should he do now? He looked around him. The houses were set back a lot further from the road and had much bigger front gardens than Sarah's.

Sarah! He had to get back to her. Was she badly hurt? Maybe she was dead! But how would he find her house?

He began to retrace his steps and after a while he arrived at a junction. Which way should he go? He didn't remember turning off on his way there, but he had been so frightened that he hadn't taken in his surroundings. He finally decided to go left but after walking for what seemed like ages, he arrived back at the junction again. He recognised it by the shape of the tree in the front garden of the end house. It looked just like a bird.

Putting his hands behind his head, he stopped, getting really worried by this time.

He saw a young man approaching. "'Scuse me, sir," he asked politely, "d'yer know where Mrs Smythe lives?"

The man shook his head. "No, sorry, young man. Is it on this street?"

Jamie looked around him. "Um…I don't know. It's near the park."

The man removed his hat and scratched his head. "The only park I know is about half a mile back there." He pointed behind him. "Down that street on your right. I'm in rather a hurry or I'd take you there myself. Do you think you'll be able to find it on your own?"

"Yes, 'spect so."

"Good day to you then, young sir," and he continued his walk.

Jamie set off again in the direction the man had pointed and, after he had gone quite a way, he saw a man lighting the lamps on the other side of the street with a long pole. He had never seen anything like that before. He watched, fascinated as the gloom was dispersed and the street lit up once more. As he stood enthralled, the lamplighter came across to him.

"Say, are you the boy that was wi' that girl who got run over?"

Jamie nodded.

"A man's bin looking for you."

Jamie's face lit up. "Was it Uncle David?"

"Nay, lad, he never told me his name. He didn't find you then?"

"No. Where was he?"

"Rait back there, near't park."

"Thanks." He began to run. After a while he thought he could see the park gates up ahead. Thank goodness. But if they were ahead of him he must have passed Sarah's house. He stopped, chewing his thumb as he looked around, puzzled. This street was quite flat so none of the houses had steps up to the front door. He felt sure he remembered steps when they had arrived. So how come he hadn't passed her house?

He carried on until he got to the gates. It looked rather dark inside. He looked back at the houses he had passed, confused. Where had Sarah's house gone?

He ventured into the park, not knowing what else to do, and sat on a bench that he could make out near the entrance. Eventually, too tired to continue any further, he lay down and fell asleep, but waking up cold during the night he crawled under a hedge where he hoped he would be warmer.

* * * *

Tillie organised the funeral with the help of two neighbours. Ruby was too distraught to do anything but sit beside the coffin where their grandmother had been laid out in her best frock and bonnet.

As Tillie looked out of the window, thinking about her son, she saw a man and a girl approaching. At first she didn't recognise the tall, handsome man, but then realised it was her brother, Matthew. He had been a gangly, spotty youth the last time she had seen him.

155

She ran out to greet him. "Matty, I'm so glad you got the message. I didn't know whether you'd be able to make it." She wrapped her arms around him.

"Yes, thank you for letting us know, we'd have been devastated if we'd missed grandmother's funeral." He indicated to the girl beside him. "Wouldn't we, Jessie?"

Tillie raised her eyebrows at her brother as the girl nodded.

"Is this your wife?" she asked, noticing the girl's rounded belly.

"Yes, it was a bit of a rushed job, I have to admit." He grimaced, his face reddening. "But as soon as she told me about the babby, I thought I'd better make an honest woman of her, so there wasn't much time to let people know."

Tillie embraced her new sister-in-law. "Good day to you, Jessie. Thank you for coming." She led them into the cottage where Ruby sat beside the coffin, stroking the old lady's cheek.

"Ruby, Matty's here." Tillie hoped that using his boyhood name might bring her out of her melancholy, but her sister looked up with a vacant expression before going back to her vigil. Tillie waited for her brother and his wife to pay their respects and then they went back outside.

"I'm quite worried about her. All she does is sit there, brooding."

As he pulled Jessie into the crook of his arm, Matthew asked, "Was she very close to Grandmother?"

"Yes, she visited her every fortnight on her afternoon off."

"And you?"

"I've only just come back to the area. I'll tell you all about it when we have a minute to spare."

"I feel guilty now for having neglected Grandmother myself."

"It's not as if you could get here and back in an afternoon, Ruby only had to walk three miles."

"It still doesn't make me feel any better, though." Jessie put a consoling arm around him, and they stood comforting each other.

"Do you know where Harry is?" Tillie asked after a few minutes. She was trying hard to be strong, and not to cry, but seeing Matthew and Jessie clinging to each other, was taking all her resilience not to do so, and even then a stray tear escaped and ran down her cheek. She quickly wiped it away with the back of her hand before any more could follow. She suddenly wished she had someone to comfort her.

"Isn't he working with you anymore?" she managed to continue.

Matthew took out his handkerchief and blew his nose. "No, he had a fall out with the head stableman over some girl, and he left, about three years ago now, I suppose it was. I haven't heard hide nor hair of him since."

"He always was a bit of a rum'un, wasn't he?"

"Yes, I thought he was settling down, but…" Matthew shrugged his shoulders and turned to Jessie. "You didn't know him, did you, darling? I think he'd left before you came."

Jessie shook her head.

"It's probably just as well, 'cos I wouldn't have got a look in if you'd met him first."

"Don't be silly," contradicted his wife, wrapping her arms around his waist. "How can you say that?"

"Because he's a right charmer, is my brother, not a bit like me."

"Don't put yourself down. It's you I love. Always have and always will." She reached up and, pulling his head down, she kissed him, making Tillie feel even more envious. She didn't know what had got into her today. Her single status didn't usually bother her. It must be the emotion of the day.

"I'm afraid I can't offer you a hot drink." She mentally pulled herself together. "We couldn't light the fire, of course, with Grandmother in there, but the lady next door is doing the honours for us. Shall we go round?"

They walked to the adjoining cottage where there were already several mourners standing around talking in muted tones.

"Ah, Tillie." Their hostess came over. "This must be the brother you were telling me about. I can certainly see a likeness."

"Yes, it is." Tillie smiled.

"Would Ruby like a drink?" the neighbour asked.

"I'll try her with one, thank you."

Taking the drink outside, she looked up and saw Nellie and Freda walking towards the cottage.

"Thank you so much," she cried, seeing the baskets of food they had brought. "I would never have been able to do this on my own. The neighbours have been wonderful but I can't expect them to—"

"Why," interrupted Nellie, "where's Ruby?"

Tillie indicated towards the inside. "In there. She hasn't left Grandmother's side since she was laid out. You'll see for yourself what a state she's in. I'm just taking her this." She held out the cup. "But she probably won't have it. I've not been able to get her to eat or drink anything. I think she blames me for her death."

"Surely not," cried Freda. "Why would she do that?"

Tillie shrugged.

"Let me take it in." Nellie put her baskets down and took the cup into Ruby as Tillie began to empty the food out onto the table.

Freda asked again, "Why do you say Ruby blames you?"

"She murmured something about Grandmamma being well before I came, and why did she die while there was only me there? Why didn't she wait 'til Ruby got back, so that she could say goodbye?"

"She's just hurting and you're the closest person to take it out on. Don't take it to heart. I'm sure she didn't mean it. At least your grandmother didn't die alone, be comforted by that."

"Yes, that's what I tell myself, but it's no consolation to Ruby." Tillie felt tears well up at the memory of her precious grandmother sitting so still in her chair.

"Just give her time."

Tillie nodded, knowing in her heart that what the cook said was true, but the thought that her sister could think that she was responsible still upset her. She decided to change the subject before she broke down.

"You haven't walked all the way, have you?" she asked, emptying some sandwiches onto a plate.

"No, Tom brought us in the pony and trap. It was a bit of a bumpy ride, however, even though I'm well padded." She rubbed her ample backside. "I'm not looking forward to the return journey. In fact, I think I'd rather walk."

Tillie grinned. "Is Tom staying for the funeral?"

"No. We didn't think we should leave the house with just Pervis there. It's John's day off, so Tom's gone straight back. He's coming to pick us up again later. You or Ruby can have my place, though."

Unpacking another basket, Tillie took out a tin mould. "You've even made a jelly. I'd better be careful how...no, you do it." Handing it over, she stood back and watched as Freda turned the jelly mould upside down onto a plate and a red wobbly rabbit appeared.

"That's marvellous," she whispered, putting her arms round the cook.

Nellie came through and put down an empty cup. "She's drunk it, but I can't get a word out of her." She pushed a plate further onto the table. "I hope there's enough food here. Any idea how many are coming?"

"The whole village, I think, and more besides. Thank you again, both of you, for all this."

"It's the least we could do." Nellie looked towards Freda who nodded in agreement. "In a way it's beneficial that the master's away, so there's less to do up at The Grange."

"Have you heard anything from him?" Tillie held her breath in the hope that she would say he would soon be home.

"Yes, actually, a letter came this morning."

She closed her eyes and, turning her back slightly, to prevent them seeing her agitation, she put her fingers up to her lips.

"It doesn't look as if he'll be back yet. Young Jamie went missing..."

Tillie gasped and felt the blood drain from her face. She could hear Nellie still talking but what she was saying was just a jumble of words drowning in cotton wool. She sat down to prevent herself from falling, clinging onto the edge of the table.

"Tillie, are you unwell?" Freda's voice sounded through the haze.

Unable to speak, she stared straight ahead.

"It must be delayed shock, after all that's happened," she heard Nellie say as her mind started to refocus.

She watched as the housekeeper took out a bottle of smelling salts from her coat pocket, saying, "Always take these to funerals, there's usually someone who needs them."

Tillie tried not to breathe too deeply as they were held under her nose, knowing how awful they smelt. Her mind cleared a little and she sighed. She had almost given herself away. She must try to be more careful. But when would the waiting be over?

"And have they found him yet?" she managed to ask. She wasn't sure she wanted to know, in case it was bad news, but before Nellie could reply she heard Matthew's voice calling her from outside so, blinking, she got up and hurried out, mumbling, "That's my brother, I'd better see what he wants."

"Ah, sis." He put out his hand towards her. "The undertakers have arrived, they're ready to start."

She took a deep breath. *Stay calm*, she told herself. *You're the oldest so you have to be brave for the others. Just concentrate on the funeral.*

"I'd better go and tell Ruby. I don't know how she's going to react," she replied as the black horse tethered to the hearse suddenly lifted its head and whinnied, making her jump.

"I'll come in with you." Taking her arm, her brother steadied her before turning to Jessie. "Do you want to wait here? I'll be out in a minute."

His wife nodded and stood back, away from the horse.

"Come on, Ruby. It's time to go." Tillie went in and nudged her.

"No, they can't take her away." Ruby dropped to her knees. "Don't let them take her."

"They have to." Matthew lifted up his younger sister and moved her away from the coffin as the undertakers approached.

Tillie tried to take her arm as they went out but her hand was pushed away. Taking a deep breath, she followed and watched the coffin being lifted onto the hearse. As they all filed behind it, Jessie came over and tucked her small hand into hers as the large procession began its way to the little church at the far end of the village.

The vicar asked if any of the family wanted to say a few words, so Matthew stood up. Tillie would have liked to say something, but didn't trust herself not to break down. She could hear Ruby weeping throughout the short service, at the other end of the bench, having declined the offer to sit next to her.

They all filed out again and gathered around the open grave. After the final prayer had been said and the last handful of soil was being thrown into the grave, she heard Matthew say in surprise, "Harry, you made it!"

Turning to the young man who approached, she recognised her youngest brother. He hadn't changed much. His thick fair hair was brushed back from his face and the beginnings of a beard sprouted through his square chin. He had grown a few feet though, so she had to crane her neck to look up at him, but, despite the difference in the colour of his hair, the main feature that struck her was the resemblance to her beloved Jamie. It was uncanny how alike they were.

She realised that he was replying to Matthew. "Yes, only just by the looks of it. Sorry I'm late. It was further than I thought."

He shook his brother's hand, and then turned to Tillie. "How are you, darling sister?"

She put her arms around him and squeezed him hard, pretending he was Jamie, too choked to speak.

He struggled out of her embrace, giving her an odd look. "And where's our baby sister, Ruby? Ah, there she is." He went over to her where she was slumped, staring into the open grave. As he put out his arm, she clutched hold of him and sobbed into his jacket. He looked at his brother above her head, his grimace showing his unease at the show of emotion.

Once they arrived back at the cottage, Tillie was handing out food when she heard Harry telling Matthew, "I had a young companion for part of the way. A delightful boy, he was, said he was trying to find his way back to his uncle's house."

Her ears pricked up. Any mention of a boy conjured up her son's face in her frustrated mind.

She continued handing out sandwiches while people all around her were talking about their memories of Alice, most of them funny ones.

"Do you remember the time she rescued that cow?" a neighbour said to her companion. "It was stuck in a dyke and she took off her dress and waded in, without a care for her own safety, or even her modesty. She was a character and a half. She'll be sorely missed." Everybody around her agreed.

Tillie went outside for some fresh air. She was unable to stop thinking about what Harry had said. Could it be her Jamie? It was too much of a coincidence though, surely...wasn't it?

"Your grandmother has had a real good send off. I'm sure she'll be pleased that so many have turned up to say farewell." Freda came out, drying her hands on her apron.

"Yes, I expect she's up there," Tillie pointed to the heavens, trying to appear calm, "looking down on us, commenting on this dress and that bonnet."

Nellie also came out. "The food's practically all gone. I knew we should have brought more. Still, it's too late now." She turned to the cook. "Your jelly was a success. They were almost fighting over it."

"Perhaps I should have made two, but carrying it all would have been a task." Freda looked up the lane. "I suppose Tom'll be here soon."

"Yes, I expect so," replied Nellie. "We'd better get the dishes packed up so that we're ready for him."

"I've told Tillie that I'm walking back." Freda rubbed her backside again. "My posterior won't stand another ride in that bone-shaker."

Nellie laughed. "I know what you mean, but I don't think I could walk that far any more. I'm not as young as I was."

Looking up the lane, Tillie put her arm round the housekeeper. "You're as young as you feel." She tried to appear normal, but inwardly, everything was in turmoil.

"Are you all right, Tillie?" Nellie asked, concern written all over her face. "You seem very distracted."

"I think it's finally getting to me, Grandmamma and everything," she replied. "I'll just go and have a word with Harry, catch up…"

She had to know.

Tillie found her brother flirting with one of the neighbour's daughters. He turned as she approached.

"And how's my big sister? I heard that you moved out of the area some time ago."

"Yes, Matthew tells me that you did as well, but you can always rely on a funeral to bring family back together, cant you?"

Get to the point, she told herself.

"You…um…said you met a young boy on your way here. Did he tell you his name?"

163

He scratched his head. "No…I don't think he did. Why?"

"It's nothing." She shrugged and turned away while her brother resumed flirting with the young girl.

Should she alert Nellie or Freda about the boy? What if it was Jamie and she had ignored it?

She turned back to Harry. "What did he look like?"

"Who?"

"This young lad you met?"

"Just…boyish, round face, about this tall." He gestured with his hand somewhere between his waist and his chest. "I didn't really take that much notice. Why?"

"It's just that…well, the master up at The Grange took in a foundling who went missing when they went to Harrogate. I just wondered whether it could be him."

"Come to think of it…he did say something about Harrogate. But I'm sure he said he was looking for his uncle's house, so he couldn't have been a foundling."

"Oh, it was just a thought."

Feeling disconsolate, she began to walk away but stopped when she heard Ruby mutter from the corner, "Jamie calls the master 'Uncle David'."

She whipped round and hurried across to her. "What did you say, Ruby?"

"Our Jamie, he calls the master Uncle…"

Tillie didn't wait to hear her finish. She ran outside, her eyes peeled, checking how far she could see, in the vain hope that her son might be in sight, and then ran back in to Harry.

"How far away from here were you?"

"Sis, why are you so…?"

"Just tell me! How far away?"

"Um…near Little Langley, I think."

Nellie came across, obviously alerted to Tillie's raised voice. "What's the matter?"

"Harry might have seen J—your boy who's gone missing." She tugged at her brother's arm. "Tell Nellie about him, Harry."

With a puzzled look, the young man raised his hands behind his head.

"I was on my way here when I came across this young lad sitting by the wayside. I asked him if he was all right and he said he was lost and looking for his uncle's house. He thought it was near Leeds so we walked together for a while until we came to a crossroads and I showed him the road to take. That's all."

A group had gathered around him by this time and everyone was bombarding him with questions.

"But didn't you think that it was odd that a boy so young should be wandering the countryside, all on his own?" Tillie was almost at breaking point.

"Well, yes, but I had to get to Grandmother's funeral, and I knew I was already late, so..." He shrugged, looking around guiltily. "Look, if I'd known who he was, I'd have brought him with me, but I didn't. I'm sorry."

Tillie put her hand on his arm. "No, I'm sorry, for shouting at you. Of course you weren't to know."

She looked at Nellie. "What are we going to do?"

"Well, we don't even know if it is Jamie, but if it is...Tom should be here soon with the pony and trap. But why are you so concerned? You don't even know the boy." She looked at Tillie, a puzzled expression on her face.

"Because...after what you told me about the master losing his son, and..." She was saved from continuing by somebody announcing that Tom was coming down the lane. Everyone poured out of the cottage and surrounded the gamekeeper before he could get down.

Nellie elbowed her way to the front and explained the situation to him.

"But it's miles from Harrogate. Surely it wouldn't be Jamie?" Tom didn't look convinced.

"But it might be, so shouldn't you go and see if you can find..." Tillie found herself getting involved again and had to stop.

Nellie gave her another odd look before agreeing. "Would you, Tom? If it is Jamie we need to find him straight away. But what is the master thinking about, letting him go missing? I just cannot understand it."

Tillie began to climb up onto the cart. "I'll come with you."

"But you don't know him, Tillie, what's the point in you going?" Nellie put her hand on her leg.

A small voice came from the back of the crowd. "I'll go." Tillie turned and saw Ruby edging her way forward.

Of course it made sense. Tillie hadn't been thinking straight again. She climbed down with a sigh and helped her sister up onto the cart.

"So where was he last seen?" Tom asked as he picked up the reins.

Harry came forward. "I may as well come with you, and show you exactly. You can drop me off there as it's on my way home."

He clambered up as the cart pulled away. "Goodbye, Tillie, Matthew, I'll keep in touch."

Tillie watched them depart, wishing with all her heart that she could have gone with them. The waiting was agonising. How could she bear it any longer?

Matthew came across to her, holding Jessie's hand. "We have to be getting off now, Tillie. I'm sorry we didn't have chance to catch up on old times. Do you think you'll be staying long?"

"I'm really not sure, Matty." She reached up and kissed him. "I'll let you know." She turned to Jessie. "Good luck with the baby. When's it due?"

"In a few weeks."

"Well, I hope everything goes well." Hugging them both again she watched them depart across the field opposite, still scanning every horizon in case her son should appear.

The neighbours filtered away as she gave up and re-entered the cottage. She helped Nellie pile up the dishes, her hands shaking. When was this nightmare going to end? After a few minutes, worried that she was going to break something, she went back outside.

Freda followed her out. "If I'm going to walk I'd better start now. Are you coming?"

"I think I'll stay here tonight." Tillie turned back to the cottage. "There's still a lot of cleaning up to do." She looked at the portly cook whose round face was showing signs of fatigue. She couldn't allow her to walk all that distance on her own. What should she do?

"And what about Nellie?" asked Freda as the housekeeper came out to join them.

The next door neighbour was shaking a rug near her door, and must have heard what they were saying.

"My son should be on his way back by now. He's been delivering potatoes to that new shop in town and I'm sure if I asked him he would take you home. He's a very kind lad, always eager to be of assistance."

She gave the rug a final shake. "Ah, here he comes now." She waved as a cart approached from the opposite direction and pulled up in front of them.

"These ladies are rather stranded," she addressed the young man. "Would you be able to give them a lift to The Grange?"

The man took off his cap and wiped his brow with a red handkerchief. "What, now? Straight away?"

"Not if it'll put you out." Nellie shook her head, but the mother took the housekeeper's arm and urged her towards the back of the cart.

"It's no problem, that's what neighbours are for, to help each other."

"There's only enough room for two, I'm afraid," the son called.

Tillie saw Freda eyeing up the small cart which looked rather dirty, and she was about to remark on it when the cook gave her a nudge. "You go with Nellie, I'll be all right."

"No, my dear," the neighbour said forcefully at the same time as Tillie protested, "No, I'll stay here and wait for Ruby and Tom."

Freda was being pushed into the cart, whether she wanted to go or not. "But surely when they find Jamie they'll take him straight home," she called.

That hadn't occurred to Tillie. She had assumed that they would return to the hamlet. Her face dropped. What should she do now? There definitely wasn't enough room for her in the little cart, the two servants were squashed as it was, and even in her dilemma she had to smile at the sight of their faces as they tried to make themselves comfortable.

"Will you be back tomorrow?" Nellie called as the cart jerked and began pulling away.

"I'm not sure. I expect so," Tillie called back.

Heaving a sigh, she re-entered the cottage, eerily quiet now everyone had gone, and picked up a photograph of her family taken the day they had gone to the seaside. How happy they had all been then. Harry was about the same age as her Jamie was now and looked so much like him.

Stroking her finger across her mother's face, tears welled up in her eyes before dropping onto the glass and she let them fall, hugging the photograph to her bosom, desperate that she would never see her son again.

After a while she recovered and began to open cupboards, thinking that she ought to begin packing up her grandmother's things, until she saw Ruby's yellow bonnet. How thrilled she had been, showing it off...was it only two days ago? Grimacing, she put it to one side to take back, but would Ruby ever want to wear it again, or would it remind her too much of her beloved grandmother?

Picking things up, and then putting them down again, so on edge that she couldn't decide what to do with what, she went back outside, searching the lane again. Her son was out there, lost and forlorn. What if Tom and Ruby didn't find him? What if they never did? Wringing her hands together before raising them to her head and pulling off her bonnet, she yanked at her hair, her face screwed up in desperation.

She couldn't just wait around, she had to get out there and find him.

Running in the direction that Tom had gone, she followed the lane as far as her lungs would allow before stopping and scanning the surrounding fields.

Catching her breath, she resumed, trotting rather than running in order to conserve her breath, especially where it was hilly, her eyes peeled, searching for the slightest movement.

Unheeding of the rough stony track, her toe caught in the hem of her dress and she fell headlong. Punching the ground in frustration, she tried to stand but her knee gave way so she crawled over to a thicket to sit on a tree stump to examine it. Pulling up her dress, she saw that her knee was bleeding as well as the side of her hand.

Wiping the blood off with her petticoat, she heard a cart approaching. Could it be Tom? She jumped up, groaning as a pain shot down her leg, but the cart passed by. It was only a young man, whistling as he drove. He didn't even notice her, hidden by the trees. She flopped down again.

After a minute or so she thought she heard a faint whimpering coming from further back inside the thicket, so she sat still, listening. No, it must have been her imagination. There was only the sound of a blackbird singing. Perhaps it had been a fox cub or a badger.

There it was again. She reached behind her and parted the trees but couldn't see anything for the thick branches, so she got up and limped further along to where there was a clearing. The whimpering got louder.

She stood stock still, unable to breathe, her eyes opening wide. Her mouth dry, her heart feeling as if it was going to burst out of her chest, she almost passed out as she saw, sitting with his back to a large oak tree, a young boy in a blue shirt.

Chapter 10

The boy looked up, startled. All Tillie's instincts yelled at her to run up and enfold him in her arms but she forced herself to remain still, not wanting to alarm him, knowing that he had lost his memory so he might not recognise her.

He sat watching her, a myriad of expressions criss-crossing his little face as she began edging closer, trying to gauge his reactions. Holding her breath, she stopped in front of him, silently holding out her arms.

A mere fraction of a second passed before he flung himself into her embrace, clinging on to her, sobbing. Tillie dropped to her knees, her legs no longer able to support her, her eyes squeezed shut, breathing in the smell of her darling boy, kissing his face, his hair, his ears.

She sat down on the ground, leaning on a tree trunk, and pulled her son onto her lap, feeling like pinching herself to make sure this was real.

He looked into her eyes. "It is you, Mama? It really is, in't it?"

"Yes, my darling, it is," she croaked, drinking in the sight of his big brown eyes and expressive mouth before wrapping her arms tightly around him.

"You came back! You came back!"

"Yes, and I promise I'll never leave you again—never ever."

He looked up into her eyes. "I lost me memory, yer know."

"Did you?"

"But I never really forgot you."

"Oh, Jamie!" was all she could reply before her eyes filled with tears.

He snuggled down into her arms. "I bin staying with Uncle David but I got lost."

Her heart was wrenched from her chest at the thought of her son wandering about once more on his own. She would spend the rest of her life making it up to him.

Eventually, as much as she would have liked to have kept him to herself, she knew that they would have to get back to The Grange and let them know that he was safe. But how would she explain herself? They would want to know why she hadn't told them about Jamie being her son.

Taking his hands in hers, she looked into his eyes. "Jamie, you're good at keeping secrets, aren't you?" He nodded. "Well, let's not tell anybody that I'm your mama. Let's keep it a special secret between you and me."

"Yes, a special secret!"

"Good boy." She patted his head. He probably wouldn't manage it for long, but it would give her some breathing space.

Examining her knee, she decided that it wasn't too bad and stood up, gingerly putting her weight onto it.

"You got blood on yer dress." Jamie pointed to a patch on her hem. "And on yer hand."

"Yes, I fell over. If I hadn't gone to sit down to recover, I wouldn't have heard you." She raised her eyes to the heavens. "Thank God I did. I couldn't have borne it much longer, not knowing where you were."

Jamie looked up at her with a strange expression and began to say, "Ruby swore..." but, covering his mouth, he shook his head before looking back at the ground.

She wondered what he had been about to say but didn't pursue it as they began walking, Jamie holding her good hand.

"Sarah got blood on her head." He looked up again and patted his temple. "Here."

"Did she?"

"Yes, in the park." He looked thoughtful. "Do you think she's dead?"

"No, I'm sure she's not." She had to reassure him, even though she hadn't the faintest idea who he was talking about.

"That's good, I like Sarah. I don't want her to be dead."

"Did you meet a nice man called Harry this morning?" she asked as she limped along the track, trying not to grimace.

"How d'yer know that?" Jamie's face was a picture. "Are you magic?"

"No, I wish I was, because then I could have found you sooner."

The pain in her knee was quite severe. It took all her resilience not to cry out as she put weight on it. Spotting a forked branch lying at the side of the track, she picked it up and tried it out as a crutch. It made things much easier.

"Is that betterer, Mama?" He put his hand up to his mouth, looking round anxiously. "Oh, I forgot."

"It's all right to call me 'Mama' when we're on our own, sweetheart, just try not to when we get home." There she was, calling it 'home' again. It really did feel like it though, but for how long? And where would they go next?

Some time later she stopped and sat down again, wondering if they were on the right track. This one led back to her grandmother's hamlet but could there be a quicker way back to The Grange?

Her knee was still bleeding so she ripped off the bottom of her petticoat and tied it round her leg while Jamie stood watching, his face screwed up in consternation.

"I hope Sarah's all right." He sat down beside her and leant his head against her.

She put her arm round his shoulders and squeezed him. "What happened?"

He jumped up again. "We nearly got knocked down by a lady in her carriage thing, and she...she..." His face puckered up as if he was going to cry.

Tillie remembered then who Sarah was. Of course, she was the master's niece. That was why he had gone to Harrogate.

"Oh, my darling, I'm sure she'll be fine."

She was intrigued as to what had happened but the sky was beginning to darken and she didn't want to spend the night outside. "Help me up. We'd better get going."

The lane they had been following was edged by hedges on each side but further along the hedges thinned out and gave way to open fields. Further down the valley Tillie could see a large house. Was it The Grange? She stopped and pointed.

"Jamie, I know you haven't been at The Grange long, but do you think that could be it?"

He peered into the growing gloominess. "Um...yes, I fink it is. There's the stables where I kept Rufus." He pointed to some outbuildings to the side of the house, looking sad again. "Uncle David says he prob'ly got caught by the hounds."

Who was Rufus? There would have such a lot to catch up on once they were back safe. She tried to hurry through the field, unheeding of the pain in her knee.

As they arrived they saw Tom and Ruby approaching in the cart.

"Jamie!" Ruby jumped down before it had chance to stop and flung her arms around him. "You're safe. We looked everywhere for you."

She looked at Tillie with a puzzled expression as Nellie came running out of the house and also wrapped her arms around the boy. "Are you all right? Let's get you inside."

Once they were sitting in the kitchen with a warm drink, Tillie explained how she had found Jamie. "I couldn't settle at the cottage, so I thought I'd go for a walk, and I came across this young man here when I fell over and had to sit down." She winked at Jamie who took another sip of his hot chocolate.

Nellie turned to the boy. "And you, sir, what on earth were you doing...?"

Jamie's head began to loll and his eyes closed.

"Never mind, you look all in, let's get you to bed. You can tell us everything tomorrow."

* * * *

A messenger arrived early the following morning as Tillie hobbled downstairs. Her knee was still paining her, but she had

173

bathed it well. She heard Pervis ask if a reply was required and, as he closed the door without letting the man in, she assumed that the answer was negative. He looked up and acknowledged her. "Morning Tillie," then proceeded towards the kitchen, so she followed him in.

Nellie took the letter and slit it open. "It's from the master. He says he received the letter we sent last evening and is relieved that Jamie is safe." She continued to read it in silence.

"Does he say if he's coming back yet?" Tillie was worried that, even though Nellie insisted she was one of the master's favourites, she would have to move on when he returned.

"He says that Annie needs him for a few more days as Victor can't get back 'til the end of the week and, oh, Sarah's had an accident."

"Jamie said something about that yesterday as we were trying to find our way home." Tillie sat down to take the strain off her knee. "Does it say how it happened?"

"No, here, read it for yourself." Nellie gave her a quizzical look as the back door opened and Tom entered, puffing on his pipe.

Pervis walked over to the range. "Looks like I'll have to make my own tea then."

Tillie had forgotten that he was there, he had been so silent, and, having satisfied herself that the letter had nothing else of consequence to impart, she jumped up, wincing slightly as she put her foot to the floor. "No, you sit yourself down. I'll make it." Picking up the kettle and pouring some water into the teapot, she swished it round before emptying it again. "Two or three spoonfuls of tea?"

"Four." Tom sat down at the table. "I like to taste my tea." He looked around. "No Freda?"

"Not yet." Nellie opened a tin of biscuits. "She was absolutely exhausted last night so she's sleeping late. We'll have to make do this morning."

"And how's the boy?"

"He's still sleeping." Nellie also sat down. Tillie had opened her mouth to say the same thing, as she had peeped in on him before coming down, but stopped herself in time.

Pervis and Tom left as soon as they had finished their drinks, leaving Tillie alone with Nellie.

Should she tell her now?

"Um...Nellie, I need to tell you about..." Where should she begin?

Drying her hands, Nellie walked over and patted her on her shoulder. "You don't have to tell me anything. Your personal affairs are no business of mine. But I have a feeling that Jamie is no stranger to you."

"Well, actually, he's..." Before she could continue, the object of their conversation came running in, still dressed in his nightshirt.

"I'm hungry, can I have some breakfast, Ma—" Jamie's eyes opened wide as a guilty flush crept up his face. He turned to the housekeeper. "I mean...Nellie?"

"I'm right, aren't I?" Nellie looked her in the eye. Tillie nodded as she crossed to her son and put her arm around his shoulder. He looked up, obviously still agitated about almost giving away the secret.

"It's all right, Jamie. I think we'd better tell Nellie, don't you?"

"Yes, it's hard keeping secrets."

"Jamie is my son—my darling, gorgeous little boy." Squeezing him tightly, she smacked a large kiss on his cheek.

Wriggling out from her embrace, he grinned. "Oh, Mama!"

"I just knew something was going on, but couldn't put my finger on it. Why on earth didn't you say something before?" Nellie stood with her hands on her hips, looking completely baffled.

"When I first heard about a boy being found, I prayed that he would be my Jamie, but when you told me he'd lost his memory, I didn't know if he would even remember me, and I felt so guilty for leaving him, I just...I don't know..." Tillie shrugged as Jamie put his arms around her waist.

"I did remember you, Mama, didn't I?"

"Yes, my darling, you did."

"Can I 'ave me sausages now?"

"You'll have to wait while I cook them." Nellie crossed towards the pantry. "So why don't you take your ma upstairs and show her where your clothes are and she can help you get washed and dressed."

"I can dress meself," he answered, but he took Tillie's hand and led her out of the room after she had filled a jug with some warm water to take up with them.

* * * *

Once he was washed and dressed they went back downstairs, and Jamie tucked into his sausages.

Nellie was putting away clean dishes from the day before as Freda still hadn't made an appearance, and she handed some to Tillie. "When are you going to tell Ruby?"

"I'll have to tell her soon because I can't see Jamie keeping the secret."

Jamie cleaned his plate. "Any more?"

"No, young man. You'll burst if you eat any more."

"But I'm still hungry."

Nellie picked up his plate. "Well, there's one slice of bread left, but perhaps your ma wants it." She looked at Tillie. "You haven't eaten yet, have you?"

"I can make do with a biscuit."

"Let's have half each." Jamie broke the bread in two. "Then we can both have some."

"That's very generous of you, love, thank you." Suppressing the urge to take him in her arms and squeeze him, Tillie sat down next to him.

"D'yer want honey on it?" he asked. "Or strawberry jam?"

"I don't mind."

"George couldn't understand how I 'membered I liked strawberry jam." Jamie spooned lashings of it onto their bread. "But I could, couldn't I, Nellie?"

The cook grinned as she wiped up some of the sticky mess he had made. "Yes, Jamie."

"Do you remember anything else?" Tillie found it hard to believe that his memory wasn't working properly. He seemed so like his normal self.

"Only the barn." He shivered and Tillie started to put out her arm, but he jumped up. "And Timmy."

"You mean Timmy who had the gypsy caravan next to ours?"

"Yes, he used to chase us."

Tillie looked aghast. "He did what?"

"Well…" He screwed up his face, obviously racking his brain. "I 'member…once we found some bad eggs and smashed them under his van." Putting his hand up to his mouth he giggled. "Poo, it didn't 'alf stink!"

"Jamie Raven, it's no wonder you got chased."

A snort behind her made her turn round. Nellie looked as if she was having trouble keeping a straight face.

"Don't encourage him!" cried Tillie, but the funny side of the story hit her as well and she had to turn her head away to prevent him from seeing her smiling.

As Nellie wiped the jam off his hands and face, Tillie asked her, "Has he been remembering things all the time?"

"No, this is the first I've heard, apart from the jam, but when he arrived here Doctor Abrahams assured us that his memory would return eventually. You seem to have sparked it off."

Tillie gasped. "He was so ill that he needed a doctor?"

"Oh yes, I'm afraid so, he was very poorly for quite a while."

Tillie grabbed Jamie and hugged him tightly, raining kisses all over his head. "Oh, my poor little boy, I hadn't realised! What did I do to you?"

177

"It don't matter." He wriggled free once more. "I forgive you."

She burst into tears at her son's innocent statement, covering her face with her hands.

"Don't cry, Mama." He tried to pull her hands away. "Please don't cry."

"I'm so sorry for what I've put you through. I'll make it up to you, I promise."

As she said this, Ruby entered. "What are you sorry for?"

Freda also came in at that point, yawning. "Why didn't you wake me?"

"Me ma's a bit sad, that's all." Jamie sat holding his mother's hand as a hushed silence descended on the kitchen. Tillie held her breath, her eyes closed, waiting to see who would be the first to speak.

It was Ruby. "I knew it, I just knew it." Tillie opened her eyes at the bitterness in her sister's voice. "I kept telling myself it couldn't be but even Grandmamma saw the likeness, and when you turned up out of the blue, looking so pretty and...and so like him, I..."

Getting up, Tillie tried to appease her forlorn sister by putting her arm round her shoulder. "Aren't you pleased that he's found his mother?" But Ruby resisted her attempts and turned away.

"But why did you have to keep it a secret?" Freda had clearly woken up properly at the news.

"Yes, why?" from Ruby.

"Because she wasn't sure what Jamie's reaction would be," Nellie began to explain.

"So you knew," accused Ruby, "and you didn't tell us?"

"She only guessed this morning," Tillie tried to defend the housekeeper and diffuse a potential eruption of bad feeling, "and I asked her to keep it quiet, just until I could explain everything properly."

Jamie had been watching the argument, evidently puzzled as to the reason. "Well, I'm glad as conkers that she's back."

He hid his face in his mother's skirts, murmuring, "I fought I weren't ever goin' to see her again."

Ruby ran over to him. "Oh, Jamie, of course we're pleased, it's just a bit of a shock."

She looked at Tillie. "Suppose you'll be taking him away now?"

"I don't know what my plans are. I haven't made any decisions yet."

"There's no rush." Nellie put her hand on Tillie's arm. "I think it would be better for the lad to stay here for a while. He doesn't need any more upheaval at the moment, and we still haven't heard how he came to be roaming the countryside on his own. What on earth was the master doing, allowing him to...?" She shook her head again in disbelief.

"And what about Sarah's accident?" Tillie prised her son from her skirt. "You were going to tell me about that, weren't you?"

Jamie looked up then, concern etched all over his face. "She had blood on her 'ead, like you got on your knee. Are you sure she's not dead?"

"No, no, she's fine," Tillie reassured him. "We had a letter from the master this morning. But wasn't she all right when you left?"

"Don't know. There weren't room for me."

Puzzled as to what he meant, Tillie looked at the others, but they looked as perplexed as she was.

"You mean there was no room at the house?" she asked, appalled.

"No, in the carriage fing what took her 'ome." His face lit up for a moment. "It were amazing in the park, all them fancy folks, 'til..." He looked down, sad again.

Freda had made a pot of tea, and as she poured it out Tillie continued, "So were you and Sarah in the park on your own?"

"George were there. He went 'ome wiv 'er but I couldn't fit in."

"So how did you get back?"

179

Jamie looked slightly abashed. "They were all shouting at me so I ran away."

"Where to?"

He shrugged.

"Where did you spend the night?"

Another shrug.

"Weren't you scared?" asked Ruby.

"A bit, but it weren't as bad as before I come here."

Tillie jumped up and enfolded him in her arms once more. "I'm so sorry, my darling boy," she said tearfully. "I'll never forgive myself for what I've put you through."

"It weren't your fault." Jamie reached up and wiped her tears. "You weren't even there."

"That's the point, I should have been, then none of this would have happened."

"You're here now, and that's all that matters." Nellie then turned to Ruby. "Don't you agree?"

The maid hesitated momentarily before saying, "Yes." as Jamie put his arms around her.

"You will still be me friend, won't yer?" he asked with a worried expression on his face.

"Of course, my little pumpkin." She gave him a huge hug.

"Pumpkin?" He pulled away and looked up at her with such a comical expression that everyone burst out laughing. The tension had been eased and Tillie breathed a sigh of relief.

"I thought about going to clear out Grandmamma's cottage this morning." Tillie looked at her sister. "I could do with your help, if you feel up to it."

Ruby shrugged. "I don't know..." she began as a gust of wind blew through the door and Sam came in.

Taking off his cap, he went up to Ruby. "I came to offer my condolences. I'm sorry to hear about your grandmother."

"Thank you," she whispered as tears began to well up in her eyes. As they fell down her cheek, he gently wiped them away before looking up in surprise as Jamie ran over to them and pulled at his sleeve.

"Jamie, I didn't see you there. How did you get back from Harrogate?"

"It's a long story," said Nellie. "Ruby can tell you about it later."

The maid looked up at the groom hopefully. "Will you walk with us to my grandmamma's cottage?"

Sam turned to Nellie, who was by this time, getting on with her chores. "Any idea when the master will be back?"

"By the end of the week, we think."

"Yes, then, I'd be pleased to escort you."

Freda was mixing some dough. "I'm sorry I wasn't up in time to make you some bread to take," she apologised. "There are some old pastries in the pantry, if you want to see what they're like."

Tillie went to find them. "They'll do," she declared as she put them in a basket, adding some biscuits and apples.

Freda added the bubbling yeast to the mixture. "I'm afraid everything else got taken for the wake yesterday, but I'll make sure there's a good nourishing meal ready for you when you return this evening."

"Thank you, Nellie."

Tillie then turned towards Jamie. "You might have to walk slowly, as my knee's still rather painful."

"Let me see." Jamie tried to lift her skirt but she pulled it down. She didn't want Sam getting any ideas.

"No, Jamie, it's impolite for a lady to show her legs."

"But has it still got blood on it?"

She shook her head indulgently. "No, it's just sore. Come on."

They set off, struggling against the strong wind, with Sam flanked by Jamie on one side, Ruby on the other and Tillie following behind. When they came to the stile, Jamie jumped over quickly.

"Do you 'member when I fell?" he asked as Ruby climbed after him, clutching her bonnet.

"Yes, I was telling Till—I mean your mama, about it…" she trailed off, her smile receding as she looked back at her sister.

Sam had stopped to help Tillie climb over and, with his hand outstretched, he froze. "You mean…?"

"Yes, she's his mother." Ruby's voice sounded bitter as she retied the ribbons on her bonnet.

"But that's wonderful news." His face beamed but then dropped as he added, "Isn't it?"

"Course it is," called Jamie, jumping up and down. "She's me ma, and Ruby's me auntie. I never had no auntie before." Swinging Ruby's hand he began singing over and over again, "I got a new auntie, I got a new auntie."

"Well, at least *he's* happy." Sam climbed after Tillie and, reaching the other side, he looked questioningly at Ruby. "I don't understand. Why aren't you?"

Ruby merely gave her usual shrug and, releasing her nephew's hand, she began to walk off. Sam hurried after her while Jamie hung back with his mother.

"Why's Auntie Ruby sad?" he asked.

"She thinks that you won't like her so much, now that I'm back."

"But I do," he exclaimed, running after the pair in front. "Auntie Ruby, I do still like you."

Ruby waited for him to catch up. "I know you do, Jamie." Picking him up, she swung him round. "And I lo…ve you."

Giggling as she set him back down, he asked, "Don't you love Mama?"

Tillie caught up and Ruby studied her face, then sighed. "Yes, of course I do." She put her hand out in a gesture of apology. "I'm sorry, it's just…"

"It's all right," Tillie accepted the apology. "Let's put it all behind us."

Sam tucked an arm in each of the sisters' and they continued their journey in a much lighter mood, with Jamie frolicking round them like a lamb.

As they approached the cottage, Ruby stopped. "I'm not sure that I can go in. I can still see her sitting there surrounded by her baskets."

Sam took her hand as her grey eyes filled with tears. "I'll stay outside with you 'til you feel ready to go in," he comforted her as the next-door neighbour turned from cleaning her window.

"Good day to you," she declared. "I wondered when you'd be back. I found your grandmother's door open last night and there didn't seem to be anybody around so I closed it."

"Oh, thank you." In her haste to find Jamie, Tillie hadn't thought about shutting the door and remembering the bonnet she had thrown off, she looked round and saw it lying in a puddle and went to pick it up. Shaking off as much water as she could, she heard Jamie being invited next door for a drink.

She entered the cottage. The atmosphere was stifling, the smell of the embalming fluid still lingering, so she opened the window and stood looking out, breathing in the fresh air, trying to be brave, as Ruby and Sam entered. Tears flowed down her sister's cheeks and her own eyes began to fill at the sight.

"I'm going to miss her so much," Ruby cried, sitting down in her grandmother's armchair and stroking the arms.

Jamie came in with a large drink. "I love that lady's lemonade. It's even betterer than Freda's."

In spite of her sorrow, Tillie had to smile at the look on her son's face. "Well, don't let Freda hear you say that."

Grinning, he finished his drink and ran out again as Ruby wiped her eyes and stood up. "Grandmamma once told me she'd written a will and put it in her writing desk, in the secret compartment." Walking over to the desk, she yanked on what looked like a solid piece of wood on the side, and, as the compartment was revealed, she pulled out an official-looking document. "Yes, this must be it."

There was a knock on the open door as Sam asked, "Don't you need a solicitor to read it?"

The neighbour came in, scoffing, "No, us poor folk around here can't afford them. We witness each other's wills so we don't end up having to pay for some rich lawyer to get the money we've scrimped and saved for."

"And it's all legal and above board?"

"Well, we've never had any bother."

"What does it say?" asked Tillie, looking over her sister's shoulder at the will.

Ruby moved away, peering at the writing and pulling faces with her mouth, before handing it over to her sister. "I don't understand all those big words. You read it."

"I can read now, Mama." Jamie had come back in, stroking a white kitten. "Uncle David and Nellie have been learning me."

"Why, that's wonderful." Tillie patted him on the head, marvelling at how much had been done for him in such a short time and, taking the document from Ruby, she began to read it aloud.

"'*This is the last will and testament of Alice Matilda Raven.*'" She looked up. "I'd forgotten I was named after her. Who were you named after, Ruby?"

"Oh, I don't know, get on with it!"

"Sorry!"

She continued, "'*I hereby bequeath all my possessions to be divided equally between my four grandchildren, Matilda, Matthew, Harry and Ruby. In the event of any dispute, I command that Matthew, being the oldest boy, has the final word.*'"

"Is that all?" asked Ruby, trying to take the will back from her sister. "No mention of her jewellery or anything?"

"No, nothing further except signatures and the like."

"How disappointing, and how are we going to decide who has what? Matthew's miles away."

"If you'd like my opinion…" The neighbour stepped forward.

"Yes, please," said the girls at the same time, smiling at each other and easing the tension between them.

"You'll need to put everything into two piles, one for things you want to keep and one for the rest, and then divide the first one into four."

"That sounds like a good idea." As the girls began taking things off the dresser, with the kitten in one hand, Jamie pointed with his free hand to a photo. "Who are them folks, Mama?"

Tillie looked at the photo showing a couple sitting sombrely, with two young men and a girl behind them. "That's my grandparents at the front, and that one there—" she indicated to one of the young men, "—that's my papa when he was younger."

"How old am I, Mama? George wanted to know, and I couldn't 'member."

"You're nearly eight. In fact, what's the date today?"

"It's July the sixteenth," said Sam.

"That means it's your birthday next week," she exclaimed.

"We'll have to have a party," cried Ruby. "And ask Freda to make some of her lovely jelly." Then, as if surprising herself at her unusual exuberance, she slumped down once more.

"We'll see what Nellie says when we get back." Patting her arm, Tillie looked around her. "But first we have this lot to sort out. How can one old lady have so many bits and pieces?"

Opening a jewellery box, Ruby took out a bright gold necklace with a big red gem dangling from it. "She often used to show this to me, it was her pride and joy. It belonged to her mother, our great grandmother, and that there is a ruby." She pointed to the sparkling jewel.

"Well, I'm sure she would want you to have it then," Tillie declared as she caressed the necklace nestling in her sister's hand. "As it's your namesake."

"But what if Matthew wants it? You know what the will said."

"I'm sure he won't object. He can have the other piece." She picked up a blue brooch that shimmered in the sunlight. "This would look lovely on Jessie, wouldn't it?"

185

"Jessie?" asked Ruby absently.

"Matthew's wife, she was with him yesterday."

"Oh yes, I was…" Ruby grimaced.

"He understood, don't worry about it. Did you know they're expecting a baby in a few weeks?"

"Oh no, I feel even worse now. I didn't even congratulate them."

"Well, we'll make a point of going over to see them soon."

"Is Matthew your brother?" Jamie began.

"Yes, Harry too, that makes them your uncles. We used to have another little brother called James, that's who you were named after, but he died when he was still a baby."

Jamie looked thoughtful for a moment. "But I've still got three uncles."

"No, Jamie, two, I thought you could count better than that."

Shifting the kitten so that he could hold up three fingers, he counted, "Uncle David, Uncle Matthew and Uncle Harry, that makes three."

"Oh yes." She was still surprised that her son was allowed to use such an intimate name. It showed how close they had become. "But, strictly speaking, Uncle David isn't…oh, never mind."

She looked around at the array of items still needing attention and turned to the old lady beside her. "I suppose you're busy today?"

"Not at all. I can help, if you'd like me to. I've done this job many a time."

"Would you be offended if I offered you some of her clothes?" Tillie asked her later as they emptied the tallboy beside the bed. "Some of these look as if they've hardly been worn and you seem a similar size to her."

Ruby picked up a black corset and held it coquettishly across her bosom, looking across at Sam from beneath her eyelashes. "I can't imagine her wearing this. It looks a bit bawdy, doesn't it?"

Sam coughed and grinned as Tillie turned to the old lady. "Would you like it?"

The elderly lady blushed. "I...no, better not. Don't want my old man getting any ideas, not at our time of life."

"Stop teasing her," admonished Ruby, also grinning. "You can have anything that's *suitable*, and take no notice of my sister, she's supposed to be the serious one, not the joker." The grin was replaced by a frown. "That used to be me..."

"It will be again, you'll see."

Ruby didn't look convinced. She stood staring out of the window, sniffing one of her grandmother's shawls before putting it around her shoulders and hugging it close to her.

"You keep the shawl," said Tillie, "and each time you wear it you can think of her."

Eventually, after eating the pastries and fruit they had brought, they sorted everything into manageable piles, and even found something for Sam, a rather rusty old penknife, with an attachment for getting stones out of horses' hooves, that he said would clean up well enough.

"It must have belonged to Grandpa," said Ruby. "I don't remember him very well, do you, Tillie?"

"No, I just remember an old man with very white hair, giving me a farthing for...I think it was my birthday or something like that. I must have been about seven. I kept that farthing right up until the fi—" She stopped, suddenly recalling that nobody else there knew about the fire, and she didn't want to remind Jamie, who was still playing with the kitten. "Anyway, I don't have it any longer. I'm afraid I'm destitute."

"What's destute?" Jamie looked up.

"I think it means your mama doesn't have any money," explained Ruby.

"I got a farthing." Putting down the cat, Jamie felt in his pocket and pulled out a shiny coin. "Sarah gev it me." He hesitated before holding it out. "You can have it, Mama."

"Oh, thank you, Jamie." Tillie hugged him again. "But you keep it. You never know when you might need it."

187

"How are you going to manage? Don't you have anything?" asked Ruby, obviously suddenly aware of her sister's plight.

Tillie shrugged her shoulders. "I pray that something will turn up."

Chapter 11

Later, as they clambered down the other side of the hill, laden with as many things as they could carry, Tillie could see a carriage in the distance, wheeling round the large drive of The Grange before drawing up at the front door.

"Oh my, that looks like the master," Sam exclaimed. "Nellie said he wasn't coming back 'til the end of the week. I'd better hurry on ahead." He ran off at full pelt, leaving a trail of cutlery behind him.

"Does that mean Uncle David's home?" asked Jamie, excitement shining from his face as he picked up some of the spoons.

Tillie stopped but Jamie grabbed her, trying to pull her forward. "Come on," he yelled, yanking at her arm.

Turning to look into her sister's face, Ruby asked, "Are you worried that you might have to leave now that the master's back?"

Tillie nodded.

"Uncle David ain't like that." Jamie looked up at her. "He never made me go away when he was cross about Rufus."

"Would you like me to go in first and explain?" asked Ruby, transferring the hatbox full of trinkets that she was carrying into her other hand.

Pushing back her shoulders and puffing out her chest, Tillie replied, "No, my darling sister, but thank you anyway. I have to face him sooner or later." Rearranging the bulging canvas bag she had been carrying, she began to run towards the house before her courage could desert her.

They entered the kitchen where they found Freda in a flap, waving her arms about.

"The master's back, and we're not at all ready for him." She pushed Ruby towards the door that led to the hallway. "Quickly, girl, run up and get changed. Oh dear, just on the day that we're behind with all the chores."

Dropping the box on the table, Ruby made for the door but she was pulled back. "On second thoughts, here, take these clean sheets and make the master's bed while you're up there. Go on, girl, don't dilly dally." She pressed a pile of bedding into Ruby's arms and gave her a shove. "And the drawing room fire isn't even made. Oh, how shall we fit everything in?"

"Let me help," Tillie intervened. "I'm not very good at making fires, but I can make a bed." She hurried out after her sister, calling behind her, "You stay there, Jamie, and sit still for a minute."

"But, Mama, I want to see Uncle David."

"Later," she heard Freda say as she ran up the stairs to catch up with Ruby.

"Which is the master's bedchamber nowadays?" she asked as she took the bedding from her.

"That one." Ruby pointed to a door on the right as she hurried towards the servant's quarters to get changed into her uniform.

Charging into the appointed room, Tillie dropped the pile of sheets onto the floor before grabbing one of them and throwing it out in front of her. As it landed on the bed, she leaned forward to smooth it out and, looking up, a surprised gasp escaped her.

"Oh!" she mouthed.

"Oh, indeed," came the deep baritone voice of her former master who stood by the washbasin, his shirt half unbuttoned, a towel in his hands.

It had not occurred to her that he would already be up there, and she stood transfixed.

"It's a while since I had a beautiful lady in my bedroom." An amused grin spread across his lips.

She blushed, feeling like a young girl caught out in a misdemeanour, and started to back out, but he continued. "You may as well finish the job you started."

"Yes…sir," she stammered, fumbling with the pillowcase.

He walked towards her. "I wasn't aware that I had engaged a new maid," he began before raising his eyebrows. "I know you, don't I? It's Tillie."

"Yes, sir," was all she could think to say again.

"Well, well!"

She continued making the bed as he stared at her.

"And what's brought you back here? Didn't you leave under unfortunate circumstances?"

Before she could reply she heard a voice outside the door.

"Uncle David, can I come in?"

She tried to get to the door, not wanting her son to interrupt before she could explain, but David beat her to it.

"Jamie," he cried, swinging open the door and lifting the boy up high in the air. "Thank goodness you're safe. I was so worried about you."

"Uncle David, is Sarah all right? She's not dead, is she?"

David put him down. "She's fine. She wanted to come and see you, but the doctor advised that she wait a while before travelling. She blamed herself for you getting lost."

Tillie watched the pair with a tinge of envy. They looked so natural together. How would she be able to take her son away?

"And you are really unscathed?" David continued.

"Am I, Mama?" Jamie turned to his mother, clearly unaware what reaction his question would create. "Am I un…whatever Uncle David said?"

Grimacing, she hardly dared to look. She saw David's body freeze before he slowly turned round to face her, his eyes wide open.

"Did he say…Mama?"

"Yes, she found me." Jamie ran over and put his arms around her.

Tillie held her breath as David studied her face for what seemed like an eternity. "I can see the resemblance."

Is that all he can say? No surprise? No recriminations?

She opened her mouth to speak but, not taking his eyes from her face, David put his hand on Jamie's shoulder and gently pushed him towards the door. "Run downstairs, Jamie, and wait for me there. I just need to speak to...your mama."

"But..."

"Do as Uncle..." Tillie could not bring herself to call her former master by his Christian name. "Do as he says, there's a good boy."

Jamie slouched out of the room, with Tillie wishing she could follow him, but she knew she had to face whatever anger or rebuke was coming her way.

David began pacing up and down. "Of course, I want to know how your son came to be roaming the countryside." He came to a stop in front of her. "But the truth is, I've become very fond of him over the past few months, and can't bear the thought of..."

He hesitated, obviously agitated, looking up at the ceiling. "What are your plans for the future?"

"I don't really have any," she whispered, wishing that she knew what he was thinking.

"Well, in that case..." Raking his hands through his hair he began pacing again. "May I enquire about your circumstances? I notice that you are not wearing a ring, but that does not always signify—"

"No, I'm not married."

"Or...intended?"

"No."

She stood watching him, pulling at her lip, until he stopped again and, taking her hands in his, blurted out, "Would you consider marrying me?"

Tillie's mouth fell open, dumbstruck. That was the last thing she had expected.

"Just for the boy's sake, you understand?"

"I..."

"I realise that some people would consider that I will be marrying below my station, but I could live with that. I've never been much of one to pander to other people's opinions."

"Oh."

"You don't have to give me your answer straightaway," he continued. "Think it over. For the boy's sake, as I said. You've already seen me in a state of undress, so we're halfway there." Picking up his jacket, he gave her an engaging smile, causing her heart to leap.

What was she doing? Just because he had proposed marriage didn't give her cause to be reacting to him in that manner. He was her master, or had been, and he had made it obvious that it would be a marriage of convenience only, so there was no point developing feelings for him.

"Well, as I said, I'll leave you to think it over. Consider, my dear, what the benefits to Jamie would be."

He walked out as Tillie collapsed on the bed, covering her face with her hands.

What a turn of events! Her, the mistress of Brightmoor? How could she accept?

But perhaps it wouldn't be such a bad idea. She was sick of having no place to call her own. But what would Nellie say? Or Ruby—how would she react? They had only just become friendly again, and she didn't want to jeopardise that friendship. No, she would have to refuse.

She got up and finished making the bed, resolved that it would not be a good idea.

But what about Jamie? a little voice in her head kept asking. *Don't you owe it to him?*

"Oh, I don't know!" She walked over to the window and saw her son playing with a dog down on the lawn while David watched him with a smile on his handsome face. He looked up but she did not want him to see her so she quickly hid behind the curtain.

"Oh Grandmamma, what should I do?" she asked, looking up at the heavens, but deep down in her heart she knew what the answer should be.

* * * *

193

My goodness, what have I done? David stood watching Jamie playing with Lady on the lawn, feeling slightly unnerved. He was not used to acting in an impetuous manner. It was not in his usual character. *I didn't know I was going to say that until the words came out. I should have just asked her to stay as his nurse or governess.*

Looking up towards his bedroom window, he thought he saw a movement and wondered if it was Tillie spying on him. She had every right to do so; he had left her in a quandary. Not just her, but himself as well.

"Look, Uncle David! Lady can do tricks." Jamie's voice brought him back to earth and he tried to concentrate on the dog's antics, but without much success.

"You carry on playing, Jamie." He turned to go back inside the house. "I have a mountain of paperwork I really must catch up on."

"But, Uncle David, you ain't see'd 'em all."

"Another time." He patted the boy's head. "Another time."

"You glad me ma's here?"

"Yes, of course."

"Me too—I membered lotsa things since she come."

"That's good. You can tell me all about them later." As he made his way in, he remembered that he hadn't asked Jamie how he had found his way back, but he was here, and that was what mattered, explanations could wait.

His dilemma could not though. How much time should he give her? If she refused, he would lose Jamie. He couldn't bear the thought of that.

And what of Christine Wilson? He had become quite fond of her, but fortunately they hadn't got as far as the courting stage, although he sensed that she had hopes in that direction. They would now be shattered.

"Oh, what a mess!" he exclaimed aloud on entering the house.

"I'm really sorry, sir." Nellie almost bumped into him as she hurried from his study laden with mops and dusters. "We weren't expecting you back so soon."

"What?" he asked absentmindedly.

"I'm sorry about the disorder, sir."

"Oh, no, I wasn't referring to that. No, something else entirely."

"Anything I can help with?"

"No, Nellie, not this time." He entered the room and poured himself a brandy. "No, I have to sort this one out myself."

Picking up the pile of letters on his desk, he flicked through them but could not summon up the inclination to read any of them. They would have to be addressed soon, but in his present state of mind he knew that he would not be able to give them his full attention.

He tipped up the glass but it was empty so he poured out another.

She must accept. Sipping this drink more slowly, he paced the room. *I shall have to be patient and try to win her round.*

He turned as he heard a knock on the door and Nellie put her head round. "Dinner's ready, sir. Would you like it in here or in the dining room?"

"I suppose I had better take it in the dining room, as usual, thank you, Nellie."

Sitting alone at the large table eating his dinner, he fanticised about having someone to share his life with again, and holding out his glass to the imaginary wife sitting opposite him, he gave a toast.

"To our new family!"

The idea was becoming increasingly attractive and he finished the meal in a positive mood. If he felt like this, surely she would too.

He looked up as he heard Jamie outside. "But I want to say goodnight to Uncle David."

"It's all right, he can come in," he called, rising from the chair. "I've finished."

Jamie came bounding in, followed more slowly by Tillie who kept her eyes cast down to the floor.

He picked Jamie up and threw him in the air to squeals of delight, all the time trying to gauge Tillie's feelings.

"Please don't get him too excited, he's just off to bed." She didn't look him in the face. "Come on, Jamie."

He put the boy down and kissed his head. He had never done so before, but he wanted to show her how much he cared for him.

Jamie reached up and hugged him. "Goodnight, Uncle David."

"Goodnight, Jamie, I'll see you in the morning." He reached out towards Tillie, but without looking up, she took her son out.

Should he have said something to her? No, not with the boy there. If she'd been ready to give him an answer, surely she would have given some indication, not ignored him like that. Had he imagined it or had she almost flinched when he'd put out his hand towards her? It wasn't boding well for a favourable reply, but perhaps, after a good night's sleep she would change her mind and realise how beneficial such an arrangement would be.

* * * *

A good night's sleep was not what Tillie enjoyed that night. In fact she hardly slept a wink. So many questions and answers.

She was still no nearer to a solution by the time dawn broke so, sick of tossing and turning, she dressed quickly and, deciding that some fresh air might help to clear her head, she crept out through the back door before anyone else was up. Breathing in the cool fresh air, she walked around the garden, listening to the birds singing their early morning chorus. What a delightful sound they made.

She stood soaking up the atmosphere as a robin hopped down and looked up at her.

"Sorry, my friend, I didn't bring any food with me," she whispered, crouching down. "But if you wait a moment I'll get you some bread." The bird appeared to understand her as it cocked its head to one side so she backed through the door and headed for the bread bin. There were bound to be a few crumbs in there that she could take.

"Feeling hungry?" a deep voice asked from behind her. She froze. What was the master doing in the kitchen at this time of the morning?

"Sorry," she murmured without turning round. "I was just...getting... " her words tapered off.

"No need to apologise...Tillie." As he said her name he lowered his voice, making it sound very seductive in the confines of the kitchen. Of course he had used it before, but now the circumstances made it sound completely different, and her stomach turned cartwheels. Blinking fast, she turned around. He was sitting at the table wearing a black silk dressing gown, looking exceedingly handsome, his hair slightly dishevelled, and holding a mug of steaming coffee.

"Drink?" he asked, holding it out to her.

She shook her head, not trusting herself to speak again.

Slowly pulling the fronts of his robe closer together, he grinned. "It seems that you're determined to catch me in a state of undress. It makes me wonder if it's deliberate."

She shook her head again, her eyes wide. "No, sir, no, not at all."

"Relax, I'm teasing you." He stared at her, the semblance of a smile on his lips, and she stared back, unwilling to break the spell.

How could she have become so sensitive to him in such a short time? Only yesterday he had been her former master—no ideas of romance would have entered her head—and suddenly here she was considering marriage to him.

She mentally shook herself. She hadn't made any decisions yet, so what was she doing standing here allowing him to think that she might have.

Freda walked in, mumbling, "Good morning," as she yawned and straightened her mop cap. She stopped, her hands still raised, exclaiming, "Oh, I didn't see you there, sir. I…um…"

"It's all right, Freda." He looked over at Tillie, adding, "I couldn't sleep," as if to let her know that he was not as composed as he appeared. "I needed a drink, so helped myself. Hope I haven't put the fire out, I did throw some logs on it."

The cook opened the range door to check but quickly closed it again when she was almost engulfed in flames. "The fire's fine." She gasped for breath. "Perhaps a few too many logs."

"Sorry." He stood up.

Tillie tried her utmost to keep her gaze lowered from his lean body but could not resist a peek from beneath her lashes. Realising that he was watching her, she turned back to the bread bin. "I was going to get some crumbs for the robin but he's probably gone now but I'll still take some just in case," she gabbled without taking a breath and, snatching a chunk of bread, she ran out before he could stop her.

Closing the door behind her, she took a deep breath. The robin had flown off so she walked round the garden and sat down on a bench in a secluded arbour, where she broke the bread and scattered the crumbs on the ground in front of her, wishing that she had someone to talk to about her predicament.

"I know," she startled a blackbird that had been pecking at the morsels and it flew off, squawking, into a tree. "I'll go and see Emily."

Rubbing her hands together to remove the few crumbs that were stuck to her palms, she went back into the house.

The kitchen was deserted. Thank goodness he wasn't still in there.

She poured herself a drink and sat wondering whether the master—she could still only call him that—would allow her to use the carriage to go to visit Emily? Perhaps it would be better to ask Tom if she could borrow the cart, or better still ask Sam to saddle a horse for her. But what should she do about Jamie? She couldn't leave him behind.

Nellie came in followed by a shamefaced Ruby, carrying a dustpan full of broken crockery. She looked up at them in enquiry.

"Don't ask." Nellie shook her head.

"It wasn't my fault." Ruby emptied the pieces into a bin. "The master wasn't looking where he was going."

"He does seem rather distracted since his return," replied the housekeeper, looking at Tillie. "Have you any idea why?"

"Me? What makes you think…?" Keeping her face diverted so as not to give herself away, she mumbled, "I'd better go and check on Jamie," and rushed out.

Surely she hadn't guessed? Not even Nellie was that wise!

Seeing Jamie in the hall, she ran to greet him.

"Mama, you're still here!" he cried, wrapping his arms around her.

"Of course, my darling." She smothered him with kisses. "I'll never leave you again. I've promised you that, haven't I?"

"But I were scared that it were a dream."

"Believe me, it's no dream. I'm back for good."

"Uncle David came to me bedroom and said I could eat me breakfast with him. P'raps you can as well."

"I don't…"

"Come on." She let him drag her into the breakfast room, as she couldn't think of a plausible excuse to refuse. But how could she sit and eat while *he* watched her?

"Sit down, young man. Ah, you've brought your mama." David looked across at Tillie.

"Uncle David, can Mama have breakfast with us too?"

"I don't see why not. Pull out a chair for her."

"I…um. I'm not really hungry," she began.

"Of course you are. You've been up a long time."

"But…"

"Just sit down, I'm not going to eat you."

She did as she was bid, feeling like a naughty girl being chastised, as Ruby entered with a rack of toast. The maid looked shocked to see her sister sitting there but said nothing.

"Could you bring some more food for Jamie and Tillie please, Ruby," David asked.

"Not for me, thanks," Tillie began, but seeing the expression on his face, she relented. "Toast will be fine."

"Can I have some of me fav'rite sausages?" asked Jamie.

"And a fresh pot of tea," from David.

"Will that be all, sir?" asked Ruby, looking at Tillie askance once more.

"Yes, thank you, Ruby."

The maid backed out.

"Fetch some more plates and cutlery, Jamie, from that sideboard," David ordered. "We can't have you eating off the table, can we?"

Jamie burst out laughing. "That would be funny, wouldn't it, Mama?"

She tried to raise a smile but, seeing David staring at her again, she merely grimaced.

"Relax." He put out his hand towards her as Jamie went to pick up some more dishes. "We're merely enjoying a meal together. It doesn't have to signify anything. I realise you may not be ready to give me the answer I'm hoping for just yet, but I can be patient and wait as long as it takes."

"But we used to, didn't we, Mama?" Jamie came back and gave out the plates.

"What's that?" asked David.

"Eat off the table."

"No, we didn't," Tillie found her voice once more, "not exactly. We sometimes had dishes of food that everyone dipped into to, but we used plates. It wasn't as uncivilised as you are making…Unc…as you are making out."

"I'd like to hear about it sometime," David began, but continued with, "but you, young man, haven't explained yet how you left Harrogate."

"Oh." Jamie grimaced as Ruby re-entered and put a plate of sizzling food in front of him. "Can I eat me sausages first?"

He received raised eyebrows from David and a slight shake of the head. "Your son can twist me round his little finger," he whispered as Ruby went out. "See what an indulgent father I would make."

She had to admit that what he said was true. Too indulgent perhaps! "I wouldn't want him to become spoiled."

"Oh no, I didn't mean that, I was merely..."

Sitting at such close proximity she noticed for the first time that his eyes were not as dark on close inspection as she had thought them to be. They had yellow flecks around the irises, which seemed to expand and contract as he spoke. She suddenly realised he had been asking her a question and was waiting for the reply.

"I beg your pardon...?" She had been so absorbed that she hadn't been paying attention. She put down the piece of toast she had been holding for the last few minutes, not trusting herself to eat it.

"No matter." He held her gaze.

"I've finished, Uncle David. Can I go now?"

She watched him drag his gaze away from her face and put a restraining arm on the boy. "Not yet, young man, you still have some explaining to do."

"Jamie's told us part of the story," she began when her son appeared to be at a loss for words. "Haven't you, darling? About being left in the park?"

He replied with a nod.

"I'm not going to be cross, Jamie," David urged. "I just want to know what happened to you."

"Is Sarah really all right?"

"Yes, I told you, she's just a bit weak. She said that you saved her life."

"You never told me that!" Tillie exclaimed.

"Well…did she really say that?"

"Yes, she did," continued David. "She told me all about the carriage charging towards you out of control and that you dragged her out of the way and saved her."

"S'pose I did. I never thought of it like that."

"Oh, my hero." Tillie kissed him, then looked across at David who was regarding her with such a look of…well, it couldn't be love, he was only interested in her son.

She cleared her throat. "But what we want to know is what happened after Sarah had been taken home."

"George said there weren't room for me, and all them folks…I couldn't stand no more…" He shrugged his shoulders, looking at them with a forlorn expression.

"So where did you go?" David asked, reaching out to him.

"I just ran 'til I couldn't run no more, then…"

"Go on."

"I asked a man where Sarah's house was, but he didn't know. Then I saw something amazing."

"What was that?"

"This man was doing magic with a stick."

Tillie looked at David to see if he could tell what the boy was talking about. He didn't look any wiser than she.

"Magic?"

"Yes, it lit up the whole street."

"Oh, you mean the lamplighter." David looked relieved, but then exclaimed, "But I asked him if he had seen you…" He ran his fingers through his hair in frustration. "Oh, I must have missed you by seconds. If only I had stayed out longer."

Tillie wanted to sooth the desperation from his troubled eyes but sat still, her hands entwined on her lap.

"So what did you do then?" She dragged her gaze back to her son.

"It got dark, so I crawled under a hedge and went to sleep…'til a big dog come and started licking me face." He smiled. "It were a lovely dog, all black."

"Was it daylight by then?"

"Um…" He puckered up his face and put his head to one side. "S'pose so. Me neck ached and me feet was cold, I remember that." He rubbed the back of his neck.

"Then what did you do?"

"I tried to find Sarah's house again but I couldn't, so I asked a man with a cart if I could have a ride. He let me sit in the back, on top of the hay. It were lovely and soft."

"But how did you know where he was going?" Tillie asked, appalled by the risks he'd had to take.

"Well, I said I needed to go to Leeds 'cos I'd heard Uncle David talk about Leeds before, so I thought it must be near here. Is it?"

David nodded with a bemused look on his face.

"But he said he weren't going nowhere near Leeds."

"I should think not, in a hay cart. It's miles from Harrogate. So what did he do?"

"He dropped me off at a crossroads, said 'good luck' and gev me an apple 'cos I said I was hungry." He forced out a burp and laughed cheekily. "Apples always make me do that."

Tillie tutted and shook her head.

"Can I take me ma to see me tree house, Uncle David?"

"You've got a tree house?" Tillie exclaimed, looking across at David who was looking back at her with an expression on his face that seemed to say, '*see how much I've done for him.*'

Her decision was getting harder and harder, or maybe easier. Perhaps she should just give in and say 'Yes'.

Jamie jumped down from his chair and tugged at her arm. "Come on, Mama. Let's go."

"But you haven't finished telling us…and…" She really wanted to go to see Emily, to get an impartial person's opinion.

David also stood up. "I'm sure the remainder of his tale can wait until later. I really do need to get on with the estate affairs. You go and spend some time with your son and…" He raised his eyebrows. "And see how he's settled in and made himself one of the family."

How could she not read the obvious innuendo? She felt as if she was being forced into a corner, but then would it be such a bad thing?

"All right, but I need to speak to you later." She saw his eyes light up and added, "About something else." His face dropped and he stalked out of the room without as much as a by your leave.

The master, or whatever I'm supposed to call him, must be serious about the proposal, she thought as she followed her son down to the woods. *But, as he said, it would only be for Jamie's sake. Could I live in a loveless marriage? I have no real idea of his feelings towards me.*

"Here it is, Mama. Do you like it?"

She was amazed, the tree house was nothing like she had envisaged. The one her brothers had played in had been much smaller. Other memories of her childhood flooded back, happy times with Matthew, Harry and Ruby. How could she deprive her own son of brothers and sisters? The thought of how that would come about made her blush until she remembered what had happened to her when Jamie had been conceived. She had purposely stayed away from any close relationships in order not to have that experience again. But if the marriage was to be one of convenience only, then that side of it might not be an issue.

"Are you coming up?"

"Yes, on my way," she called as she climbed up the ladder. "My, what a grand place."

"Here, you can sit on my cushion." Opening a box that was hidden under a blanket, Jamie took out some pictures and proudly showed them to her.

"You drew these?" she asked in amazement, receiving a nod in reply. Back at the gypsy camp he had been left to run wild as she had always been too busy trying to make a living to teach him anything. She studied the pictures, enthralled at the expressions on the faces of some of his subjects.

"This one's me fav'rite." He showed her one he had drawn of Lady. "She's a dog."

"So I see." She smiled.

"Sam says she's gonner have pups."

"Really?"

"And I might be able to keep one for me very own."

Yet another trap to keep her here!

"I'm gonner call him Rufie, after me pet fox what died."

She sat looking at the pictures while he explained who or what they all were, until she heard a voice from below.

"Hey, you up there!"

Jamie peered down the stairwell. "It's Auntie Ruby."

Ruby's head popped up over the lintel. "Nellie asked me to bring you some drinks and cake. The master said you'd be thirsty." She gave her sister a sidelong glance. "He seems to have taken an interest in you since you came back, doesn't he?"

Tillie tried to appear noncommittal. "Does he?"

"It's 'cos she's me ma." Jamie poured out some lemonade and drank it lustily. "That was good." He grinned before wiping his mouth with his sleeve.

The sisters smiled as he poured out another and drank half of it before handing the beaker over to Tillie.

"Thank you." She drank it in one gulp. Even her sister had noticed the extra attention she was receiving from her master. She would have to ask him to temper it down until she made her decision.

"You want some, Auntie Ruby?" He filled the beaker once more, emptying the bottle. "No, lad, you have it. I've got to be getting back."

"Sure you can't say a while longer?" asked Tillie, eager to be friendly.

"No, I've still got so many chores to finish."

"I could help you. I feel really guilty, you doing all that hard work and me lazing away down here."

"But, Mama..."

"It's all right, honestly," Ruby replied. "I've been doing it so long, I'm used to it."

"I know that, but I'm sure you could do with an extra hand now and again. Tell you what, if Jamie doesn't mind staying here for a while and doing some more drawings for me, I'll come back with you and get stuck in. We'll get those chores done in half the time. Eh, Jamie?"

"All right," he conceded, and then chirped up, "I'll draw you a surprise."

"That would be lovely." She leaned over and kissed the top of his head.

Ruby had already descended the ladder and was walking away so Tillie hurried down and ran to catch up with her.

"You don't have to do this." Her sister kept her head down. "I'm sure you'd much rather stay with your son."

"I want to. Ruby, stop a minute." She slowed down, putting her hand on her sister's arm. "Are you still out of sorts with me?"

As usual all she received in reply was a shrug and a downcast face.

"Please don't be. You seemed so happy to see me when I first arrived. What changed?"

Ruby looked up at her and opened her mouth, seemingly about to say something, but closed it again without doing so.

"Was it when you found out I was Jamie's mother...because that doesn't stop me, or him, loving you any less?"

Her sister kicked at the dead leaves, her lips pursed. "No?"

"Of course not." She held her at arm's length, looking deeply into her eyes. "Oh, Ruby, I shouldn't have run off, leaving you like that, all those years ago. You were so young. It's all my fault. Can you ever forgive me?"

After a moment Ruby put her arms around her and hugged her. "I'm sorry, I just get so...so uncertain of things. I can't seem to make sense of my feelings sometimes."

"Well, I'm here to change all that, if you'll let me," she replied as they began walking again.

"Does that mean you're staying?"

She tried to think of a non-committal reply, but as they came in sight of the house she saw a carriage drawn up outside.

"That'll be the master's new lady friend, Christine...Wilson, I think her name is," explained Ruby. "Rumour has it that they are to be married before long," she continued, clearly unaware of the shocked effect her innocent statement was having on her sister. "You'll understand why when you see her. She's the prettiest lady I ever did see, besides you, of course." She turned with a smile and stopped. "Are you all right, you've gone very pale?"

"Just a bit of indigestion. I'll be fine in a minute." Tillie took a deep breath, trying to take in what she had just heard. How could he propose marriage to her if he was already engaged to this...beautiful Christine person?

Ruby looked at her with concern written all over her face. "Are you sure that's all it is?"

She nodded. "Honestly, I'm fine. Come on. I'm interested to see this paragon of beauty." She pulled her sister's arm and hurried on.

Chapter 12

Nellie met them as they entered through the back door. "Ah, Ruby, just in time. Take this tray of tea in to the master. He's got company."

"Yes, we saw the carriage. Is it Miss Wilson and her sister?"

"Yes, now hurry up about it."

"Let me take it in." Tillie rubbed her hands down the side of her dress. "I should very much like to meet the lady."

Test the opposition, she thought as she picked up the tray before anyone could object.

"Well, if you..." She was already out of the room before Nellie could finish the sentence.

Being out of the habit of carrying a tray full of heavy cups and saucers together with a teapot and milk jug, she almost dropped it trying to open the door.

"Come in," David sounded rather irritated.

Managing to adjust the tray, she walked in.

"Just put it down there, Ru..." The look on his face when he saw that it wasn't the parlour maid was comical. He had his jacket tails in his hands, obviously about to sit down, but stood bolt upright, his mouth open.

"This isn't the usual maid," one of the ladies scrutinised Tillie's face, "and she isn't even dressed like one."

"This is Tillie," was the gruff reply. "She's..."

"I'm Ruby's sister...ma'am." *Mustn't forget her manners.*

"And how long have you been here?" A warmer voice spoke from the other end of the couch.

Tillie straightened and turned towards the speaker who had previously not been in her line of vision. This must be the one. She was certainly beautiful, with her blonde curls peeping out from under a little green hat.

"Not long."

How could she compete with that vision of loveliness?

"Tillie used to work here some years ago," David had found his voice, "and has recently returned."

"Would you like me to pour the tea?" she asked in the sweetest voice she could muster. "Sir?" If he wanted them to think she was the new maid, then so be it.

"And I have asked her to marry me!"

A shocked silence pervaded the room. Jumping up in alarm, Tillie poured hot tea all over her hand. She ran out, perversely not feeling any pain, but not wanting to see the looks on the ladies' faces.

She ran into the kitchen, fortunately empty, and plunged her hand into the bowl of water in the sink, followed almost immediately by David.

"Get back to your visitors!" she cried. "Leave me alone."

"Please." He tried to touch her but she shrugged his hand off.

"What's going on?" Freda came out of the pantry carrying some apples.

"I've scalded my hand, that's all."

David looked from one to the other and walked out without saying another word.

"Here, let me look at it." The cook went across and examined her hand. "It doesn't look that bad."

Tillie burst into tears.

"Is it that painful?"

"No…it's not that. Oh, I don't know what to do."

"About what?"

"Oh…nothing." She wiped her eyes with her apron and dabbed at her hand where a small blister was appearing.

"You'd better put a bit of butter on that. That's what I always do. I'm forever catching my arms on the oven, look." The cook rolled up her sleeve and showed her a row of scars.

As Tillie did as she was told, Jamie came running in. "Have you finished…?" he asked, stopping in his tracks. "Why're you putting butter on yer hand?"

"I've scalded myself on some hot tea."

He walked over and peered at the burn. "Ugh, does it hurt?"

"A bit."

"I done you a picture." He held up the paper in his hands. It was obviously a drawing of her, although not a very flattering one. "Do you like it?"

"It's the best picture I've ever seen." She put her hands around him, careful not to get any of the butter on his clothes, as Freda went out of the back door to empty some slops.

"Can I show it to Uncle David?"

"Not now, sweetheart. He's got company."

"No he ain't. I just see'd the carriage pull away. They've gone."

"Well, I don't think he—"

"Uncle David." He ran across to the very person they had been discussing, who was coming through the door. "Do yer like me picture of me ma?"

"Lovely, Jamie." He didn't look at the picture, but across at Tillie. She resolutely kept her gaze down, although she could still see him through her lashes.

"Run and play now. I need to speak to your mother."

"Can I play with Lady?"

"That sounds like a good idea."

The boy ran out, calling for the dog and David purposely closed the door behind him.

Tillie tried to get past him to re-open it. "He—"

He put his hands on either side of her shoulders. "Tillie, look at me. I apologise for blurting it out like that."

"But, what must they have thought?"

"Well, they did seem to be rather non-plussed." He grinned but she was still angry at him.

"But I didn't think you would tell anybody until I gave you a reply." As he raised his arms, combing his hair with his fingers, she continued, "And I still haven't done so."

"I know, and I don't mean to put you under any pressure."

"It doesn't seem that way to me."

"I can only apologise again."

She heard Nellie coming down the corridor talking to Ruby so she moved away.

"So, if you're sure your hand is all right," David said, loudly enough for them to hear as he went outside, passing Freda on her way back in.

"The master's acting very strange lately." Freda looked back at him as she rinsed her hands at the sink before fetching some potatoes from the pantry. "Why has he started using the kitchen door?"

"I think he went to find Jamie," gabbled Tillie. "Actually, I needed to ask him a favour," she added as she ran out after him.

He hadn't gone far. He was showing Jamie how to throw a stick for Lady to fetch. She ducked behind a hedge and watched them. They seemed so in tune with each other that any unknowing bystander would think they actually were father and son. But if he had been contemplating marriage to that vision of beauty who had just left...?

She desperately needed someone to talk to, and the best person would be Emily.

But how could she get there?

The dog came barking up to her and destroyed her reverie. She could hide no longer.

"Mama, what you doing in the bushes?" Jamie had followed the dog.

"I...um...wasn't..." She emerged, rather dishevelled, with a tear in her dress where it had caught on a protruding branch.

He burst out laughing. "Your hair's all messy." He turned to his benefactor who had followed him. "Look at Mama, Uncle David. Don't she look funny?"

She couldn't bear to see the derision she knew would be on his face, so she tried to push past him.

"I...need to clean myself up. Please excuse me."

"I like the tousled look, it's more natural."

She looked up in surprise and saw an amused smile on his face as he reached over and tucked a stray russet curl behind her ear. His gaze mesmerised her for a second but she had to keep focused.

Dragging her eyes from his, she pushed back her shoulders and began to leave.

"Come and play," Jamie yelled over his shoulder, already running after the dog. "It's great fun."

"Yes, why not?" David stood aside to let her pass. "You've already ruined your dress, and your hair can't come to any more harm." With raised eyebrows, he took her hand and led her onto the lawn.

"Watch this, Mama." Jamie threw a ball into the air and as it descended Lady caught it. "You 'ave a go."

Jamie took the ball from the dog's mouth and threw it to her. She put out her hands to catch it but missed and overbalanced, falling right into David's arms.

"I knew you'd fall for me one day," he whispered in her ear, "but didn't dare hope it would be so soon."

"Stop it!" she cried, regaining her dignity and brushing herself down. "Just stop it. I know what you're—"

"Why're you shouting at Uncle David?" Jamie came running up.

"Your mama thought she was going to fall, but I saved her. She was just a little... *scared*." He turned to her with an expression of feigned innocence. "Weren't you, my dear? A little fearful of what might be."

"Please don't..."

"I bet Sarah were scared when I saved her—" Jamie began, but an enormous toad hopping down the path diverted his attention. "Hey, what's that?"

Lady began to bark at the creature and he yanked at her. "Lady, leave it."

"It's only a toad, Jamie. It won't hurt her."

"But she looks like she's goner eat it."

"I don't think it would taste very nice." David grinned at the antics of the dog and the boy, and Tillie couldn't prevent a smile from creeping over her face. While her son's attention was diverted, she plucked up the courage to ask, "I would like to go and see a very good friend who lives in Welton. She's the vicar's wife, and I thought she might be able to give me some... And I was wondering if...that is..."

He merely stood watching her, his brows raised, not helping her in the least.

"I...Stop looking at me like that," she whispered.

"Like what?" He acted as if he didn't know what she meant, continuing to regard her in the same manner.

Jamie's yell of disappointment broke up their conversation. "Aw, it's hopped away into the bushes. D'yer think it'll come back out?"

"I doubt it." David didn't take his eyes off Tillie.

Jamie suddenly turned round and asked, "Where's Maisie?"

Tillie's jaw dropped. She didn't know what to say.

"I just remembered her when I saw the toad."

"That's not a very nice thing to say."

He giggled. "D'yer member that pet frog what she found? Well, it weren't really a pet. It were dead."

She looked at David and could see him grinning again. "No, go on."

"We put it in a tin, with leaves, 'cos Maisie said that if we kept it warm it might bring it back to life, but it didn't. We even tried feeding it. If we pressed its mouth at the sides it opened, like this." He demonstrated by pressing in his cheeks and opening his own mouth.

She was finding it hard to keep a straight face. "And what happened to it?" she managed to ask.

"Mrs Curtis said it were smelly...and...where is Maisie?"

"I don't know, darling." What could she tell him?

"I 'spose she's with Lucy."

Should she tell him now? But would it harm his returning memory? It was imperative she went to see Emily for some advice as soon as possible. She turned to David. "About what I was saying earlier…please could I—?"

"I'm intrigued to hear more of your previous life but, yes, I have some business to attend to near Welton so, if you would like, I could drop you both off and pick you up when I've finished."

* * * *

"Tillie," Emily exclaimed in surprise, drying her hands with her apron. "How lovely to see you. This must be—"

"Yes, Emily. This is my Jamie."

"Do come in."

Tillie waved to David to let him know that he could carry on, for he had waited to make sure that there was somebody in before leaving. As the carriage drew away, Jamie asked, "Is Uncle David leaving us, Mama? I don't want to live here. I want to stay with him."

"It's all right, Jamie, he'll be coming back for us later." Emily and Tillie exchanged glances as he followed them into the house.

"But I wanted to go with him," he said truculently.

"He has to go and see someone and couldn't take you," she explained.

"Would you like some lemonade, Jamie?" asked Emily.

She received a nod in reply.

He drank the fizzy drink and then burped. "Them bubbles always gets up me nose," he laughed, his former gloom evaporated.

Tillie shook her head. "Please excuse my son. He seems to have forgotten his manners."

"That's all right." Emily smiled.

Jamie walked over to stroke a ginger cat that was curled up on a chair at the other side of the kitchen. "Can we go and see Mrs Curtis? I like her."

"So you haven't told him yet?" Emily whispered.

Tillie shook her head. "No, I didn't know whether he'd be able to take it in," she whispered back.

"And Maisie?" he continued without looking up.

Emily jumped up. "I've been making some enquiries and I think I might have found Maisie!"

"You have?"

"She weren't lost, were she?" Jamie came across to stand next to his mother. "Oh, I 'member now. She ran outta the barn, and she never come back, did she?"

Tillie put her arm around him as she turned to Emily. "Where do you think she is?"

"There's a farmer a few miles west of here who has about thirteen children, and apparently they took in a young girl who they found wandering alone about the same time as...you know what. I'm told that she hasn't spoken a word yet, but she seems to have settled in with them quite happily. They've called her 'Mary' because she can't tell them her name, and it was Christmas time. Luckily, it sounds very much like 'Maisie'."

"Is she about six years old?"

"That I don't know. I haven't had chance to get to see her as I only found out yesterday."

"Oh, thank you, thank you." Tillie stood up and hugged her friend. "You don't know what it means to me, to know that she's safe and well."

"Can we go and see her?" Jamie stroked the cat again.

"Not today, I'm afraid. But we'll have to ask...Uncle David another day."

"You're staying around then?" Emily placed a pot of tea on the table and took down a tin of biscuits from the shelf, offering them to Jamie who took out a whole handful.

"Don't be greedy. That's far too many," Tillie admonished him.

"But I'm hungry."

"Put some back, please. What must Mrs Thompson think of you?"

He looked at Emily as if to gauge her reaction. Her lips were pursed which made her look rather angry, but Tillie knew it was to keep a straight face. He obviously didn't realise that as he put two of the biscuits back in the tin.

Tillie took one herself, and nibbling it, she replied to Emily's earlier question. "Well, actually that's partly why I've come to see you. I could do with a word..." she mouthed the rest of the sentence, "*in private.*"

Emily nodded and then clutched her belly. "Oh, Junior's really active again. Still takes me by surprise sometimes."

"I'm so sorry, I hadn't even asked how you were."

"I'm sure you had other things on your mind. I'm really—well—blooming, as Edward says."

"And how is the vicar?"

"Oh, bearing up, as usual. But you haven't come here to talk about us." She turned to Jamie. "Do you know how to play with a spinning top?"

"One o' them with a stick with string on the end?"

"Yes, I think I have one in here somewhere. It was mine when I was a little girl." She rummaged in the sideboard and produced a battered brown top that had the remnants of pictures barely visible around the sides. "Come on, let's go out into the garden and you can show us how good you are."

They all went outside and, after a shaky start, Jamie was soon running around, spinning the top with ease. Emily took the opportunity to murmur, "So? What's developed?"

"You're not going to believe this..."

"Try me."

"Mr Dalton, my previous master, the man my son calls 'Uncle David', has only asked me to marry him."

"What?" Emily cried out before putting her hand over her mouth. Jamie looked across but carried on playing. "When was this?"

"As soon as he arrived back home. He was away, and Jamie with him, at his sister's, when I arrived."

"And what did you say?"

"I haven't yet. You see there are complications. He said it was only for Jamie's sake, which I can quite understand, and could probably live with, but there's this beautiful lady he's supposed to be practically betrothed to."

"Oh."

"You see my dilemma?"

"But, why would he propose to you if he's engaged to this woman?"

"That's what I can't understand. Then, to make matters worse...he actually told her, while I was in the room, that he had asked me to marry him. What do you think about that?"

"That he can't be as enamoured of her as you think."

Tillie looked at Emily with a frown. "But..."

"Who told you that he was engaged to her?"

"My sister, Ruby. Coincidence has it that The Grange is where I used to be employed as a maid. It's where Ruby and I went to work when our mother died, and she's still there."

"My, that is a coincidence. But is your sister...how can I put this? Would she be reliably informed?"

Tillie had to think about that. Ruby was renowned for getting the wrong end of the stick occasionally. She pursed her lips, tapping her fingers against her chin.

"I hadn't thought about that...possibly not."

"There you are then. Why don't you ask—whatever you call him now—what he really thinks?"

"I couldn't do that, no, that would be far too impertinent." She raised her eyes to the sky. "I don't know what to call him, what to think about him, what to...I can't stop thinking of him as anything but my master."

"And what reply would you like to give him?" Emily asked.

"I do find him attractive, although I keep telling myself that I shouldn't, and I know it would be the best thing for Jamie."

"So?"

"But he doesn't love me."

"He could learn to. You have to do as your heart tells you."

Tillie smiled before enfolding Emily in a hug.

"So you've made up your mind?" her friend asked.

"I...think so. But she's so pretty..."

"So are you, my dear. And anyway, looks aren't everything, you know. Look at my Edward."

"But he's like a big cuddly bear." They both laughed as Jamie came running over.

"Have you got aught else I can play with?"

"Don't keep bothering Mrs Thompson, Jamie."

"It's no bother. I need to get into practice for when Junior here—" Emily patted her belly, "—makes an appearance."

"When's Uncle David coming back?"

"When he's finished his business." Tillie put her arm around his shoulder. "Just have some patience."

Jamie heaved a sigh and ran off down the lawn which was surrounded by shrubs, flower borders and tall trees, making a graceful backdrop as they swayed in the breeze.

"There's a swing on that tree down at the bottom," called Emily.

He ran over, jumped on it and began to push himself with his feet but was not getting very high. "Push me, Mama!" he called.

"Coming, darling."

As they walked down to him, Emily remarked, "He seems to have taken to his *Uncle David*, doesn't he?"

"Yes, that's my main problem. How could I disrupt his life again?"

"You don't have to."

"I know. But me...the mistress of The Grange?"

"Push me high. I want to go right up to the sky," Jamie called as they reached him. She pushed with both hands but couldn't satisfy him. He wanted to go higher and higher. She found she was enjoying herself, releasing some of her innermost frustrations in the energy she was using, so she put all her strength into it.

Pretend it's David, she thought. *Harder, harder.*

"Be careful, I don't know if it's safe to go too high," she vaguely heard Emily saying behind her, but ignoring her, she pushed again.

Suddenly, she was aware that something was wrong. Emily was shouting, "Stop!" Stop!"

Looking up, she could see the rope that was attached to the branch was untwining near the top. She stood transfixed as it snapped and in slow motion she saw her son hurtling through the air and landing in a heap a few yards away. She sped towards him, crying, "Jamie! Jamie!"

He was lying crumpled in a heap, murmuring, "I flew, Mama. I flew!"

She looked up at Emily who had caught up. "Do something, Emily. Please!"

Her friend bent down and examined the boy who was starting to squirm. "Don't move, Jamie. Stay still while I check you over."

She ran her hands over his arms and legs. "Do you hurt anywhere?"

"Not sure."

She looked up at Tillie. "I can't see any blood or feel anything broken, thank God."

Tillie let out a huge sigh of relief. For a split second back there she had had visions of her son...

"I found this gentleman on the doorstep, vainly knocking on the door," the booming voice of the vicar came from behind them. "It's no wonder he couldn't make anyone hear..." He suddenly seemed to become aware that something was wrong and hurried towards them, with David following.

Bursting into tears, Tillie ran towards David.

"What's happened...?" he began before thrusting her aside and bending down to look at the boy still lying on the ground.

"The swing broke," she said over his shoulder.

"And I flew," repeated Jamie, trying to sit up.

"He doesn't appear to have come to any harm, miraculously," said Emily, rubbing her belly again.

"Are you all right?" asked her husband, putting his arm around her.

"Yes, yes. Junior's just kicking again."

David was still kneeling down, trying vainly to prevent Jamie from getting up. "Stay where you are, boy. We need to know if you've hurt anything."

Tillie knelt down on the other side, stroking his head. David looked across at the offending swing, now dangling lopsidedly, then at her. "What were you thinking of, letting him play on a dangerous swing?"

"Pray, don't be angry at Tillie," Emily intervened. "It was entirely my fault, I should have realised that it wouldn't be safe. It hasn't been used for so long. I must take full responsibility."

"Can I get up now?" Jamie tried to stand. Tillie hovered around him whilst David helped him up.

"How do you feel?" she asked.

"Me 'ead feels a bit funny."

"I'm not surprised. I can't believe you haven't broken anything." Tillie felt his forehead.

"We'll get him home and I'll call Doctor Abrahams to check him over." David picked Jamie up and carried him across the lawn.

They all followed, and Emily put her hand in Tillie's. "I'm so sorry."

"Emily, it was not your fault. Please don't cut yourself up about it. It's not good for the baby."

"She's right, my dear," agreed Edward. "Accidents do happen. It wasn't anybody's fault."

His wife looked at him with tears in her eyes. "But I should have—"

"Uh-uh…" Tillie lifted her finger, using the same expression her friend had used on her when they had first met, in her kitchen.

Emily smiled ruefully.

They rounded the corner of the house and saw Jamie being lifted into the carriage.

Raising his eyebrows, Edward said, "I suppose introductions will have to wait."

Tillie pulled a face as David climbed up in silence onto the driver's seat.

"Yes, please forgive his bad manners." Scrambling inside, she wrapped her arm around Jamie to make sure he didn't loll about, and before she could turn to say goodbye the carriage pulled away so quickly that her head was forced back, so she merely put up her hand and waved.

Jamie lay with his head resting on her lap and she was forced to cling onto the side with her free hand to prevent herself from falling sideways, whilst gripping Jamie with the other.

She thought about calling out to David to slow down but felt it was not her position to do so. He hadn't seemed in a very good disposition so she didn't want to antagonise him.

No wonder his wife and son had been thrown out if he had been driving so recklessly that day they had been killed. She wondered whether he thought about her much. Supposedly, three years was long enough to get over someone. He had appeared very much in love with her, she remembered, as another jolt caused her to grip more tightly.

At last they were within sight of The Grange and she could feel them slowing down. She felt a nervous wreck, her hair in disarray, and she heaved a sigh of relief as they slowed to a halt at the front door.

David immediately jumped down and yanked open the carriage door, before reaching in to grab Jamie.

"Get Doctor Abrahams," he barked to Pervis, who had appeared at the door. "Straightaway."

Tillie jumped down and ran after him. She tried to pull at his sleeve but he pushed her with his elbow.

"Please, he's my son," she cried, but he merely carried on inside, and mounted the stairs two at a time. She followed, almost tripping up when she caught her foot in her dress, and saw Nellie appear at the top of the stairs.

"Out of the way." He brushed past the housekeeper into his bedroom.

"What's the matter?" asked Nellie, following him inside. Tillie caught up as he placed the sleeping child onto the bed. She stood at the door, out of breath, her chest heaving.

"Ask her." David looked across at her with such venom in his eyes that she was taken aback. But that was her son, her baby, lying there on the bed. She had every right to be there. She moved closer and saw Jamie stir.

"Mama," he squeaked.

"I'm here, darling." Taking his hand, she looked at David as if to say, 'see, it's me he wants.'

"Is anyone going to tell me what happened?" asked Nellie, still standing near the door.

"I flew, didn't I?" Jamie opened his eyes.

"Well, it certainly looked like it," Tillie replied, trying not to notice the disdainful look on David's face, but wanting to humour her son. If that's what he thought he had done, why should she disillusion him?

She turned to Nellie. "He fell off a swing."

"More than *fell off*," spluttered David. "He was almost killed."

"That's a bit of an exaggeration." She had felt exactly the same at the time it happened, but didn't want him to know that, so tried to play down the enormity of it.

Nellie moved towards the bed and touched Jamie's forehead. "Is he hurt?"

"We're not sure, so I've called for Doctor Abrahams," David said before walking over to look out of the window.

"He seems all right to me," said Nellie.

"I'm hungry." Jamie sat up.

Tillie and Nellie smiled but David remained with his back to them, seemingly unamused.

"He can't be too badly hurt, probably just shaken up." Nellie put her hand to his forehead.

David replied without turning round. "Well, he's staying where he is until he's been examined by the doctor."

"Shall I bring him up some soup?" asked Nellie.

"I'll do it," said Tillie, eager to show her motherly concern.

"And some bread," called Jamie as she went out.

She ran downstairs, meeting Ruby on the way. "I thought we were going to finish emptying Grandmamma's cottage today. Where've you been?"

Tillie stopped. She had completely forgotten, with everything that had happened since the previous day. "Oh, Ruby, I'm so sorry."

"I'd arranged it with Nellie."

"Do you mind if we go tomorrow? Jamie's been hurt and we're waiting for the doctor…"

"Jamie? Where is he?" Her sister began running back upstairs.

"He's in…the master's…bedroom."

Ruby looked back in surprise but turned round and carried on up.

"Nellie's with him, and the master." She didn't want her sister barging in and being embarrassed when she found him in there. Ruby slowed down, clearly reluctant to continue.

"Do you think…? Perhaps I'd better not…"

"I'm sure he won't mind. I'm just going down to get Jamie some soup."

"I'll come and help you." She turned and came back down. "What happened to Jamie then?"

Tillie explained as they approached the kitchen and then had to repeat it again to Freda.

"I'd heard that you'd both gone out with the master, but didn't know where you'd gone," Ruby sulked as they waited for the soup that Freda had fetched from the cold slab in the pantry to warm through.

Tillie hadn't thought to inform her of her plan to visit Emily. She realised there were going to be so many more considerations that had not previously occurred to her, if she was going to stay, but she had promised her sister that she would make up for lost time, so she was another concern to be mentally put on her list of pros and cons.

"I just wanted to let my new friend Emily know that I'd found Jamie. She was the one who helped me find him."

Her sister still looked dejected at being excluded, but Freda said to her, "Tillie doesn't have to let you know about everything that she does, Ruby. You can't expect her to report to you before she goes anywhere."

"I know. I didn't mean...I just..." She looked up with a pitiful expression.

"We'll soon get the balance right. Come on, let's take this up to Jamie. You carry the bread."

The doctor arrived as they entered the hall so they hung back and let him precede them upstairs. David sprang to attention as they all entered the bedroom and gave a brief explanation of what had occurred, giving Tillie another of his disdainful looks. The doctor gave Jamie a thorough examination and pronounced, "He'll have a few bruises by the morning and will probably be a bit sore, but thankfully he doesn't seem to have sustained any serious injury."

Everyone let out a sigh of relief. "And how's the memory?"

"I've remembered all sorts o' things since me ma come," Jamie beamed. "Can I have me soup now?"

The doctor moved aside as Tillie put the tray down in front of him. "So you're his mother?"

Tillie nodded. She could feel David's eyes boring into her but daren't look up at him. *He's probably thinking Jamie was better off before I came*, she thought miserably. *But at least I didn't lose him in the park, so Mr High and Mighty can just get down from his high horse and...*

"I'm pleased to hear it," the doctor continued. "Are you staying long, because I think the boy should remain for a while yet, for his own well-being? That is if it's all right with you, sir?"

He turned to David who raised his eyebrows at her. "My thoughts exactly," he replied, unsmiling, not taking his eyes off her.

She didn't know what to say. Everyone was looking at her expecting an answer.

Ruby piped up, "Yes, you are staying, aren't you, Tillie? You told me you were."

"It looks like it then." She daren't look at David again. He might change his mind about wanting to marry her after today's fiasco.

Chapter 13

"But I want to learn Lady some more tricks." Jamie was confined to bed the following morning, much to his disgust.

"Perhaps later." As Tillie straightened his bedclothes, she tried to work out how to tell him that she was to return to her grandmother's cottage without taking him. He was covered in bruises, the worst one being the one that almost closed his right eye. Freda had put a piece of steak on it earlier, to bring out the bruising, so it shone black and blue.

"But I don't like it in here." He had remained in David's bed for the night as he had fallen asleep almost as soon as the doctor had left. Goodness knows where the master had slept. He had left on business early so she hadn't had time to speak to him.

She looked around the room. It was rather stark and almost devoid of personal belongings. Picking up a silver hairbrush from beside the washbowl, she removed a black hair that had become entwined in the bristles. Maybe soon she would be married to its owner, unless, as she had wondered the previous evening, he had changed his mind.

"Please, Mama, can I go to me own room? I can do some drawing or somat."

"I suppose so. Wait two minutes while I find Auntie Ruby to help me carry you."

"I can walk meself." Before she could stop him he had pushed back the covers and jumped out of the huge bed, landing in a heap on the floor.

"Ouch!"

"What did I tell you?" She dropped the hairbrush and ran to help him up. "So independent!"

But that was how you brought him up, to be a free spirit, so what do you expect? Hearing a movement outside the door, she called out, "Is that you, Ruby? Can you come and help me a minute?"

She managed to get Jamie back onto the bed. "He wants to go back to his own bed. Would you help me carry him?"

"I think he ought to stay where he is," a stern voice came from behind her. She closed her eyes and began to count to ten. Her father had taught her to do that as a child. Having had a bad temper, he had said that it was the best way to prevent oneself from speaking rashly.

"Uncle David!" Jamie was clearly pleased to see him.

"How are you feeling today, young man?" He approached the bed and stood close beside her. She remained rigid, not knowing whether to stay or move away.

"A bit sore."

"That's a shiner you've got. Here, let me find a mirror to show you." Going across to the washstand he picked up the partner to the hairbrush, and then bent down and picked something up.

"What's my hairbrush doing on the floor?"

"Mama was looking at it."

"She was, was she?" She daren't turn round. What would he be thinking now? Trying to think of a plausible excuse, she looked up as he got level with her and saw an amused smile on his lips.

"Let me look, then." Jamie reached out for the mirror. David handed it to the boy without taking his eyes from her.

"It don't look like me, do it?"

He was forced to look away then. "No, it doesn't."

Jamie twisted the mirror this way and that, sticking out his tongue and pulling faces into it.

Tillie took the opportunity to move across and straighten the bed again. She needed to bring up the subject of her grandmother's belongings but was not sure how to.

"I—" she began at the same time as David said, "We—"

She stopped, but he continued, "Sorry, you first…"

"I…um…don't know if you heard about our…Ruby's and my grandmother?"

"No, what about her?"

227

Jamie put down the mirror, looking up with a sad expression. "She died."

"No, I didn't know that. When?"

Comforting Jamie with her hand on his shoulder, Tillie took a deep breath. She had come to terms with her grandmother's death but speaking about it aloud brought a lump to her throat. "The funeral was the day before you came home," she managed to utter in a croaky voice.

"Why didn't someone tell me? No wonder you've been..." He walked over to take her hands in his. "I'm so sorry. If I had known I would not have bothered you..."

"She were my grandmamma too." Jamie pulled at his sleeve, before trying to climb down off the bed again.

"Yes, of course she was." David put him back onto the bed. "But you need to stay where you are."

"Can't I get up? Pleeease?"

"What do you think, Mama?" David asked.

She had recovered her composure again. "Well, I think he ought to say in bed, at least in his own bedroom." She hesitated. "I um...I need to go and finish sorting out my grandmother's things and I don't think Jamie would be able to manage the trip."

"No, he definitely would not." David picked up the energetic boy. "Right then, young man, let's get you to your own room and see what we can find for you to do. I'll stay with you until your mama returns." Lifting him onto his shoulders, he started for the door, and then turned round. "Coming, Mama?"

* * * *

David instructed Sam to take Tillie and Ruby in the pony and trap so that they could bring back what was to be stored for distributing to Matthew and Harry at a later date. It was not so traumatic this time and they were soon on their way back. Tillie let Ruby climb onto the front seat with Sam whilst she climbed into the back, surrounded by pots and pans and furniture. Ruby's secret smile had not eluded her when she had sat next to the groom and Tillie was pleased for her. The girl deserved a little happiness. Perhaps something would develop and she would find romance with Sam.

She sighed. What about herself? Would she find it? She still didn't know how David thought of her.

"David," she whispered. Could she ever bring herself to call him that? She repeated his name over and over again in a low voice, knowing that the pair in front would not be able to hear her, and liked the sound of it on her lips. If Jamie could say it so naturally, then surely she could come to do so also.

Suddenly, as they rounded a sharp bend in the road, a pan fell on top of her, banging her on the head. She yelped, causing Ruby to turn round.

"Whoa," her sister called. "Everything's going to fall."

As the cart came to a halt, Tillie felt the pile around her begin to shift. She held up her arms to protect herself as she was engulfed in boxes, some of them with sharp edges that dug into her skin.

She could hear Ruby and Sam's muffled voices calling her, but couldn't see anything. She was in darkness. Pushing aside what she could feel was a large tea chest wedged on her shoulder, she tried to disentangle herself from the blanket or whatever it was that was covering her.

"Tillie, Tillie! Are you there?" she could hear Ruby's anxious voice and, despite her predicament, she had to smile. Where else could she be?

"Yes, Ruby, I'm here somewhere."

A ray of light brightened the gloom and Sam's face peered in. "You all right, miss?"

"I think so. Just a bit battered."

"Oh, Tillie!" Ruby's face was now visible as well.

Sam pulled away some of the items covering her and she was able to move her arms to pull herself up. Her leg was trapped but she yanked it free and Sam helped her out.

She shook herself as Ruby fussed round her. "You sure you're all right?"

"Just a bit bruised."

Ruby looked into her face. "Jamie'll be pleased."

Tillie looked at her sister in amazement. "I beg your pardon?"

"You've got a shiner to match his."

She winced as she put her hand up to her face and felt the bruise above her eye.

"It's a good job we're nearly home." Sam looked around them. "If I ran directly across this field I could take a shortcut and get help."

Ruby shook her head. "No, it would make more sense for me to go across the field, and you take Tillie back in the trap." She turned to her sister. "Do you think you can climb up?"

Helping her up, Ruby then scampered off as Tillie put her hand up to her aching forehead.

"You sure you're all right, miss?"

"Just get me home, please." As he drove she could sense him looking anxiously at her every now and again but he said nothing more.

As they approached the house, the front door opened and David ran out. Ruby must have already arrived. Before the cart had quite stopped he had reached up and lifted her down and, carrying her into the house, deposited her on the large comfy sofa in the lounge, kneeling beside her as Nellie came hurrying in.

"Let me look at you. Are you badly hurt?" David's concerned face betrayed…what did it betray? She knew it wasn't love. No, he was just worried about her because she was Jamie's mother, and whatever happened to her affected her son.

"Just a bit bruised. I'll be fine. Please don't fuss."

"What a family! You and your son! I'm going to have to take more care of you both in future."

She tried to sit up. "How is Jamie?"

Nellie came closer. "He's just having a nap. We let him get up for a while earlier. He wanted to wait for you but his little eyes couldn't stay open any longer, bless him."

Sam had remained at the door. "Please, sir, what should I do with the trap?"

Ruby had been hovering close to Tillie and she walked across and stood beside him.

"Yes, sir, what should we do with all my grandmamma's things? I expect half of them'll be smashed."

David looked from her to her sister. "How do you feel about leaving them in the old stable for tonight?"

Tillie nodded. "I just don't have the energy to be doing anything about them right now. I'll leave it with you, Ruby."

Her sister hesitated. "I'll go with Sam and have a quick look at them."

Nodding before closing her eyes and leaning back on the sofa, she heard Nellie say, "I'll bring you something to eat on a tray."

"I'm not really hungry."

"I think you ought to try something light." David was still fussing over her when all she wanted was to be left in peace.

"All right." If it meant she could get to her bed sooner. "But don't forget Ruby."

"I won't. I'll have something ready for her and Sam in the kitchen, as soon as they return." Nellie went out and closed the door behind her.

David took her hand in his, and, turning it over, he gently lifted her palm to his lips. What was he doing? She must be having hallucinations! Had the bang on her head been worse than she had thought?

"My dearest girl, what am I going to do with you?"

She tried to look away, not knowing what to say, but his dark eyes kept her gaze for what seemed like forever and eventually she had to break the spell before she gave herself away. Butterflies danced in her stomach and not from hunger. Squeezing her eyes shut and suppressing a groan, she realised she was falling in love with him. But she mustn't let him find out. If she accepted his proposal it was to be for Jamie's sake, wasn't it?

She was saved by Nellie returning with her meal. David jumped up and dragged a small table across for her to place it on, before making for the door. "I'll leave you to eat in peace." He grinned. "Jamie will be so made up when he sees your matching black eye."

"That's what Ruby said. I'm glad you all think it's so funny."

He merely grinned again and went out.

Nellie made sure she was comfortable and followed him out. At last she was alone to contemplate her feelings. She ate mechanically, not really noticing what was going into her mouth.

What was she going to do? She had accepted the fact that when he repeated his proposal—that is, if he ever did repeat it—she was going to accept. But it was going to be so difficult to keep her newly realised love hidden.

* * * *

Both the invalids had recovered by Jamie's birthday, although they still had matching yellow rings around their eyes. He was up earlier than usual, only just giving Tillie time to get downstairs to help Freda cut his toast into animal shapes.

"Oh!" He picked up the first piece. "Can I bite the head off first?"

"Jamie Raven, you have a sadistic streak. I don't know where you inherited it, certainly not from me."

"I hope not." A deep voice behind her made her jump. She seemed to be doing that a lot lately. Almost every time he spoke, in fact.

David reached forward and picked up a piece of toast and asked Jamie, "Mind if I try one? What's this, a pig or a goat?"

"Silly, it's a cat."

"So it is." He placed it in his mouth. "It doesn't taste like one."

Jamie giggled. "'Ow d'yer know? You've never eat a cat."

David tickled him under the arm. "I have now, so I'll know in future." He straightened up. "A little bird tells me it's your birthday. Many happy returns." He shook his hand. "And as it's a special day I've decided that we're all going on a picnic."

"What, all of us? Even Auntie Ruby?"

Ruby had just entered and was setting out her master's breakfast tray. She looked up in surprise. "Me as well?"

"Yes, everyone. That's if it can be arranged at such short notice." He gestured towards Freda and Nellie who both nodded vigorously.

"I'll bake some cakes." The cook rushed into the pantry to get the ingredients.

Tillie gave her son a big hug. "Happy birthday, darling. When you've finished your breakfast there are some presents for you to open in the lounge."

"Can't I open them now?" He tried to push past her to get to the door.

"No, breakfast first."

"What pwesents ish there?" She could scarcely understand him as he stuffed more toast into his mouth.

"You'll find out. And don't speak with your mouth full. You've been told about that."

His shamefaced look had her shaking her head and, looking up, she saw David watching her with a smile on his face. He looked just like an indulgent father. She couldn't help but smile in return.

"What would you like us to prepare, sir?" Nellie began taking out baskets and tablecloths from the pantry.

"Oh, whatever you think. I'll leave it up to you good ladies."

Ruby clapped her hands in delight. "I haven't been on a picnic since I was a little girl. Do you remember that time Ma and Pa took us all to the seaside, Tillie? We had a picnic then, didn't we? That was the best day of my life."

"Yes, and Harry fell into the sea and got soaking wet." They laughed and Ruby ruffled her nephew's hair.

"You remind me of your Uncle Harry when he was a boy, Jamie. He was always getting into scrapes, just like you."

"I like Uncle Harry. Can he come on the picnic with us?"

"There isn't time to let him know about it, darling. And anyway, he probably wouldn't be able to have the time off."

"Would I be able to ask Sam to come?" Ruby turned to her master with a sheepish look.

"Why not? I'm feeling generous today. The more the merrier." Tillie had never seen David look so exuberant. "The sun's shining and the outdoors beckons."

Ruby straightened her apron and smoothed her hair before running out to find the groom.

"Where shall we be going for it, sir?" Freda pounded dough energetically.

David watched her, apparently bemused. "That looks like hard work."

"It's nothing, sir. I'm used to it." She turned the dough over and kneaded it some more. "It ought to keep my figure in trim, but, as you see…" She looked down at her spreading waistline and laughed. "It doesn't." Everyone grinned.

"Anyway, to answer your question…I think the top meadow would be a good place. It's been left fallow this year, and there are some lovely views from there." David looked at Tillie as if he especially wanted her to know this information. She couldn't think why and merely nodded.

"Sounds nice," she said tamely.

"I've finished, can I open me presents now?" Jamie jumped down from the table, his face covered with jam.

"Hold your horses." Grabbing him, Tillie quickly wiped it clean. "Come on then."

Taking his hand, she proceeded towards the door, followed by David – rather more closely than etiquette allowed – but she didn't want to make a scene so tried to hurry forward to get away from his supple body. This didn't work, he merely kept up, pace for pace. She thought to stop completely, but realised that would bring him into even closer contact, so she just tried to ignore him. As they reached the lounge door she turned round and glared at him. He just raised his eyebrows and looked innocent, then grinned and held out his hands as if to ask what he had done wrong.

Jamie had run in ahead of them and was squealing in delight. Giving David one more glare, she found her son trying to undo the string on the largest parcel. Being too impatient to untie the bow, he had pulled it into a knot.

"Let me help." David had overtaken her and he reached over to take it. Tillie watched as he also tried. *He's just a big kid really*, she thought as he stuck out his tongue in concentration. *I shall end up with two boys.*

"Give it to me." With Jamie jumping up and down in excitement beside her, she took the parcel and quickly untied the knot.

"I wonder what it could be." She held it out for him to finish unwrapping. He tore the brown paper off and held up a box with pictures of trains on the lid.

"It's a train." Taking out the carriages one by one, he placed them on the carpet. "Thank you, Mama."

"I didn't buy it." She looked at David who was bending down to show him how to connect the carriages. "I couldn't afford such a present."

David looked up at her with a peculiar expression in his dark eyes. "It's from me."

"You shouldn't have…"

"I didn't buy it. It used to belong to my son Frederick and has been lying in the attic since he died, so I thought…" He shrugged.

She didn't know what to say. Touched, she knelt down next to him and put her hand on his. He smiled into her eyes as he wound up the engine and they all watched in glee as the train chugged around the room. When it stopped, Jamie put his arms around David.

"Thank you, Uncle David. It's the best toy I ever had."

Tillie wondered whether the generous act had been genuinely to please her son or to get into her good books, but seeing the look of affection on his face as he cuddled him she felt guilty at even considering it.

"Aren't you going to open the others?" She hoped he wouldn't be disappointed with the meagre gift she had made him. It wouldn't compare to the train set, or even come close, but without any money of her own, it was all she could manage.

He ran over and began to open the remainder of the parcels: a bright red scarf from Ruby, marbles from Sam, a little hand-carved fox from Tom that had him clapping his hands in glee, a blue shirt from Nellie, and, from Freda, a gingerbread man with a green ribbon around its neck and buttons down its jacket.

The final present was hers. She waited with baited breath as he opened it. Would he like it? "This one's from me."

"What it is?" He tore off the last piece of paper and she helped him unfold the board and smooth it out flat.

"It's a game, called 'snakes and ladders'. You throw the dice and move your piece forward. If you land on a ladder you go up and if you land on a snake you go back down. Here, let me show you." As they played the game she recalled how she had been up nearly all night painting the pictures on the board. She had made the dice out of cardboard and the moving pieces were different coloured pebbles she had found in the garden.

"I won! Can we play again, with Uncle David, this time?" She had felt David watching her again as she had been playing, but had tried to ignore him. As he took his turn and moved up a ladder, he asked quietly in her ear. "Have you made this?"

She nodded.

"I hadn't realised I was going to get such a talented wi—"

She shook her head vehemently to prevent him saying anything in front of the boy. She still hadn't given him an answer. She jumped up, pleading with him with her eyes.

"Sit down, Mama, we haven't finished the game, and I'm winning." Jamie looked up at her, so, kneeling down again, she took her turn, landing on a snake.

"Ha, ha. I told you I'd win."

David landed on another ladder and moved up to the top row.

"You haven't won yet, young man."

Much to his disgust, Jamie's next turn took him down a snake, and the game was won with David's next move as he threw a six and finished.

"Aw, that's not fair!"

"You invited me to play. You shouldn't participate if you're not prepared to lose." He ruffled Jamie's hair before walking away.

"Can't we have another game, so I can win?" Jamie called.

"Another day."

Tillie hurried after David. "That wasn't very kind, especially on his birthday."

"Life isn't always kind, my dear. He has to learn that." He opened his study door. "I have some work I must attend to before the picnic." He closed the door behind him, effectively shutting her out.

She shook her head. Would she ever understand his seesawing moods? She heard the clockwork train start up again and went back into the lounge to play with her son.

* * * *

"Can Tom come too?" Making their way to the picnic site, Jamie had run on ahead with Lady and had bumped into the gamekeeper and Bridie. The two dogs did not very often come into contact and were having a good sniff at each other.

"Yes, if he wants." David had regained his good humour.

"Here then, Tom, you can help carry some of these baskets." Freda struggled up the path and handed him one of the heaviest ones she had been having trouble with.

"Give me the other one as well. I may as well carry them both."

They carried on up to the top of the hill and Sam opened the gate and waited for everyone to go through before closing it again behind them.

Tillie caught up with Jamie and looked around. The most beautiful sight beheld her. The valley below seemed to stretch for miles. She could see verdant green fields, some with cows and sheep grazing, others with golden wheat waving in the breeze, all interspersed with copses of green trees, and a blue stream winding its way down the middle. A skylark rose from the meadow, its melodious song increasing the peaceful atmosphere.

"Do you like the view?" David whispered in her ear.

"Mm, it's beautiful." She didn't look round, as she couldn't take her eyes off the scene before her. Each time she blinked she saw a different aspect of it.

"You could be mistress of all this…"

Closing her eyes and holding her breath, she felt at one with the ambience of the scene before her. A bee buzzed nearby and a gentle breeze wafted the scent of fragrant wild flowers towards her.

Before she could comment, Jamie's voice drifted over to her. "Mama, come and sit next to me." Opening her eyes once more, she saw him pat the blanket next to him. Lady tried to sit there but he shooed her away. "No, Lady. That's for Mama. You sit over there."

She glanced back at David before silently going across to sit by her son. He hadn't actually repeated his proposal so what could she say?

Nellie and Freda were emptying the baskets. They laid out plates full of cold meats, cheese, veal and ham pies, salad, and for dessert there was fruit, cake and biscuits.

"What would you like to drink, Jamie? Ginger beer or lemonade?" Ruby was in charge of the drinks.

"Ginger beer."

Tillie looked at him with raised eyebrows.

"Please."

"You, Tillie? We've got ale?"

"I think I'll stick to ginger beer as well, please." She glanced across at David and thought she saw him mouth the word 'coward', so quickly looked away again to give the impression she hadn't seen it. She couldn't even contemplate the idea of getting tipsy. She had to have all her faculties intact.

They spent a happy half hour eating and chatting. David joined in with the banter, not at all behaving as a master, but as one of them. Occasionally Tillie caught him looking at her in a peculiar fashion, but she tried to act normally, as if he were just her master.

"Can we play a game now?" Jamie's exuberance was not abated.

"Yes, let's play cricket." Ruby was up on her feet in a flash and opening the bag containing the equipment. "I'll bowl."

"No. I want to be bowler." Pushing her out of the way, Jamie grabbed the ball and began to practise over arm moves.

"I'll decide who plays where." David stood up and took the ball from him.

"Well, can I bat first then?"

"I suppose so, as it's your birthday."

Tom picked up the mallet and began to bang the wickets into the hard ground.

Jamie started running round. "I bet I score the most runs, 'cos I can run real fast."

"We'll see about that, Master Jamie." Sam paced out the length of the pitch and stood where the other wicket was to go as Tom joined him and knocked it in. "I'm a pretty good batsman myself."

David held out the ball to Tillie. "Would you like to bowl first?"

As he put the ball into her hand, his fingers caressed her wrist. She glared but he merely smiled his enigmatic smile and walked over to act as wicketkeeper.

"Aren't you playing, Nellie?" Jamie called.

The housekeeper got up slowly and rubbed her back. "I'll stand here and catch any balls that come this way."

"What about you, Freda?"

The cook shook her head and remained sitting on the blanket. "No thank you, I'll just watch."

Everyone was in place so Tillie threw the ball. It didn't even reach halfway down the pitch.

"Mama, don't you know how to bowl?" Jamie walked forward and pushed it back to her with the bat. "You have to throw it hard."

David was grinning at her from behind the wicket. *I'll wipe that grin off his face.* She walked back a few paces, took a run up, and let fly. The ball flew through the air and right over her son's head. David had to jump up and reach out, almost falling over in his bid to catch the ball.

"Mama, you're s'posed to aim at me bat."

"Sorry."

"Here, let me show you." David came over and put his arms around her from behind. She could feel the length of his warm body against her back and found it difficult to breath. He raised her arm with his and threw the ball. It bounced halfway along the pitch and as Jamie lifted his bat to hit it, it rolled underneath and hit the wicket.

"Aw, that's not fair," the boy wailed. "That don't count."

"Now see what you've done," Tillie hissed, as David unglued himself from her and moved away, holding up his arms.

"All right, that was just a practice to show your mother how it should be done. Perhaps she'll get it right now."

He raised his eyebrows at her before walking back to his position and the game continued. Every time she looked up to throw the ball she had to try not to look at his face, tried to concentrate on the bat in her son's hand and eventually got into a pattern. Jamie scored twenty runs before Tom caught him out and as nobody else could match that by the end of the game he was declared the winner, much to his obvious delight as he whooped and danced around the pitch.

The remainder of the afternoon was spent playing various other games and Tillie tried not to get too close to David or to be on his team. His physical presence unnerved her. She had never felt this way before and wasn't sure how to handle it.

She felt sure that he was aware of how he was affecting her, by his facial expressions and the small intimate touches that he seemed to go out of his way to make. She hoped that nobody else noticed but once she looked up and saw Nellie watching her with a knowing glint in her eye. Nothing much got past the wily housekeeper. She was bound to find out in due course.

Eventually, it was time to pack up and return home.

"I wish we could stay here forever." Jamie dragged his tired legs back down the hill.

"I've had the best day of me life."

Tillie put her arm around his shoulders. She could see David well ahead of them so could relax. Should she ask her son what he would think if they were to marry? She didn't need his permission, of course, and she felt certain that he would approve, but she did not want to upset his applecart. He had experienced so much upheaval in the last year or so.

"Are you going to marry Uncle David?" he suddenly asked, as if he had read her mind.

"What makes you...?" Jumping back she looked anxiously at the people in front, hoping that nobody had heard. They all carried on down the path, seemingly oblivious. Ruby was chatting away to Sam, Tom was helping Freda along whilst Nellie was marching ahead in the lead with the master. "Why do you say that?"

"'Cos then I'd have a papa. Ruby says everyone has a papa, but I ain't never had one."

"Would you like it if I did?"

"You bet!"

"We'll have to see then. But don't tell anyone, will you? Do you think you could keep it a secret?"

"Like before?" He looked thoughtful. "But can I tell Uncle David, 'cos he ought to know?"

"No, no, not yet. Just don't mention it to anyone at all until I say."

"All right. What we 'aving fer supper?"

She had to laugh. His mind could switch from one subject to another in the shake of a lamb's tail. Unlike her. All she could think about was this proposal. The sooner she gave her answer, the sooner she could get on with her life. The next time David said anything at all in that vein she would say 'yes'. Perhaps she would have chance to speak to him tonight. Having finally made the decision, she resolutely walked on, her head held high.

* * * *

Tillie went in search of David as soon as the picnic baskets had been emptied and put away. Pervis informed her that the master had gone out on business and would not return until late.

Drat! She might have lost her nerve by the morning.

She ate her supper in the kitchen with Jamie who was exhausted, barely able to finish his meal before his eyes began to close, so she took him up to bed early.

"Are you happy here?" She needed to be certain.

He lifted his nightshirt over his head and, as his head popped out, said sleepily, "Yes, Mama, but it'd be even better if Maisie were 'ere." He climbed into bed and she tucked him in. "And Lucy."

Should she tell him now? He was so tired though that he probably wouldn't take it in. Perhaps that was the best time. He had to be told sometime.

"Jamie, I need to tell you something…" No, she couldn't spoil his birthday. It would wait. She realised that he was asleep anyway, so she kissed his forehead and crept out.

Should she try to get in touch with Maisie? It would make her son happy but, if she was settled in, it might disrupt her. On the other hand, it might help her. The poor little orphan needed stability, so she was probably better off left where she was.

She lay in bed, tossing and turning. So many decisions to be made. When she finally fell asleep, nightmares haunted her, of a young girl in the rain, sitting on a swing and spinning round at great speed, before spiralling upwards and out of sight.

She awoke in a sweat and sat bolt upright, gulping in mouthfuls of air, before lying back down, exhausted. She tried to get back to sleep but it eluded her, so, after a while she pushed aside the covers, got up and walked over to the small window and opened the curtains. It was almost daylight. Being in one of the servant's rooms at the top of the house, she had a panoramic view of the estate at the back of the house. It was, in fact, her old room that she had occupied when she had lived there before, so its familiarity made it feel very much like home.

Something moving in the distance caught her eye. She strained to see what it was. It looked like a horse. Yes, it was. Whoever was riding it looked like he was chasing demons. Perhaps it was a highwayman, on the lookout for unwary travellers, his saddlebags full of plundered booty. Or a poacher. But no, they didn't usually ride horses. Horse and rider disappeared into the woods so she turned back into the room, her interest dissipated.

It was too early to go downstairs so, taking a writing pad and pencil out of her top drawer, she sat down and began to write a letter to Becky, the baker who had saved her life. She thanked her profusely for all her help, explained that she had found Jamie and that she was to be married to her master.

She stopped, chewing the end of the pencil. Perhaps that was being a bit presumptuous, as he had not actually repeated his proposal, but what the hell? Now it was down in black and white it seemed more real. Signing off, she opened the drawer to look for an envelope, but there wasn't one. She would have to go downstairs and find one in the drawing room bureau.

There wouldn't be anybody else up yet, she wouldn't need to get dressed, so, putting on her wrap from the back of the door, she tiptoed down the stairs.

Just as she got to the hallway the front door opened, and a gush of cold air hit her. She gasped as David marched in, panting and obviously out of breath. He pulled up with such an astonished look on his face that she had to smile. He stood as if transfixed, staring at her, before closing the door behind him.

She suddenly realised her dressing gown was not fastened, so quickly wrapped the belt around her. Why didn't he say something?

"I…" they both began at the same time.

"Pray, excuse me. I've been out riding." He looked down at his mud-spattered trousers and boots.

So that's who it was. No highwayman or poacher, after all. "So early?"

"Yes, I needed to clear my head. And what's got you out of your bed at such an hour? In such a—?" He gestured towards her clothes, or rather lack of them.

"I…um…needed an envelope…for a letter." She pulled her robe tighter.

"Oh." He tapped his boots with his riding crop.

"But while there's nobody else about…I, um, did want to have a word with you…"

"Well, let me go and get changed and I shall be all yours in an instant." He hurried up the stairs before she could reply.

Should she get dressed herself? She might as well get the envelope first. She entered the drawing room and, after opening the curtains, went across to the bureau. It was locked. Of course it would be! There was a family photograph on top of it. She picked it up and took it over to the sofa where she sat down and studied it. The boy, Frederick, looked so happy. Even though it was a formal photograph with all three of them sitting down, she could see a twinkle in his eye. She wondered whether he had been anything like her own son in character. Was that why David had taken to Jamie so well, or was it because he was so different? Ah, Elizabeth, she had always been beautiful, but she looked stunningly so in the picture, with just the faintest of smiles on her lips. And David. He looked quite austere, not even the hint of one on his.

"I wonder what it would be like to be kissed by them," she murmured softly as she stroked them, pouting her own lips in an exaggerated gesture.

"Would you like to find out?" a seductive voice whispered in her ear. She jumped up, almost dropping the photograph.

"I would be happy to oblige." The twinkle that had looked so cute on the son looked ominous on the father as he turned her round to face him.

She tried to move away but her muscles had seized up and she could only stare as his lips descended towards hers. It was only the merest of touches, a soft feathering of skin on skin, but it had her senses reeling. He pulled back slightly as if to gauge her reaction. She could see the yellow flecks in his eyes momentarily before her lips were being caressed once more. So softly, no pressure, just a smooth encircling of his mouth on hers. She felt his tongue lick at the soft tissue inside her lips, and pushed forward, wanting more, but he pulled away, leaving her feeling bereft and frustrated.

Opening her eyes, she saw that he was grinning at her. She was still too stunned to speak.

He looked so cool and collected. The kiss had evidently not affected him. She pulled away, gathering her robe around her once more. In the heat of the moment she hadn't realised it had come adrift again.

If only she could tell what he was thinking.

"What was it you wanted to speak to me about?" He took the photograph out of her hand and looked at it.

"She was very beautiful, wasn't she?" she asked.

"Uh?"

"Elizabeth. She…"

He looked up then. "Yes, she was." He placed the picture back on the bureau. "But she wasn't perfect."

Tillie's eyes opened wide in surprise. She had never heard any criticism of her mistress before, from anyone. "But..?"

He walked back and put his hands on her shoulders, looking deeply into her eyes. "Everyone has their faults, my dear, even my beloved wife."

Why did he have to look at her like that? Her knees were turning to jelly. She looked at his expressive lips. Was he going to kiss her again?

"Have you made your decision yet?"

"What?"

"Do I have to get down on my knee and propose in the customary manner?"

"Oh, that."

"Yes, that." Suddenly, he was kneeling on the floor in front of her, and, taking her hand in his, he asked solemnly, "Matilda Raven, will you do me the honour of becoming my wife?"

Before she could reply, the door opened and Nellie came in, stopping short and almost dropping the basket of clean cutlery in her hand.

"Well?" Ignoring the interruption, David remained on his knees, looking up at Tillie and stroking her wrist.

Tillie looked at Nellie then back at him. "Yes, yes," she cried. "Yes, I will."

"About time." Nellie rushed over as David stood up and they were both enfolded in her arms. "I had a feeling this was on the cards. I'm so happy for you both." She clapped her hands together. "Oh, a wedding to prepare! Wait 'til the others hear, they'll be just as thrilled." She hesitated. "What do you think Ruby will make of it?"

"I don't know. She's been one of the stumbling blocks as to why I haven't given an answer earlier."

"You mean...? This isn't the first proposal?"

Tillie looked rather sheepish as David said, "No, it isn't, I proposed to her the night I returned from Harrogate."

Nellie shook her head as she looked at Tillie. "And you've taken all this time to reply?"

"Well, there were so many things to consider, Ruby being one of them. And...I thought everyone would look down on me, saying I wasn't good enough."

David raised her hand to his lips. "They will have me to deal with if they do."

"But you said—"

"I distinctly recall what I said and regret it profusely. It's no wonder you've taken so long to give me your reply, thinking I felt that way."

Nellie grinned. "Well, I'm sure you'll have no problem with your son. Jamie'll be delighted."

"You're right there. I've already sounded him out."

"Really?" David was the uncertain one now. "What did he say?"

She didn't have time to reply.

"Mama, where are you?" Jamie called from the hall.

"In here, Jamie."

Her son ran in and stopped, cocking his head to one side. "Can I tell Uncle David the secret now?"

"What secret's that?" David asked.

"Can I, Mama? Can I?"

"It isn't a secret any longer, Jamie. You can tell the whole world now."

"Yes!" He jumped up and down, squealing in delight.

David was still baffled. "What is this secret?"

"Mama said it was a secret that she was going to marry you."

"So, how long has it been since you've known your decision but not thought to inform me?" David turned to Tillie, rubbing his chin in feigned umbrage.

"Only yesterday. I wanted to tell you last night, but you'd gone out."

He looked slightly mollified.

"Can I go and tell Auntie Ruby?"

Ruby appeared at the door, her arms full of firewood. She looked surprised at seeing so many people in the room. "Tell me what?"

"I'll tell her, Jamie." Tillie put out a hand to restrain him before walking over to her sister. She was still uncertain as to how Ruby was going to react, so tried to pick her words carefully. "Put down the wood first."

The maid did as she was bid and looked around anxiously. "It's not bad news, is it?"

"No, no. Well at least I don't think so. The truth is, I...that is..."

"Mama and Uncle David's going to get wed." Jamie ran up to her and grabbed her hand.

"Jamie, I asked you to let me tell her." Tillie was annoyed at her son for blurting it out like that.

"But I couldn't wait."

"It doesn't matter who told me."

Tillie tried to gauge her sister's reaction. Was she happy about it? Her expression didn't give anything away. Everyone seemed to be holding their breath as she looked from one person to the other.

Unsmiling, she bowed her head. "Congratulations," she murmured before going over to kneel at the fireplace.

Tillie was still none the wiser and was about to go over to her sister until she saw Nellie shaking her head. "Leave her," she mouthed.

She looked at David who shrugged.

Jamie was clearly unaware of the undercurrents. "I'm going to have a papa, now, Auntie Ruby." He tugged at her sleeve but she remained on her haunches, her back to the room, fiddling with a log.

Turning back, he picked up the photograph that Tillie had left on the sofa. "Who's that boy? It ain't George, is it?"

David took the picture from him. "No, that's my son Frederick."

Jamie's mouth dropped open.

"He died."

"Oh!" The boy looked at the image again. "And is that his mama?"

David nodded.

"So…so…?" He looked at Tillie, his face wrinkled in dismay.

"She died also, Jamie. There was an accident." She didn't dare look at David. He had never mentioned the accident to her, she only knew what Nellie had told her, so she didn't know how he felt about it, or whether he still blamed himself.

"That's all right then."

"Jamie!"

"I thought…that you wouldn't be able to get wed, if Uncle David was still…and then he wouldn't be me papa…"

"That's all right, Jamie. I understand." David put an arm round him. "Is that the most important thing to you? That I should be your papa?"

"Yes." His face lit up. "'Tis."

"Then so be it."

Tillie stuck out her bottom lip, pretending to be offended. "So, you don't care about me then?"

Jamie wrapped his arms around her legs. "Course I do, Mama. But I love Uncle David as well."

Ruby turned round, the log still in her hands, and he ran over to her. "You as well, Auntie Ruby."

Chapter 14

"It doesn't look as if too many things are broken. Plenty of things have survived." Tillie picked up a chipped cup and put it on the pile for discarding. Ruby walked over and picked it up again. "That was her favourite cup."

"I'm sorry. You still miss her, don't you?"

"Yes."

She gave her sister a hug before resuming the task. "What about this? I don't remember putting this in?" She held up a battered hairbrush.

"I did. I used to brush her hair with it sometimes, when she was feeling low."

"Well, you have it then, Ruby. You didn't keep much yourself, did you?"

"I didn't want to look...you know? Matty needs stuff more than me."

"Oh, Ruby! You're just as important as anyone else. Was there anything else you added to his pile that you would have liked to keep?"

"Only her blanket." She must have known exactly where it was for she reached in and pulled out the multi-coloured patchwork straightaway. She put it up to her face and sniffed it. "I can still smell her," she said before bursting into tears.

Tillie waited for the tears to subside. "If this is too painful..."

"No, I'm all right now."

Jamie came bounding in with Lady barking at his side. "Mama, guess what?" He didn't wait to see if she could. "Uncle David says he's gonna take me on a train."

"On a train? When?"

"Next week. You can come as well."

"Where to?"

"Dunno, the seaside, or summat." He ran back out without waiting to see her reaction.

She had seen the large, dirty machines puffing out smoke as they lumbered across the peaceful countryside, but had never had any inclination to go for a ride on one. "Well, Ruby, what do you think of that?"

Her sister gave her usual shrug.

Tillie tucked a stray curl behind her ear. "But we have this lot to sort through first." She delved into the nearest box and pulled out more broken items.

"Oh dear, Matthew would have liked this."

"What is it?"

"It is, or was, a horse." She looked pensive. "It looks like the one Mama used to have on her dresser."

Ruby nodded. "It is."

"But how did grandmother get it?"

"I gave it to her. It was the only thing I had to remind me of Mama, but one day gran said she liked horses, so I gave it her."

"Oh, Ruby! You're such a kind girl. And now it's in pieces."

Another shrug and Ruby carried on taking items out of a tea chest.

Tillie sighed. Would her sister ever gain any self-confidence and realise her own worth? Guilt welled up inside her again at having left her without a second thought.

Jamie reappeared. "Sam's coming. I told him you were in here."

Ruby stood up and straightened her apron and cap. Her eyes wide, she looked towards the door as Sam entered.

"Good day to you, ladies."

"Hello, Sam." Tillie remained kneeling on the floor, watching her sister wringing her hands.

"Can I be of any assistance?" The groom doffed his cap.

"Well, you could shift that box of things that are either broken or of no use, if you would, so that we can get to the others."

"Certainly." He moved the box with ease and turned towards Ruby who still hadn't spoken, and touched her mop cap. "Not got your new bonnet on today then?"

She looked down coyly and half smiled. "No, silly, I only wear that to go out in."

"Well...I was wondering...Would you like to wear it Saturday night to the village dance?"

"But I'm not going to..."

"I'm asking you to go with me. That's if it's all right..." He turned to Tillie.

"I'll have to check with the master, but I'm sure it'll be fine. It's time she went out and enjoyed herself."

"But Nellie..." Ruby didn't look sure.

"I'll deal with Nellie."

"Can I go too?" Jamie was running round in circles with Lady, kicking up dust. He sneezed.

"It's no wonder you're sneezing. Go outside if you want to run about. And no, children don't go to dances."

"Why not?"

"Because they're for adults. Now go outside and play before we all start sneezing."

He ran out singing, "I'm going on a trai...ain, I'm going on a trai...ain."

Tillie shook her head. "Have you heard this nonsense, Sam? The master only wants to take him on a train ride."

"Sounds like a good idea to me. I've only ever been on one once. It was a bit smoky, but great fun."

Tillie pulled a face, still unconvinced, and then remembered that Jamie had mentioned the seaside. Ruby had reminded her of the day their parents had taken the family. It had been a truly wonderful day.

"I'll leave you ladies to your unpacking. Good day." Sam departed after giving Ruby a cheeky wink.

The maid was still obviously uncertain. "Do you really think I'll be allowed to go with him?"

"Yes, Ruby. It's about time you went out and had some fun."

"But I've never been to a dance before. I won't know what to do." She wrinkled her nose and sneezed. "And anyway, I don't have anything to wear."

"Oh, I hadn't thought of that. I'm sure we'll be able to alter one of your..." She suddenly remembered the pink striped muslin dress that Becky had given her. She had taken it out of the tapestry bag and hung it up but had never had an occasion to wear it. "I know just the dress. It'll need taking in as you're slighter than me, but that shouldn't be a problem."

"What dress is that?"

"You'll see. I'll show you later. Come on, or we'll still be in here sorting through this lot, come Saturday."

* * * *

Tillie sat at the bureau in the drawing room, pondering over who she could invite to the wedding. "I've only got Matthew, Jessie and Harry, besides everyone here, so could I invite Emily and Edward?"

David put down his newspaper. "You can invite whomsoever you wish, my dear."

"And Becky?" He nodded. Earlier on that day, when they had been out walking with Jamie, she had told him about the prison, and everything that had happened since. She didn't want to keep any secrets from him. If they were to be married she wanted complete openness, at least on her part. She understood that men might have things they would not want to disclose to their wives, but she hoped that David would always be honest with her. "Are you going to write your list?"

"I already have, it's in the top drawer." He picked up his newspaper again, seemingly having lost interest. Opening the drawer, she rummaged for what could be his list. Discarding the top piece of paper as it only had three names on it, she rifled through the rest of the paraphernalia in the drawer.

"Well, I can't find it."

Sighing, he put down his paper and stood up. "It should be there. I wrote it out as soon as I asked you to marry me."

"So, you were that sure of me, were you?"

He shrugged, grinning, as he crossed over and held up the first piece of paper she had found.

Her eyes opened wide. "But you've only got three names on it."

"Well, actually, if you add Victor, Sarah and George to Annie, that makes six."

She was puzzled. Surely he had more friends than Major Wallace and Charlie Hodges, the Huntsman?

"You said you wanted a quiet wedding with just a few friends and close family, so I've conformed to your wishes." He sat back down, leaving her confused. Since she had agreed to marry him he had stopped flirting with her, had only really spoken when spoken to, and she wasn't sure how to get back the camaraderie they seemed to have had before.

She sat chewing the end of her pencil, unsure how to broach the subject that had been worrying her. "I...um..."

Looking up, she saw that he was watching her. He kept her gaze for a moment, the blueness of his eyes seeming even deeper in the soft glow of candlelight. He raised his eyebrows questioningly.

"I..."

"Come on, girl, out with it." The moment had vanished. He was back to his cold self.

"I don't have any money to buy a wedding dress," she blurted out quickly before her courage left her.

"It's all in hand. Nellie's offered to make it. Didn't she tell you?"

"No." Taking a deep breath, she wondered what other arrangements she was unaware of. It would have been nice to have been told earlier, instead of worrying herself silly over it. Had she done the right thing in agreeing to this marriage?

Would she have any control over her life? And would David ever come to love her as she loved him?

She laughed to herself. To think that she had been concerned that she wouldn't be able to hide her love from him! He never came close enough anymore for her to betray herself.

"What's funny?"

She hadn't realised that she had chuckled out loud. "Nothing, nothing at all."

He picked up his newspaper again and she got up from her chair. "Good night. I'm going to bed."

"Good night, my dear. Sweet dreams."

She wondered what he would do if she went over and kissed him but his head was firmly ensconced in the newspaper so she went out without another word.

Little did she know that David had been thinking along similar lines. He would have loved to have kissed her but knew that he would have trouble controlling himself once he started, so it was safer to appear uninterested. He found it hard to believe how quickly he had come to fall in love with her. What he had felt for Christine was nothing compared to how he felt for his future bride. The sooner the wedding came, the better.

* * * *

"It's big, innit?" Jamie stared up at the large train in awe. "Are we really gonner have a ride on it?"

"That's what we've come for, Jamie." David showed the tickets to the guard and stood aside for Jamie and Tillie to board the train before him.

Tillie felt grand, dressed in the new brown suit that David had ordered to be made for the trip. She was amazed at how quickly the seamstress had been able to make it up, never having been very adroit at sewing herself.

Picking up her skirt, fearful of getting it dirty, she climbed the step. She was still not convinced that this was a good idea, but her son was so excited that she had to go along with it, for his sake, even though she had a hundred and one things to do in preparation for the wedding.

"Where're we going again?" Jamie peered out of the window as the fields and trees went rushing past.

"To Scarborough, to see the sea."

"Have I ever see'd the sea before, Mama?"

"No, Jamie, you haven't."

"What will we do when we get there?"

She didn't know, so she looked at David who said, "We'll walk along the beach and take in the invigorating sea air."

"Oh." Jamie turned back to watch the fast moving countryside through the window, leaving her to examine her surroundings. It was not at all as she had imagined. The seats were clean and comfortable, they had the compartment to themselves, and once they were on the way a waiter had brought them some drinks.

"Does everyone get treated like this?"

"They do in the first class carriage that we're in."

That explained it. She might have known that David would only have the best treatment. She would have to get used to it once they were married.

"Well, what do you think? You didn't seem very enthusiastic when I first mentioned it." David looked at her with that enigmatic smile he often used on her.

She smiled in return. "I have to admit it's very pleasurable. I'm glad I came." He didn't lower his eyes, but remained staring at her. She couldn't take her gaze from his, but sat wondering what he was actually thinking, his expression giving nothing away, as the dimness of the light in the carriage hid any meaning in his eyes.

Finally, he raised his eyebrows as if to goad her into some sort of action, but before she could act Jamie jumped down from the seat, clapping his hands in excitement. "I think we're there. Look, we're stopping."

"So we are."

"That didn't take long, did it?" Standing up, Tillie smoothed down her skirt and reached over to tidy her son's hair, before David opened the door and they alighted onto the platform, along with all the other passengers that she hadn't realised the train contained. People bustled and jostled them so she grabbed Jamie's hand, wary of having him swept away on a mass tide of heaving humanity.

"Keep close together," she heard David say behind her, before he took hold of her other hand and guided her off the platform and out of the station.

"Phew, what a crush. I'm glad to have got out in one piece."

"Yes, are you all right, my dear?"

"I think so." He was still holding her hand and, apparently absent-mindedly, stroking her wrist. Did he realise he was doing it? She had no inclination to stop him. She was enjoying it too much.

Jamie seemed a trifle subdued at the experience and stood looking around him. "Where's the sea?" he asked after a while.

"This way." David led the way to the beach.

"Caw, look at all that water!" Jamie's astonished face was a picture. Tillie had to smile. It was a sunny day and there were people in striped bathing suits wading into the sea while others swam around, seemingly having a good time.

"Can I go in?" Jamie began to unbutton his jacket.

"I'm afraid not, my lad, not today. We haven't brought any costumes."

"Aw!" He refastened his button. "Look over there, Mama." Tillie looked out to see what he was pointing at. "There's boats. Can we go on a boat, Uncle David?"

"I think we might be able to do that later. What does Mama say?"

Tillie hesitated. "We won't get wet, will we?" She didn't want to spoil her new clothes.

David smiled. "Of course not, my dear. Do you think I would put my soon-to-be family in such a predicament?"

She shook her head.

"Can I have one of them, Uncle David?" Jamie pointed to a small boy sitting on the sand, eating an ice cream.

They walked over to the ice cream seller. Tillie tried to keep her skirt from catching in the sand, without success, so eventually gave up.

After eating his ice cream, Jamie began to take off his shoes and socks. "Can I just go in the water like them other kids? I promise I won't get me clothes wet," he asked as he rolled up his trouser legs, copying other people who were doing the same thing.

"You'll be the one who has to walk about in wet clothes if you do," David called after him, but he didn't wait for a reply before running ahead towards the incoming sea, leaving the adults alone.

Closing her eyes, Tillie felt a gentle breeze ruffling the ribbons on her bonnet as she raised her face to the sun and breathed in the sea air, poking out her tongue and licking her lips to taste the saltiness of it.

"They say it's very beneficial." David husky voice made her open her eyes and she saw him watching her once more.

"What is?"

"The sea air." He cleared his throat and looked away. "Are you so provocative intentionally, or is it all innocence?"

She hadn't the faintest idea what he was talking about. "What do you mean?"

He moved away, running his fingers through his hair.

"David?" She tugged at his sleeve, unknowing why he was acting so.

"Forget I said anything."

"But…"

"I said *forget it*." He yanked his arm from her grasp and walked away, leaving her in a state of utter confusion. Would she ever understand this irritating, changeable man?

She watched Jamie paddling in the breakwaters. At least he hadn't been witness to David's bad temper. She wanted to go after David, but, looking back, she saw that he had stopped a short distance away and had turned round, looking at her with his lips pursed, before coming back and taking her hand in his.

"I'm sorry, my darling." It was the first time he had used the endearment.

Seeing the distress on his face, she brought his hands up to her lips. "Don't spoil such a beautiful day. For Jamie's sake, let's pretend nothing happened." She didn't really know what had occurred, but put it to the back of her mind as Jamie came running up, his trouser legs wet through.

"Uncle David, can we go on the boat now?" He looked down and grimaced.

"You may well pull a face, young man. I think we'll have to wait until you're dry."

"Can I play in the sand, then? That boy over there said I could lend his spade."

"You mean *borrow* his spade, Jamie."

"That's what I said." He ran across to a young lad who was building a sandcastle with what was probably his younger sister, and began digging.

Enjoying the sunshine and watching the little girl, Tillie's thoughts wandered to the future. Would Jamie ever have a young sister, or brother? Perhaps he would have two or three, or even four. A large family would be nice. She would have to broach the subject once they were married, definitely not today, the mood her future husband was in, although he seemed his normal self once more.

But perhaps he didn't want any more children. She would have to find ways to change his mind, if that was so. Uneducated in the ways of lovemaking, she wasn't sure how she would go about this, but felt certain that she could find out. There had been other men in her life over the past eight years but she had never let them into the secret recesses of her mind or body. Mrs Curtis's son had come the closest, and she would probably have given in before much longer, if he hadn't gone away again. Blushing at the way her mind was beginning to veer, she cleared her throat.

"Are you all right, my dear? Not coming down with a cold?" David led her towards a bench that an elderly couple had just vacated, and they sat down.

"No, no…" She couldn't very well explain what she had been thinking about. "Thank you for bringing us here today, David." She liked the sound of his name spoken aloud.

"Look, my dear, I'm really sorry about back there."

"There's no need to apologise, David." She accentuated his name this time, the more to enjoy it.

"I wanted today to be so special. I wanted to show you what a good father I could be."

"It is special. Look at Jamie. He's having the time of his life."

David sighed.

"And so am I. Truthfully, it's a grand day out." She stood up. "And it hasn't finished yet. Come on, his trousers must be dry by now. Let's find that boat."

After the boat ride they had luncheon in a secrete café set back from the promenade. On the way out Jamie saw a poster advertising a freak show. "Oh, look at them people. Are they real?" The pictures of some of the performers in the show didn't look like real people at all. "Can we go and see them, Mama?"

Tillie studied the picture with revulsion. How could anyone pay to look at these poor creatures? One picture showed a lady covered in hair, looking more like a gorilla than a woman. Another was a man with huge lumps all over his head, and another was so tiny he was billed as *The Smallest Man on Earth*.

She shuddered. "No, Jamie, I don't think we should exploit these people by going to gape at them."

He turned to David. "Please can we, Uncle David?"

"No, not if your mama says not." She gave him a grateful smile for backing her up, but then he surprised her by saying, "But this is how these people make their living. If the public didn't pay to see them, they would have no means of support, because who would employ someone looking like that?"

She hadn't thought of it like that, but she still couldn't bring herself to go and watch them.

David took out his watch. "Anyway, it's almost time we made our way back to the station to catch our train."

"Aw, not yet!"

"I'm afraid so."

"But we're having such a good time."

"All good things must come to an end, young man." He bent and tickled Jamie in the ribs. The boy giggled.

"He always was ticklish." Tillie grinned.

"So're you, Mama," he chuckled as David tickled him again.

"Oh, she is, is she?" He regarded her with a mischievous look.

Realising his intentions, she tried to back away, but he grabbed her round the waist. His hands began to slide upwards towards her ribs, and then he stopped, his smile fading. Clearing his throat, he adjusted his tie and turned away.

Tillie straightened her bonnet. Had he realised he was making an exhibition of himself in public? Was that why he had stopped so suddenly? Or was it because he couldn't bear to touch her so intimately? Shaking her head in bewilderment, she grabbed Jamie's hand and hurried to join him.

A large gathering drew their attention and, getting closer, they saw a barrel organist with a monkey that he was allowing children to stroke.

"Can I go and stroke it, Mama?" Jamie looked round to ask.

"If your Uncle David thinks we have time." She knew she sounded rather more curt than she intended, but the day seemed to have lost its sparkle.

"If you're very quick about it." David also spoke abruptly. Jamie didn't appear to have noticed though and ran over to the barrel organ.

They stood side by side watching him in silence. With a discreet glance out of the corner of her eye, she could see David standing as stiff as a board, his back like a ram-rod, his lips pressed tightly together.

The sun went behind a cloud and the breeze increased in strength. She shivered, pulling her shawl tightly around her. David must have noticed as he turned and tucked one of the curls that had escaped from her bonnet, behind her ear. Silent and unsmiling, his hand still on her cheek, he stood looking into her eyes for a moment before turning away again.

She didn't know how much longer she could take this erratic behaviour. She walked up to Jamie and took his hand. "Come on, we have to go now."

"Just one more minute, Mama. In't the monkey sweet?"

"Yes, he's very cute, but it's time to leave."

"Bye, bye, monkey."

She dragged him away as David caught up with them.

"Don't you want to stroke him, Uncle David?"

"No, Jamie, not the monkey."

Tillie picked up on the innuendo. She glanced up at him to see if he had meant what she thought he had meant, but he was looking straight ahead and marching on purposefully. Perhaps she had read too much into it. Shaking her head, she followed him with Jamie rattling on beside her about what a wonderful day he had had.

* * * *

A few days later, taking a break from organising wedding arrangements with Nellie, Tillie decided to go for a walk. Jamie had gone down to his tree house, armed with his usual books and lemonade, and David was out on business on the estate somewhere, so she had time to enjoy some peace. During all the time she had spent alone after leaving the prison, she had never thought that she would ever seek solitude for its own sake, but the events of the past weeks had been like living in a tornado, and all she wanted was to gather her thoughts and put things into perspective.

She passed Sam, rubbing down one of the horses, and waved. Not being in the mood for conversation, she carried on, reminded of her sister. She had never seen her so animated. All she could talk about was the dance that very evening. The pink striped dress had been duly altered and now fitted her perfectly.

"I can't wear this, it's much too nice," Ruby had said when she had shown it to her. "And anyway, wouldn't it make more sense to save it for your wedding?"

"You're having a new dress made for the wedding. You're going to be my chief bridesmaid. I can't have you wearing an old hand-me-down."

"Oh, but are you sure?"

"Ruby, my dearest sister, it's you I want at my side when I get married. If you don't want a new dress, then come naked, if you wish. In fact, everyone could come naked."

"Oh, Tillie, don't be so daft." She had looked pensive. "You do want to marry the master, don't you?"

"Yes, of course."

Of course she did, but it just seemed as if she had no control over her life anymore. Having had to fend for herself for the past eight years or so, she was finding it difficult to adjust to having things done for her, even sometimes without being consulted.

"Stop your whinging!" she told herself as she sat down on a log and took off her bonnet. A smile crept over her face as she recalled her mother saying that. What would *she* have had to say about the present state of affairs? She raised her face to the azure sky above.

"Mama, are you watching? I am doing the right thing, aren't I?"

A gentle breeze ruffled her curls as if in response and a peace descended upon her. Closing her eyes, she gave herself up to the sun beaming down on her, and listened to the singing of the larks as they soared above her, seemingly also giving their approval.

Eventually, her usual good mood restored, she put her bonnet back on and began to make her way back, deciding to call on Jamie in his tree house on the way.

As she entered a field, she thought she heard voices and strange beating noises. A dog suddenly ran out from behind a hedge, just as a male pheasant flew over her, followed by a female. The loud crack of a gun startled her and she saw the first bird plummet to the ground to one side of her. She jumped back in alarm. Another shot rang out. This time she didn't see anything fall, but she felt a sharp pain in her shoulder. Looking down, she saw a red patch spread across the bodice of her blue dress. She heard a scream and realised that it must have been her own, before everything went black.

* * * *

"Mama, please wake up!" Was that Jamie sobbing? Where was she?

She could feel someone holding her hand and caressing her wrist. It felt so good. Then she remembered the sound of the gun shot and flinched. She opened her eyes but couldn't focus. Everything looked blurred.

"I've given her some laudanum, so she shouldn't be in any pain." Who could that be? She didn't really care who it was. She felt as if she was floating.

"Mama, are you awake now?" That was definitely Jamie.

"Um," was all she could manage to answer.

"Oh, my darling, we were so worried." Who was that? The blurriness cleared somewhat and a dark face with sapphire-blue eyes came into view.

It's the master. How good of him to come.

Grey eyes with tears streaming down from them, replaced the blue ones. "Oh, Tillie, thank God you're alive." Ruby, her dear sister. But of course she was alive.

She smiled as sweetly as she could. "I'm fine." Why did her own voice sound so slow and so odd?

"There doesn't seem to be any lasting damage. A few days in bed and she'll be as right as rain." That voice again, it must be the doctor.

"Thank God for that." The master again. Was it him stroking her wrist? Why would he be doing that?

"I'll call in again tomorrow, just to make sure she's all right."

"Thank you, doctor." She'd been right.

She tried to sit up. "I need to…" She couldn't stay lounging in bed all day.

"You don't need to do anything, except recover. Stay where you are."

"But…"

"My darling girl, do as you're told." That was the second time he had called her 'darling'. What was he thinking of?

Then the grogginess in her head cleared and her memory returned. She was going to marry him! Her eyes opened wide and she tried to sit up again. What was she doing lying here when there were so many arrangements yet to be finalised?

"I have to…"

"Whatever you think you have to do can wait."

"But, the wedding…"

"Will she be betterer, Uncle David? For the wedding?" Jamie had come round to her other side and was stroking her face. "You will still be getting wed, won't yer?"

"Certainly, Jamie, the doctor didn't seem too worried about your mama's injury. It's only superficial."

"It don't look super to me."

"Nor me." Ruby was still hovering around, trying to get closer.

"It means the shot didn't go deep, he was able to get it out."

"Can I have a look?"

"No, Jamie."

"When you've finished talking about me like I'm not here…" Tillie's eyes felt very drowsy and all she wanted to do was snuggle down into the sheets and sleep.

"Sorry, my darling." There it was again, the last word she heard before drifting off into a soft swirling world of blues and pinks that enveloped her in a warm cloud of comfort.

Chapter 15

A warm hand smoothed Tillie's sweat-soaked hair from her brow. She reached up and took hold of it.

"You've slept for over twenty hours. How are you feeling now?" The voice sounded familiar. She tried to focus on the hand she was holding, but it didn't give her any clues. Through the haze a face looked at her rather oddly. It looked like...

Her eyes opened widely as she remembered once more.

"Why am I still in bed?" She tried to push him away and sit up.

"You had a nasty accident. You need to recuperate."

"But..."

"Look, my darling..." She would never tire of him calling her that. She relaxed and lay back. "I was so scared when I saw your lifeless body lying there on the grass. I really thought for a moment that I was going to lose you. I don't think I could have borne that."

"Because then you might lose Jamie."

"No, you silly goose, because I love you."

What had he said? He couldn't possibly mean that.

"You...?" She looked at him in disbelief.

"Yes, I love you, I love you." He turned her hand over and pressed feathery kisses on her palm.

"But you only wanted to marry me for Jamie's sake." Her own voice sounded husky as goose pimples spread up her body at the touch of his lips.

"I know that's what I said, and perhaps it was true at the time, but I have since come to get to know you better, and realised that I love you with all my heart." He looked deeply into her eyes, an anxious expression on his face. "Maybe one day you'll grow to love me in return."

"Maybe..." she teased.

"But I could..." He began to kiss her wrist. "Show you..." His mouth travelled up her arm. "How..." Her stomach began to tighten. "How to love me…" His lips reached the hollow of her neck. "As I love you."

Her breath caught in her throat. She couldn't reply, however much she wanted to declare her own love. His lips had now reached the side of her mouth and their touch was destroying her equilibrium. If she hadn't been lying down her legs would have buckled as her whole body felt as if it was made of jelly. She lay back, revelling in the sensations his mouth was causing. Suddenly, just as she was about to turn her face so that her own lips made contact with his, he pulled back.

He cleared his throat. "You will, one day." He stood up.

Why had he stopped, and what did he mean? Could he not tell how she felt? Did he think that, because she hadn't actually declared herself, she was immune to his advances?

"But…"

"It's all right, my dear. I won't impose myself on you any longer. Just get some rest. Jamie will be in to see you before long, I'm sure."

It suddenly dawned on her how dishevelled he looked. He hadn't even shaved. She had been aware of his prickly chin as it had rather enhanced his kisses. Had he been at her bedside all night long? She saw the dark circles under his eyes.

"David." She reached out to him but the austere look on his face told her that the moment of intimacy had vanished. "Thank you," she said tamely.

He crossed over to the door and she couldn't define the look he gave her as he glanced back. "Rest," he ordered. Then he was gone, closing the door behind him.

Why hadn't she said how much she cared for him? He must still think that she was only marrying him for Jamie's sake. She pushed back the bed covers, intending to run after him and put him straight, but the pain in her shoulder stopped her.

She had, for a moment, forgotten why she was lying there, bandaged up like a mummy. She felt underneath her nightdress and found that she was wearing nothing else, not even any underwear. Had David undressed her? A blush rose from her throat to the top of her face at the thought, as the door opened again and she thought he had returned. But it was Nellie, with a bowl of Freda's famous broth.

"You're looking rather flushed." Nellie put the tray on her lap. "Perhaps I ought to call Doctor Abrahams to come earlier."

"No, no, please don't. I'm fine now." It must have been Nellie who had undressed her. "Honestly."

"The master stayed up with you all night, he was so concerned for you." She had been right about that then.

"I hope he's gone to catch up on some sleep now."

"No, he called in to say that you were awake and to ask if I would bring you something to eat. Then he went out. I saw him cantering off on Starlight as I came past the landing window." She gave Tillie a thoughtful look. "Is everything all right between the pair of you?"

Tillie couldn't keep her gaze, and lifted the spoon to her mouth, pretending to be absorbed in her food. "This is delicious."

"I'm sure it is, but you haven't answered my question."

"Yes, why shouldn't it be?"

"You do know you're doing the right thing, don't you?"

She put down the spoon and smiled. "Yes, Jamie needs a father, and they get on so well."

"But what about you...your feelings?"

Picking up the spoon again, she took another mouthful. "I love him, I really do, and he says he loves me."

"Well, that's wonderful...but I can sense a 'but' coming on."

"I...I haven't actually told him so yet."

"Why not?"

"The moment never seems to be right."

"You need to find the moment, lass. The master needs to know he's loved. He's always been like that. Don't delay too long." She picked up the tray as Tillie heard footsteps running along the landing.

"Mama, are you betterer now?" Jamie ran in and launched himself onto the bed.

"Be careful, young man! Your mama's still hurt, she doesn't need you attacking her," Nellie admonished him rather more severely than usual.

He climbed down sheepishly. "Sorry, Mama."

Tillie reached over and kissed him. "Here." She patted a space at her side. "You can sit beside me. What have you been up to?"

* * * *

Three days later Tillie had still not found the right moment. David had popped in a few times to check on her but hadn't stayed any length of time. The day of the wedding was looming and the doctor had pronounced that she would be fit enough, as long as she did not exert herself too much.

"You look ravishing," Ruby was giving her opinion on the almost finished wedding dress that Nellie was helping Tillie try on. "I don't know how he'll be able to keep his hands off you!"

"It's a bit hard to fasten the buttons, with the bandage in the way, but we'll have a rough idea of how it will look." Nellie stuck another pin into the soft material.

Tillie let her fingers linger on the smooth silk fabric. The dress was beyond her wildest dreams, ivory in colour, full-skirted and ruffled, but tight at the v-shaped waistline, with little buttons running down from the neck.

"I hope I shall have the bandage removed by the middle of the week. We'll be able to have a proper fitting then."

Nellie seemed as if she was agreeing, but because her mouth was full of pins, the sound came out as a grunt.

Ruby laughed before looking at her sister expectantly. "Tillie...?"

"Yes?"

"I…um…" She turned away. "Never mind."

"Come on, Ruby, what were you going to ask?"

"No, it's too cheeky."

"You've intrigued me now." Tillie half turned. "Ouch!" she yelled as a pin missed its mark and jabbed her in the leg.

"Well, if you will keep wriggling." Nellie clearly had no sympathy for her.

Ruby took a deep breath. "What I was wondering was…would I be able to borrow your wedding dress when you've finished with it?"

"Oh, Ruby! Has Sam proposed?"

"Well, not exactly."

"He either has or he hasn't."

"I'm hoping he will."

Tillie smiled but didn't move as she knew that she would exact Nellie's wrath if she did.

"Of course, my darling sister, you can borrow whatever you like, when the time does come." She suddenly remembered the dance that Sam was taking her to. "How was it at the dance…? Oh no, it was the day I had the accident, wasn't it? Did you still go?"

Ruby shook her head.

"I can't believe I've been so wrapped up in my own affairs I haven't even asked you about it before."

"That's all right. I didn't expect you to. You were quite poorly, after all."

"That's no excuse for neglecting you."

"Really, Tillie, don't beat yourself up about it. Sam's asked me to go this Saturday instead."

"Well, to make up for my negligence you can borrow my bonnet, if you wish. The one Emily gave me. It'll match the pink dress better. In fact, I shall give it to you."

"No, Tillie, that's too much."

"I insist."

"For goodness sake, Ruby, just accept." Nellie had removed the pins from her mouth and had obviously had enough of the sisters arguing. "Shouldn't you be cleaning the windows?"

Ruby slouched out of the room.

"That was my fault." Tillie tried to make amends for her sister. "Don't be too hard on her."

"I know, but just because you're marrying the master doesn't give her the right to shirk her duties at every opportune moment."

Jamie was next for a fitting. He was going to be the ring-bearer, and was to be decked out in a little Lord Fauntleroy suit of pale blue satin with collar and cuffs of lace.

"Do I 'ave to wear this, Mama?" He did not seem too enthralled at the frilly outfit. "It's so…girlish."

"You do want to look right, don't you, darling, for my wedding?

"Yes, but, why can't I wear my new brown suit what Uncle David brought me?"

"Because you're to be a pageboy, and this is what pageboys wear."

He stood glumly through the fitting, his bottom lip stuck out. "I bet George won't have to wear a stupid suit like this."

"Well, actually, he is, just the same as yours." She had told him that George was also going to be a pageboy, much to his disgust.

"You'll have to get on with George at the wedding, for your mama's sake." Nellie was having difficulty pinning the material while Jamie wriggled.

He shifted his position. "Will I be related to him and Sarah, when you're married?"

"I suppose you will, once Uncle David has officially adopted you. You do want him to adopt you, don't you, like we talked about before?"

"Oh yes. He'll be me proper pa then, won't he?"

Nellie rose from her bent position, rubbing her back. "All finished, young man. Let's take it off. I'll soon have it sewn."

"Why won't you let me help, Nellie? I feel so useless just watching you doing all the work." Tillie tried to help her son out of his costume, but had to give up.

"I can manage, Mama."

"Well, I know one thing you could do." Nellie put the unused pins back into the pincushion.

"Anything."

"You could ask Freda to make me a nice cup of tea."

"Oh, Nellie, is that all?"

"That's all I'm letting you do. You still need to rest. You do want to be fully recovered for the wedding, don't you?"

"Of course. I bow to your better judgement, as usual."

"So you should, now get downstairs and find me that drink." Nellie shooed her out of the door as Jamie put on his play clothes. "Oh, and if you see Ruby, tell her to come for her fitting."

* * * *

"Thank you so much, Doctor Abrahams, for everything."

The bandages had finally been removed and Tillie flexed her shoulder. It was still quite sore, though, and she had to hide a grimace for fear that David would keep her confined to the house even longer if he knew it still hurt.

She would be able to try on her wedding dress properly when Nellie was free. It was the most beautiful dress she had ever seen, and she got it out of its wraps repeatedly, just to gaze at it. The housekeeper had given in and allowed her to help with the sewing of Jamie's outfit, as she had been desperate to be involved, but it would have been bad luck to have made her own dress.

Some time later she sat down at her dressing table, clad only in her bodice and petticoat, trying out different hairstyles in front of the mirror. She was holding her hair up when a tap on the door made her jump

"May I come in?" David popped his head hesitantly round the door.

"I…um…yes, of course." She lowered her hands, thinking to cover herself up.

Walking in, he studied her through the mirror. "You look beautiful with your hair loose like that." Closing his eyes, he picked up a handful and smelled it, before clearing his throat and standing back.

"I have something for you to wear for the wedding." He held out a bright blue satin box.

She smiled. Whatever was in the box wouldn't cover much of her.

He opened the lid and she gasped. Inside was the most striking necklace she had ever seen. It glistened and sparkled in the sun's rays as if it was alive. Diamonds and pearls alternated in droplets from the chain that was also encrusted in diamonds.

"Do you like it?"

"It's heavenly."

Reaching forward, he placed the necklace round her throat before lifting her hair from her neck and fastening it. She stroked it, before turning round.

"No, don't turn. Let me look at you in the mirror." He put his hands on her shoulders. She tried not to flinch when he caught the sore area. She did not want to spoil the moment by being a cry baby.

She could hardly tear her eyes away from the sparkling jewels. "Is it really for me?"

"Of course."

"But…it's so beautiful."

"A beautiful necklace for a beautiful bride." He bent down and pressed his lips to her neck. She closed her eyes as sensations began to invade her, but he stopped abruptly and stood upright.

"I'm glad you like it, my dear. It belonged to my mother. My father gave it to her on their wedding day. "

She reached up and unfastened the clasp, carefully putting it back in the box which she placed in the bottom drawer of the dressing table. Reaching up to take his hands, she rose from her chair. "Thank you, David. It's the most gorgeous thing I've ever had."

Suddenly, she was in his arms, his hands stroking her hair. She could feel his heart beating wildly and her own following suit. She could scarcely breathe, he was holding her so tightly. Closing her eyes, she leant against his heaving chest. His hold loosened, and his hands lowered to her waist moving up and down, caressing her sides, before cupping her breasts. She gasped. Nothing had prepared her for such a sensation.

The sound must have penetrated his mind as he paused.

"Don't stop," she whispered, pushing her breasts forward towards his retreating hands. He hesitated briefly before cupping them again and pressing his lips to her neck. Arching her back for him to get better access, she wanted more. She bit her lip as his hand found its way under her bodice and found her aroused nipple, rolling it gently between his fingers before enfolding her entire breast.

She closed her eyes, wishing she could get out of the bodice so that he could have full access, and had to grab onto his jacket, feeling as if her legs were going to give way. Then he lifted her up and carried her over to the bed. As she lay there, awaiting more, she heard voices outside the door.

Jumping up, she heard David moan as he ran his fingers through his hair, and, grabbing her robe, she quickly put it round her as Jamie came rushing in.

"Mama…" Looking at David, obviously surprised to see him there, he hesitated for a brief moment, before going across to put one arm round Tillie and then he pulled David towards him with the other, and stood with his head resting against them.

She looked up at David and smiled. The passion may have waned but the love shone from his eyes as he pushed his lips forward in imitation of a kiss.

"Both me mama and me nearly-papa together." Jamie clung onto them even tighter, unaware of them making love with their facial expressions above him. "I'm so happy."

David pulled away first. "I'm pleased to hear that, young man. As to your mama...?" His raised eyebrows questioned her.

"Yes, me too. I couldn't be happier."

"That's settled then." David turned to the door. "But I must leave you now. As usual there's work to do." Turning back, he blew her another kiss.

* * * *

Tillie adjusted one of the flowers entwined in her headdress one more time. Their faint aroma drifted down to assuage her nostrils. Closing her eyes, she took a deep breath.

She could hear Matthew trying to organise the procession into the little church. "Jamie, stop prancing around and stand still. You'll drop the ring off the cushion in a minute, and George, stand next to Jamie, not behind him."

It felt surreal to feel so calm with all the goings on around her. Feeling as if she was floating in a bubble, she turned her head and watched as Ruby almost dropped her posy of flowers as she bent to tie the lace on her new boots.

Smiling as she fingered the necklace David had given her, she mentally checked that she hadn't forgotten anything, and silently recited the age-old rhyme:

> *Something old, something new,*
> *Something borrowed, something blue.*

She had found a small pin broach amongst her grandmother's things for the 'something old'. She wished the dear old lady could have seen her now, and sent up a silent prayer for her to keep watch over the day's proceedings.

Nellie and Freda had bought her some little pearl earrings for the 'something new'. They matched the necklace perfectly.

276

The 'something borrowed' was a hair slide that she had found in one of the drawers in her bedroom, and a small blue bow stitched onto her garter completed the list.

Through the haze of her veil she could make out Sarah, dressed in a miniature copy of Ruby's high-necked blue dress, trying to look composed, while George was poking out his tongue at Jamie, obviously trying to goad him into doing exactly what Matthew had warned against.

And there was little Maisie, also in a blue dress, her thumb in her mouth, clinging onto Sarah with her free hand. Emily had got in touch with the family who had taken her in and the little girl had been to visit The Grange to see Jamie. She had begun to speak and was now known as Mary Maisie.

"Are we all ready then?" Matty, her dear brother who was to give her away, took her hand. "Are *you* ready, Tillie?"

She nodded, suddenly feeling very nervous as she pulled up her long white gloves. Her legs began to shake as she took the first step towards the open door.

Was she really doing the right thing? Of course she was. Too late now for doubts!

As they entered, a hush came over the whispering crowd as the harpist began playing the wedding music.

A sea of smiling faces looked round at her. She could see Emily half way down the church, very heavily pregnant, and Edward standing at the altar ready to perform the service. Becky was there also. She had shut up shop for the day in order to be there. Harry was with his new sweetheart, she couldn't remember her name, and Victor was next to a smiling Annie.

Then he turned. The top hat shielded his blue eyes but couldn't hide his lop-sided grin.

Did she really deserve to feel so happy? she thought, taking in David's lithe body in a grey suit and ruffled shirt.

The service flew by in a miasma of blurred images. Afterwards she remembered speaking her vows but not much else. The ring on her finger proved that nothing had gone awry, and Jamie hadn't dropped it.

She was married, was now signing her name in the register as Matilda Anne Raven for the very last time. She could scarcely believe it.

They walked out of the church to cheers and were showered with rice for good luck. She might need some of that. She was now mistress of The Grange and the Brightmoor Estate. How thrilled her mama and papa would have been. If only they could have seen her now.

David lifted her veil and kissed her gently. "Hello, Mrs Dalton."

"Hello, husband."

He kissed her again, this time more urgently, before looking into her eyes and smiling broadly. He didn't appear to be embarrassed at showing such affection in public. Victor spoke to him and he looked away but kept tight hold of her hand.

She smiled across at Matthew. How like their father he was becoming. Jessie stood beside him, trying to placate her baby boy who was obviously ready for his next feed. The photographer was having trouble getting everybody in line, as most of the guests had never had their photograph taken before so weren't sure what to do, but he soon organised them into a manageable group.

Eventually she and David were greeting the guests at the front door, after being whisked away from the church in the carriage drawn by four white stallions, their manes and tails decorated with large white plumes of feathers. She had felt like the queen, waving to all those familiar faces and once they had rounded the bend, leaving them all behind, David had taken her in his arms and kissed her passionately.

"I love you, Mrs Matilda Ann Dalton," he had said with true emotion shining in his eyes. "And I'm going to ensure that you always know it."

"And I love you too, David Harding Dalton, you've made me the happiest woman on earth."

He then kissed her again and it was fortunate that they arrived at the house when they did, or things could have been very embarrassing.

EPILOGUE

Tillie looked down at the twins sleeping peacefully for what seemed like the first time. As they had been so small she had had an easy birth, but her milk had refused to come through until today so they had been very fretful. Now, however, everything was going to be all right. She wouldn't need the wet nurse Nellie had lined up, she would be able to do it all herself.

She sat back against the pillows, closing her eyes and savouring the silence, broken only by occasional little grunts or suckling sounds from the crib.

Her wildest dreams had come true. She thought she had been the happiest woman on earth on her wedding day but that had been nothing compared to what she felt today.

The door opened and she saw David peer round.

"I didn't know if you'd be asleep," he whispered, walking over to the cradle where the girls slept side by side, curled up in their cocoons. He gently touched the cheek of one of them. "I hope I'll be able to tell them apart soon. At the moment I can't say which one's Alice or which one's Amelia."

Smiling indulgently, Tillie leaned over and pointed to one of the babies. "That one's Alice. You can tell by the tiny birthmark on her neck."

David peered into the crib. "I can't see her neck, let alone a birthmark, she's so wrapped up."

"Well, next time I'm feeding her I'll show you."

His eyes lit up as his hand reached out to her breast, but she nudged it away. "They're out of bounds for the time being, only for feeding the babies."

Reluctantly, he stood back, grimacing.

"But I'll make sure I make it up to you as soon as I can." She pulled his head down and gave him a lingering kiss. "I don't want to waste a moment longer than necessary either."

They were interrupted by the joyful voice of her son as Jamie came running into the room.

Her family was now complete. Unless, of course, Mother Nature had other plans.

About The Author

Married to Don for 40 years, 5 children and 7 grandchildren. Born in Sussex, England, the middle child of 9. Now living in Derbyshire. Changed junior schools 7 times before going to convent boarding school in Alton, Hampshire at age of 10 and staying there till age of 18.

Interests are: reading, playing Scrabble, singing, religious activities, family get-togethers, gardening.

Lightning Source UK Ltd.
Milton Keynes UK
07 March 2011
168812UK00001B/1/P

9 781877 546501